Bound by Flames

Bound by Flames

LOVE AND MAGIC - BOOK FOUR

Pix Pentham

Contents

To all who may need to hear it, I am so glad you're still here.

Content Warnings:

Bound by Flames contains descriptions of behavior and feelings caused by major depressive episodes, mentions of suicide/ideation (non-detailed), explicit sexual content (bondage, primal, voyeurism, knotting, shifted and part-shifted), depictions of accidental limb amputation, house fire, non-consensual drink spiking (no untoward sexual treatment of unconscious persons), non-consensual physical restraint of FMC by MC (one incident, non-sexual), and depictions of survivor's guilt.

Take care of yourselves and happy reading!

Preface

Love and Magic is designed as a series of standalone novels, each one containing the story of one couple, and can be read out of order. However, some of their stories are interconnected and may contain spoilers for earlier books. *Bound by Flames* begins at the approximate halfway point of *Spiritbound*, and thus contains some spoilers for Rose and Spider's story. If this doesn't bother you, read on! Happy reading!

1

"Hettie, you slugabed, wake *up*!"

Hettie groaned, tugging her pillow over her head. She rolled away from the door where her obnoxious coworker stood. Little claws scraped her skin as two chicken feet fought for balance on her back.

"Oh, Hettie, get out of bed already! I've been calling you!"

"Go away, Avery," Hettie groaned.

Cold air washed over her as her blankets were yanked away. Indignant chicken noises split her ears as her pillow was snatched away too.

"Come on, I need you to watch the shop for a little bit!"

That sentence was a better wake-up call than being doused with a bucket of ice water. Hettie sat up and glared at the senior apprentice, who was unbothered as she threw open the curtains on her little, round window. Sunlight bounced off her sheet of shiny red hair.

"*You're* supposed to be working the counter this morning, Avery," Hettie growled, "I'm coming in to rotate stock this afternoon."

"Well," Avery began with saccharine sweetness, "now *you're* watching the shop."

"Where are *you* going, then?"

"*The Dragonflower* sailed into the marina this morning. Nastia and I want to go down and watch the lords disembark." Hettie noticed that Avery had her "man-catching" corset on, the one that lifted her tits nearly up to her throat.

"Nastia too?" Hettie frowned, "You know Crystal doesn't want me manning the shop alone." For good reason, not that the two of them understood. For weeks they'd been teasing Hettie about being babied by the two women who owned the shop.

"Crystal doesn't have to know. This is her day off. She and Poppy won't even be in today. They went to the market for supplies and you know they'll turn it into an all-day thing."

"Avery..." Hettie sighed.

"Please," Avery wheedled, "I'll make the next batch of bruise-balm. And we'll bring you back lunch." She folded her hands together, pleading.

"You're going to leave whether I agree or not," Hettie grumbled.

Avery flashed her a grin, "So you might as well watch the shop so neither of us gets in trouble. Hurry up, we're leaving in fifteen minutes." She tossed Hettie's apron at the bed and scurried out. Hettie shrugged aside the apron with a huff.

The nerve of her.

Hettie snagged her glasses from the bedside table and shoved the round frames up the bridge of her nose. She scooted to the edge of the bed, casting a rueful glance at the speckled white chicken resettling by the footboard.

"Sorry, Didi," Hettie murmured apologetically. She reached out to pet the bird on the head and received a sharp peck for her troubles. Hettie shook out her hand and gave Didi a glum look. "That's fair."

With a heavy sigh, Hettie stood so she could tug on her shop uniform. It was a simple white shirt and red skirt, and the apron she tied over top was brown, emblazoned with the poppy and crystal logo of *Pollimer's Potions*. She'd been apprenticed to the same magic shop since she graduated from the Arcane University in town a few years prior. Poppy and Crystal were the married couple that owned the shop, and they'd been incredibly kind to Hettie, given her circumstances.

Hettie tied back her thicket of dark, ashy curls with a red sash, careful not to pinch the fabric, or her hair, in the joints of her mechanical right hand – a souvenir of a childhood accident. She'd been far too young to remember the house fire that had taken her limb, but for as long as she could remember she'd had one variation or another of this half-magic, half-metal construct instead of a flesh and bone arm up to the elbow. It could do most anything a natural hand could do, though she had no sense of feeling in it. She had no memories of anything before that night to remind her of having two natural hands, so she didn't miss it.

She did a quick spin in front of the mirror to make sure

everything was as it should be, and tightened the tie on her apron a bit to accentuate the dip in her plump waist.

"Come on, Didi," Hettie carefully scooped up the bird with her right arm so when she pecked it didn't hurt. She didn't want to leave her up here where she could get into all kinds of unsupervised mischief. The apprentices lived above the shop, so her room was littered with many half-finished projects that would be dangerous for a little beak to poke into.

"There you are!" Nastia, the other apprentice and Avery's partner in crime, crowed when Hettie tromped down the stairs into the back room, "Ugh, you and that chicken. Can't you have a normal pet? Get a cat or something."

Hettie ignored Nastia and set Didi into her nesting box in the corner. She was well used to Nastia's jabs about her chicken. She ignored them for the most part. Truthfully, Didi was not what Hettie would have picked if she had a choice. She wasn't even a pet, not really.

She was an accident. The first of many.

"Leave her be, Nastia," Avery shooed her fellow senior apprentice towards the shop, "She's watching the counter for us after all."

Nastia rolled her eyes, "We'll only be gone a little while. We probably won't even get any customers. Most people will be watching the ships in the marina."

"You'd better hope Crystal and Poppy don't find out about this," Hettie fixed her glasses, already pulling jars from the upper shelves. If she was going to be stuck watching the shop, she might as well get started on her afternoon's work.

"They *won't*," Avery insisted, "Not unless *someone* tattles on us."

Hettie scowled over at her. "You know it won't be me. Just bring me something from that little deli on Kingfisher Street on your way back."

The two of them chimed a hasty agreement and scrambled out through the shop. Hettie took a deep breath as the air settled in their absence, trying to calm her nerves. It wouldn't do for her to get worked up now. Bad things happened when she let her emotions get the best of her.

It had started just after her graduation. It was just little things at first, items moving or disappearing when she was stressed, strange lights and flickers at the corners of her eyes – odd, but nothing to cause her alarm.

Little did she know, those were just the warning signs that she was losing control.

The real doozy came when she... well... came.

She'd had plenty of partners through her university days, but they'd all been lazy or incompetent enough that her pleasure had never been their objective. Encounter after encounter left her disappointed and unsatisfied.

That is, until Cordelia.

She'd met her at Oros's Festival, a year and a half ago. A radiant, red-headed half-elf busking on a street corner. She'd noticed Hettie staring and had winked at her, and that was enough for Hettie to be hooked like a fish. They'd spent the rest of the night together, strolling through the festival grounds and dancing in the square before hiding away in Cordelia's room at the inn.

Her touch had been like magic over Hettie's skin. It was like nothing she'd ever felt before. One second she was writhing under Cordelia's mouth, and the next she was climaxing, and a flash of light filled the room. When she could see again, Cordelia was gone, and there was a chicken left in her place.

Or, more accurately, Cordelia *was* the chicken, and had been ever since. She'd frantically brought her to Crystal and Poppy, sobbing and panicking. Every witchlight in the shop had exploded in a burst of blue flame and glass, and three shelves collapsed, their contents slicking the floor, hissing and boiling where they combined. When they got her calmed down, the random, poltergeist-like damages stopped as well. No matter what the three of them tried, Cordelia remained a chicken. Not a single reverse spell or dispelling charm had any effect. So, Hettie had taken care of 'Didi' ever since.

Through a series of misfortunes since then, they'd discovered that strong emotions triggered these strange bouts of magical chaos. Fear was the quickest to trigger it, and Hettie hadn't so much as flirted with anyone since the incident for fear of starting a chicken collection. It was why they didn't want Hettie working the shop alone, with nobody around to help her manage the fallout of this strange new nature of her magic.

She ought to flip the 'open' sign on the front door and hide in the work room until the senior apprentices came back, but that would activate the anti-thief wards, which in turn would alert Crystal, and then they would all be in trouble. No, she'd just hope nobody came in while she was alone.

That hope was ill-placed, it turned out.

The bell chimed up front almost an hour after they left her alone, just as she was thinking she was in the clear. Dread pinned all her limbs in place, and for a long moment Hettie wondered if they'd just go away if she waited long enough.

But no, she could hear the impatient huff of a customer

with no intention of leaving empty-handed. Hettie wiped the clammy chill from her palms on her apron, steeled herself, and stepped through the curtained doorway into the shop.

Hettie's breath caught in her throat at the sight of the man waiting at the counter.

He was tall, much taller than her, and a skein of silky black hair drifted around his shoulders. The black and gold fabric draped around him did nothing to hide the fact that he was corded in ropy, lithe muscle. Four black horns curled back from his temples, and his eyes when they flicked over to her were gold, with slit pupils like a cat.

He was incredibly attractive, with a strong, square jaw and smooth bronze skin, though there was something a little *off* about him. His expression as he eyed her up and down was neutral, but the look in his eyes was deadened, dull.

"Good afternoon," she greeted politely, when she could get words past the glue-trap of her tongue. Magic eddied and swirled in her belly like fog creeping over a marsh. She hoped this interaction wouldn't take long.

"I need a thieves' trap," the man told her without preamble, his voice a thunderous rumble that she felt deep in her chest.

"Y-yes, of course." She was flustered, by his attitude and good looks and by the magic buzzing over her skin. She collected the spell from beneath the counter – a freeze-movement stasis curse laid on a convincingly real-looking gem-studded necklace. A discerning eye would know that the jewels were just cut glass, and the metal not real gold, but the idea was that a thief in the midst of a heist would likely be grabbing indiscriminately. She wrapped it in a little box along with the token to deactivate it after it had been triggered, but before she could name a price he slid six gold coins the size of her palm across the counter.

"I hope these will cover it."

Hettie gaped at the antique coins, worth, she had to guess, at least twice their weight in current currency, and more than three times what his purchase was worth. She nodded numbly.

"I can't give you change-"

"Keep it," he interrupted.

Without further preamble, the man slid the box from her palm, his fingers brushing over her own. There was a spark of something between their hands, a flicker of something just for a moment in the man's dead eyes, and then he was gone.

That spark was probably nothing, Hettie told herself. It definitely wasn't her suddenly-out-of-control magic messing with the spell in the box. It was just a coincidence.

For just a second, it had seemed like something in his touch had called to her, but that was crazy.

She just had to hope that everything would be fine. And that none of the events from the day would come back to haunt her.

2

APPROXIMATELY SIX MONTHS LATER

Gyl watched from one of his towers as the construct-driven carriage disappeared down the path. He already felt the pressing emptiness of his massive home. He wasn't very old by dragon standards, but he had lived a very long time. Alone, for most of it. He wasn't built to be alone. Though most dragons did just fine on their own, and some even preferred it, he was… struggling.

What an entertaining diversion catching that thief had turned out to be. He'd expected to just be solving the frustrating problem of a greasy little rat too bold to get away with his little rat thievery just one time, but that was not how things turned out at all.

The trap he'd purchased malfunctioned, and the thief had been caught in stasis, even after he deactivated it. He didn't find out until scant hours ago that it was because the spell had split the man's soul from his body.

While brooding in his nest like usual, he'd smelled an intruder in his treasure vault. When he'd gone to investigate, he found only a flustered, plump little morsel talking to an invisible ghost, who'd turned out to be his original thief. Upon leading her to the rat's body, she'd restored him to his former self, and they'd invited Gyl to watch their rather *exuberant* reunion.

It had awoken something in him.

He'd been numb to the world for so long that he couldn't remember the last time he'd been interested in any sort of intimate physical activities. He'd forgotten what it was like to be *interested*. If they'd invited him into the bed he had no doubt he would have participated with *gusto*. As it was, he was feeling a trace of his old fire flaming in his blood, burning even after he'd self-completed while watching them.

A sudden itching, nagging urge had been plaguing him since then. He wanted to go to town, though not to follow the amorous couple. No, something else was tugging at him, like an invisible thread pulled taut through his heart, urging him to follow.

So he'd go to town, he decided. Though he'd have to wait until the carriage returned. A sad thought, that a dragon his age should be so dependent on a mortal method of transport.

Every dragon had a mortal form they could shift into, in addition to their more regal beast forms. While he'd never be mistaken for human, that form allowed him to do business with other bipedal races. Gyl had been wearing his mortal form for far too long, and once he'd built his palatial house and firmly ensconced himself into both mountain and lonely despair, he found he no longer had access to his beast form.

He was stuck.

He'd never heard of a dragon having such a problem. There was no precedent for someone getting stuck in their mortal form, not that he'd heard of anyway. He had no avenue for assistance, and had not cared enough to seek answers. Perhaps, now that he was feeling a little more awake, he could seek them out.

For now, he'd follow this strange call to go down to Serpent's Bay. It took a few hours for the carriage to return, but return it did, magic-propelled wheels bouncing along the road.

Thankfully, since his servants were metal constructs, the extra work would not burden the carriage's valet.

He made each of their metal bodies with his own hands. He'd studied their craft for a long time, though he could not enchant them himself. It had been a while since he'd worked on anything, given his state in recent years, but each of the dozen or so constructs that kept his castle in working order were a by-product of his own artistry – alive in the sense that they walked and followed orders, but they were not exactly sentient.

The one that sat in the driver's seat of the carriage was one of his favorites. The plates on its arms and legs had been engraved with scenes of wild horses running through mountains, and it was draped in a protective cloak with a row of tassels down the back made to represent a horse's mane. It just nodded when Gyl ordered it to turn back around and be prepared to head back to the city.

As the carriage trundled down the hill, the tension on that thread pulling on him eased a little. Whatever was calling him to town, he was getting closer to it.

He'd start at the magic shop where he'd been sold the dud trap. And then he'd find whatever this urge was leading him to.

3

Hettie sighed from behind the counter, chin propped in her metal hand, staring out the open front door at the hustle and bustle of the festival being set up on the street.

"What are you pouting for?" Nastia huffed from between the shelves to her right. She had a little crate perched on her hip and was stocking a shelf with one hand. "The festival starts in half an hour!"

"I'm not going," Hettie groused. She tapped one metal finger against the side of her glasses absently.

"You can't tell me you're going to spend Oros's festival holed up in your room again?" Avery leaned against the counter on the other side.

"Live a little, Hettie," Nastia plopped the empty crate on the counter, "Come out with us. You're, what, twenty-three? And you already act like an old maid."

Across the shop, a gray-blonde head peered at her from between the shelves, eyebrows raised in a warning look. Crystal had already told her she wasn't allowed to go to the festival. Hettie resented the reminder. She knew it wasn't wise to go out right now.

She'd been having more incidents with just her normal magic casting. Lately even smaller spells were blowing up in her face, sometimes when she was completely calm. She was rapidly losing control of her magic, and between the booze and the dancing and the crowds, there was a high chance she'd have another incident.

"No, thank you," Hettie declined politely, "I've got studying to do for my senior apprentice trials."

"You're no fun," Nastia groaned.

"Be nice, Nas," Avery scolded. She turned to Hettie and gave her a sympathetic smile, "You're sure? Your test isn't for another couple of months."

"Maybe next time," Hettie shrugged, casting a sideways glance over at Crystal.

"Yeah, right," Nastia snorted.

"Don't be a bitch, Nas. Hettie works hard. She's dedicated," Avery scolded. Nastia made an indignant sound, but she dropped it. Hettie's heart warmed towards the redhead. They weren't close, but Avery wasn't catty by nature. She'd never been afraid to correct Nastia when she was being petty – which was all the time – even though the girl was her best friend.

"Why don't you two head out early?" Crystal told them as she approached the counter, "Hettie and I will close up the shop."

They didn't need to be told twice. The two of them yanked

off their shop aprons and raced into the back rooms. Their footsteps thundered overhead as they ran upstairs to their rooms to change.

"Must be nice," Hettie sighed glumly.

"I know it's rotten," Crystal patted her arm sympathetically, "but we just can't risk it."

"I've hurt enough people," Hettie agreed. Her eyes flicked over to the box on the counter where Didi was nestled, head tucked to chest for a nap.

Crystal gave her arm a squeeze, "Poppy and I will bring you back some festival treats."

"Thanks," Hettie attempted a smile, but she was sure it fell short. It was a kind gesture, but eating fried festival food cold and sad in her room did not sound like an equivalent consolation prize.

"Do you have something to keep your mind off things while we're gone? It'll be easier if you stay busy," Crystal asked as she crossed to the shop door and flipped the sign on the window to 'CLOSED.'

"I'll do some extra cleaning down here, I guess," Hettie shrugged. She didn't realize how much of her free time she spent practicing her magic until it was no longer safe to do so. She'd worked and studied so hard for so long, and for what? For her passion to start ruining her life? To have wasted all those years of schooling? To live alone forever because her magic might harm anyone she got too close to?

She tried not to see the pitying look on Crystal's face. The older woman took off her own apron and hung it on a peg by the door. As one of the owners, she didn't wear the red and white shopgirl uniform, but rather a cream apron and a serviceable dress and jacket in a deep burgundy that brought out the trace of strawberry that still lingered in her hair.

"If that's what you want to do, dear, you know I won't complain. I'll give you a little extra for the work." Crystal crossed to the front door and pulled it closed, muffling the ambient noise from outside.

"Just take it out of what I owe you for damages," Hettie shook her head forlornly. She'd started two fires in the last week alone just trying to light candles with her magic, an easier feat than conjuring witchlights, but she couldn't even do that without consequence anymore. Avery and Nastia were starting to notice the disturbances, and it was getting harder to play off her accidents as clumsiness. She'd begged Crystal and Poppy to let her keep her problems a secret out of sheer embarrassment, but at this rate they would need to be told soon for their own safety.

"We'll get to the bottom of this, love," Crystal returned to the counter and squeezed her shoulder. "Hopefully the university will get back to us this week, and they'll be able to do something to help you."

Eventually. They'd been petitioning the Arcane University for help for months, and nobody had gotten back to them yet. It was always like that. Given the sheer number of petitions they received, it took a while for one to get pushed through. Once it did, she had no doubt they would take up her case.

Hettie shivered. She was going to be put on display like a bug and studied. She'd been at that university, she'd know. Once they got hold of an anomaly, it was passed around the departments and tested to exhaustion until it was either broken or its mystery solved.

Hettie was hoping for the latter.

"We're going out!" came the twin cries of the seniors as they clomped down the stairs. They got stuck together in the doorway for a moment before they broke free, fluttering outfits catching on corners as they rounded the counter. Their eagerness for Hettie to join them was entirely forgotten, as they didn't so much as cast a glance backward at her as they darted out the front door, shop bell jangling clamorously even after the door swung closed behind them.

Crystal shook her head, "I had hoped they'd grow out of this over-exuberance, but it only seems to worsen as the years go on."

"Don't be silly, Crys," a familiar sweet voice chimed from the doorway behind them, "we were much the same at their age."

Poppy, the shop's other owner, stepped through the curtain that separated the shop from the back rooms. Her ginger hair was streaked with gray, and her figure was nearly as wide as she was tall – which was not very. Poppy always said she had a touch of gnome blood in her, and that was why she measured exactly four feet tall, and where she got her green thumb.

"Surely not I," Crystal sniffed disdainfully.

"Even you. Remember when you were so eager to leave for the winter fair that you left an entire cauldron of vitality booster on the fire and ruined it?"

"I've no memory of this," Crystal shook her head, though her cheeks were turning pink.

"Just be easy on them." Poppy winked at her wife and partner. "Hettie, darling, will you be alright here alone for the night?"

"Just fine," Hettie replied woodenly. Her belly boiled with jealousy as Crystal tucked Poppy under her arm and planted a kiss on the top of her head. She didn't used to be so bitter. She'd once thought their public displays of affection adorable, something to strive for. She wasn't made to be alone, but her condition was forcing it upon her.

"If you're sure, we'll be going too. I like to get our offerings done before the bonfire gets too crowded." The two of them clasped hands, and then they, too, walked out of the shop.

Hettie felt the emptiness of the building close in on her. It seemed even more oppressive with the noise ramping up outside. She glanced over at Didi, who'd woken with the bell from the shop door closing and was now eyeing her warily with beady black eyes.

"I deserve this," she told Didi bitterly. Her eyes burned, and she swiped angrily at her leaking tears with her left hand.

She felt a fluffy body bump into her elbow. Hettie glanced down, surprised, to see Didi had hopped out of her box and had pressed her feathered little body into her side. She was clucking softly, rubbing the sides of her head against Hettie's arm.

"It's okay if you hate me," Hettie murmured, lowering her hand to stroke her feathered neck, "You don't have to be sweet just because I'm miserable." But despite her words, she was grateful for the comfort. Didi had been warming up to her lately, and while Hettie was sad that it was necessary, she needed it.

She spent a few minutes wallowing in self-pity, crying and petting this sympathetic girl-turned-chicken, before she dried her face and grabbed the broom. If she let herself get too sad, she risked another incident regardless of whether or not she stayed home. She could already feel the buzz of magic under her skin.

So she got busy. She swept the shop from back to front, shifting furniture and dusting shelves and products with a rag. The seniors must have been slacking in their closing duties, because she had a sizable pile of dust ready to sweep out the front door. Hettie opened the door to sweep it out into the street...

And was faced by a familiar dark-haired, quad-horned man looming over her, hand raised as if he'd been about to try the door.

Hettie recognized him immediately, of course. How could she not? She'd been nervous about that trap she'd sold him for months, hoping it hadn't killed him – or worse, pissed him off.

"S-sorry, sir, we're closed for the holiday," she stammered. She tried to tamp down her rising panic, but she could already feel the broom handle vibrating against her palm. So much for being incident-free tonight.

Right away she could tell something was different about him. His hand lowered to his side and he stared down at her, face creasing into a frown. Whereas before he seemed to look right through her, now she felt like he saw her all too well. Those gold coins he had for eyes that were dull and lifeless on his last visit were bright and full of fire, and when he saw her his face tightened into a collection of hard lines.

He stepped into her, towering over her – gods he was *tall*. She took a step back reflexively, and he followed, ducking his head to get beneath the doorframe.

"You're the shop girl who sold me the trap." His voice was a low, gravelly hum. His slit pupils widened into dark wells as his nostrils flared.

Two years ago she'd have stood her ground. At her top form, she'd have been able to handle any nonsense that arose from a disgruntled customer. Now...

"L-look, I'm sorry if it malfunctioned. I'll give you a refund, and –"

"Who hurt you?" He took another step forward. Automatically, she stepped back.

"What?" What was he talking about? She was getting too scared. She needed to calm down, but he just looked so angry. She could feel her magic rising to tighten around her windpipe like a fist.

"You've been crying," he stated simply, though the heat in his voice could cut through ice like a hot wire. He reached out and hooked a finger under her chin, tilting her head back and leaning close to peer at her eyes, which must have still been red and puffy if he could tell she'd been bawling her eyes out.

Hettie jerked back, "Don't touch me!" She didn't even know this guy. Her heart was pounding, and magic was rolling in spiky waves through her limbs. She needed to get a grip.

The broomstick in her hand twisted, the top of it flopping over her wrist. It curled and looped over her forearm, tightening and constricting. The wood grain pattern shifted into diamonds of black and brown scales, and the bristled end of the broom shriveled and condensed into a wedge-shaped head with a forked, flickering tongue.

Hettie shrieked and shook her arm. The snake hissed and loosened its hold, falling to the floor in loose coils. Hettie, panicked, glanced between the reptile on the ground and the man in the doorway who was suddenly eyeing her with a much different look, one of rapt fascination.

"Very interesting," he hummed as he, too, looked at the snake on the ground.

She could hear bottles and charms rattling on shelves as she passed them, backing slowly away from this intense stranger. She was losing control, rapidly, and if she stayed here she might bring the whole shop down around her.

"You need to go," she told him shakily, "It's for your own good."

"I don't think I will," he followed her step for step, skirting the snake on the floor, "I came here for answers and found them, plus much more."

There was a snap of glass and the hiss of potions oozing out of their bottles and dripping down shelves. Hettie took a choked breath and decided that taking a risk was better than destroying the entire shop. If she could get out into the street, she could probably lose him in the crowd. She spun around and ran. She darted around the counter and pushed through the curtain into the back room. Before she could reach the back door, a hand clamped around her arm, yanking her back.

She was thrust bodily into the work table and bent over it, one hand capturing her wrists and pinning them on the table, the other holding her down by the shoulder. Sparks fountained from her hands, leaving scorch-marks on the wood where they landed, yet they skittered harmlessly over this stranger's skin.

"What are you?" Hettie panted. Her glasses dug into the bridge of her nose, pressed upward by her cheek mashed to the tabletop.

"Are you done running?" the stranger growled, ignoring her question. He grunted, twitching behind her, and irate clucking accompanied by the sound of buffeting wings filled the room.

"Please don't hurt her!" Hettie cried. What was Cordelia thinking? She was a little chicken, and this was a huge, scary man.

"Is this thing your pet?" he asked. She didn't answer. She could feel the bitter tang of magic in her mouth and was afraid of what might come out if she did. He sighed, lifting the hand from her shoulder. There was the sound of squeaky hinges, and then the muffling of Didi's noises as this man shut her in a nearby cabinet.

"What do you want from me?" She couldn't hold the words back anymore, and they came out half-sob. Green flames spewed from her lips, spraying across the wooden work table. She gasped, flinching at the lick of heat against her face.

"You have no control over this, do you?" His voice was thoughtful as he ran his free hand over the flames, collecting them in his palm before closing his fist and extinguishing them. All that was left was a burn on the table and an acrid curl of smoke.

"How are you not injured?" Her voice shook but was blessedly free of flame. The magic had been expressed for the moment.

"My ilk are resistant to most magics, and the kind you're using tends to invigorate us."

"The kind *I'm* using?" she squeaked. Was this not just her normal magic going haywire? Whatever it was, it felt like a colony of ants crawling under her skin, and it was going to break free if things continued in this manner. It collected in the places where his hands touched her, the ants condensing and buzzing like wasps. Her magic was turning inward and was building inside her.

Yet all of the outward effects had ceased. The cabinets had stopped rattling, and the rows of jars above her head were silent. It was like his touch contained it, even if it was overflowing from her. She could feel it pressing in on her even now, constricting her consciousness. Her vision was starting to narrow.

"I don't have control," she gasped, finally answering his earlier question.

"Relax," his voice sounded both very close and far away, like he was speaking through water right next to her ear, "I think I can help you."

She didn't have time to decide if she believed him, because no sooner had he spoken the words than she lost control of her body. She felt herself go slack seconds before the darkness closed in over her.

Gyl caught the girl as she collapsed, scooping her up and laying her out on the table gently.

Things had gotten out of hand. He hadn't meant to frighten her, but she was going to harm herself or someone else if she kept running with her magic leaking all over the place like that.

Gyl tucked a wayward curl back under her red scarf, stroking her cheek gently with the back of his hand. Their skin was almost the same color, hers a slightly lighter shade of tawny brown, his with an undertone of gold from his dragon coloring. She was quite plump, and, judging by the way her clothing settled around her, generous of flesh in all his favorite places. Perched on the curved bridge of her nose was a pair of round, gold-rimmed spectacles, knocked askew in their struggle. He straightened them for her. And then he took a moment to examine the bit that most intrigued him.

The arm.

Her right arm was made of brass. Interlocking plates with delicate hinges and wires threaded through them to help them function – a limb construct, not unlike the ones he made himself, though this one was solely function, with no decoration to speak of. He bunched up her sleeve on that arm, to examine where metal met flesh just above the elbow. Peeking above the juncture were threads of scar tissue where her original injury had healed.

What a fascinating, delightful creature.

The moment she'd opened the door, that nagging tug in his chest had ceased. *She* was what he'd been called back here for, and he had some idea why. That call had likely been hounding him since his first visit to this shop, but he'd been so dead to the world that he hadn't noticed it – and probably wouldn't have cared if he had.

This magic was of the very old variety, brimming with chaos energy. He hadn't heard tale of someone who could wield magic like this in some time, let alone in quantities this large. He thought they'd all vanished long ago. The energy flaring within her had settled down, but when he touched her he could still feel it, swirling beneath the surface. She was saturated, inundated with it, and she had no way to regulate it. How long had this been going on? Since that day he'd bought the trap? Before that even? He violently wished he had paid attention last time he was here. He could have saved her a lot of grief.

Additionally, how hadn't he noticed how pretty she was when he was here before? She had a soft, round face when she wasn't frowning, and her hair was a fan of raven curls loose enough to loop easily around his large fingers with room to spare. When he took a deep breath, he caught the smell of sage, cloves, and woodsmoke beneath the acrid scent of her fear, fading quickly now that she was unconscious.

Maybe it wasn't just the magic in her that called him back.

Gyl didn't know what to do. He couldn't just leave her here, not like this. She was a danger in her current state. She needed to be taught to control it, by someone who wouldn't be harmed by it.

She might not choose to go with him once she woke, not after he'd scared her like that. He thought guiltily about how he'd pinned her against the table. She hadn't deserved that, but he'd panicked, and he was out of practice dealing with humans.

You did just fine flirting with Rose, he scolded himself. But that was different, almost reflexive. She'd lost her fear of him in an instant and had been much easier to handle. This girl... goddess, he didn't even know her name. But he was determined to help her, whether she wanted it or not.

He'd just take her, then. While she was out. He could make up for it later. He hoped. Probably.

A noise below him jerked him to his senses. The chicken, throwing a fit in the cupboard. He opened the door, only to be accosted by a flurry of feathers and a buffeting of beak and claws.

"Easy now, bird," Gyl huffed with exasperation, "I'm not going to hurt her." He captured the hen easily, pinning her wings to her sides with both hands so she couldn't hurt herself. He held her facing him, and peered down into her little beady eyes.

Now that he knew what to look for, he could feel the threads of that chaos magic thrumming through the little body. Whatever she was now, she had once been something else, that much he knew. Exactly what, he couldn't tell, but he had a feeling it was one of the variety of creatures that walked upon two legs.

"I'm taking her with me, for her own safety." He felt a little silly talking to a chicken, but it was worth a shot. "I want to help her. You can come, if you like, but either way I expect you to behave and stop pecking me, alright?"

He tested his theory by setting the hen down. She stood there, staring up at him and clucking indignantly, but she did, in fact, stop assaulting his ankles.

Gyl scooped up the girl once more. Her plumpness may have been a challenging heft for a human man, but he carried the strength of his dragon shape even in his mortal form. Her frame was an easy lift for him. He brought her back up into the front of the shop and paused at the counter. The snake had slithered off somewhere, and there was a growing puddle of potions on the floor.

This could be dangerous for the little bird. He turned to see if the chicken was following. She was, right on his heels. He knelt, still holding the girl, and settled her on his thighs for a moment.

"Given the unidentified puddle of magic potion on the

ground, and the missing scaly friend, perhaps you'd better hitch a ride out to my carriage, hm?"

The chicken gave a thoughtful little coo, then flapped her wings and took a giant hop. Gyl flinched when her wings buffeted his face, but she wasn't attacking him, merely finding a perch on his broad shoulder. He could feel her claws prick his skin as she settled down.

"Right. Hold on tight."

His carriage was right outside. If he was quick, and acted naturally, he could get to it and get it rolling before anyone even questioned what was happening. The bustle of the festival picking up would be enough of a distraction.

He didn't give himself time to think about it. He shouldered the door open, walking briskly but not running to where his carriage waited.

The construct opened the door for him, and as he set the girl on one of the benches he barked, "Home, quickly!"

He heard someone shout behind him, but the carriage was already rocking forward as he pulled the door shut.

The chicken hopped to the free seat, and Gyl lifted the girl's head so he could sit with her top half propped in his lap. He told himself it was so he could hold her steady on the trip home, but there was the added perk of feeling her body pressed against his. He watched out the back window, looking for suspicious activity.

They were not followed.

4

Hettie woke in a cloud. There was sunshine warming her face, and she was practically floating in an abundance of soft white bedding, feeling practically weightless.

When she cracked her eyes, a little feathered head hovered over her face.

"Cordelia?" she croaked. At the sight of the chicken, the memory of the night before came rushing back to her. She sat bolt upright, knocking Didi aside. She squawked angrily at being nearly knocked over, but Hettie righted her quickly, patting her until she settled.

Hettie squinted at her fuzzy surroundings and realized she wasn't wearing her glasses. She spotted their gold glint on the table beside the bed and crushed them onto her nose, blinking as the world came into focus.

She was still in her shopgirl uniform, sans the headscarf,

which was also on the bedside table. She felt a flush of relief that she had maintained at least that bit of privacy.

The room was made of stone, bare of much but functional furniture – bed, end table, wardrobe – though both the bed and the window were draped with sheer white-on-white embroidered curtains. There were two doors, one slightly open that led to a bathroom, and one closed that must be an exit.

"Where are we?" she asked Didi, knowing she couldn't answer, "And how did we get here?"

Hettie scooted to the edge of the bed, dangling her bare feet over the side. Her toes sank into a plush fur rug that covered the floor beside the bed. It was soft as a rabbit, but she'd never seen a rabbit as big as this pelt.

There came a knock on the door. It swung open before Hettie could call out. Through the doorway sidled a form in a robe, carrying a tray. The robe was soft green velvet, embroidered in places with flowers and vines in cream and gold. Where its limbs poked out of the sleeves, the sun from the window glinted off bright silver panels decorated with swirling flowers done in enamel paint. As it grew closer, Hettie could see its face under the hood was a flat mask of flowers in the same style, with no discernible facial features.

A construct, and a very artfully done one at that. Hettie could faintly feel against her skin the hum of the magic that propelled it as it set the laden tray down on the side table.

The smell wafted up over Hettie, and her stomach let out an empty rumble. The tray was full of food - fluffy eggs, bacon, oatmeal studded with fruit, pastries, and two pitchers of juice. It was entirely too much food for her alone.

"Thank you," she told it reflexively. It nodded before

shuffling over to the bathroom door. It disappeared inside, and a moment later Hettie heard the sound of running water.

Hettie was still a little groggy, but now she was thoroughly confused. Her last memory was of being captured by that stranger, and now she was being pampered.

Had she had a complete meltdown before she passed out? Did the university come to collect her? She had no idea where she was, let alone who'd rescued her from that feral stranger.

I think I can help you.

Maybe it wasn't the university that had come for her.

Uneasiness aside, she was being well taken care of for the moment. Not to mention whoever it was had the consideration to bring Didi along. Hettie tipped some of the oatmeal into another dish and put it down on the bed for the bird to pick and peck at it. Hettie ate her fill, and by the time she was full, the construct was waiting patiently in the doorway with a towel over its arm. When Hettie set her plate aside to let Didi peck at the rest, it beckoned her forward.

She didn't see the harm in it. Why feed her and let her recover in a soft, warm bed if they had nefarious plans for her, right? She followed the construct into the bathroom, and was immediately surrounded by the sweet scent of bath oils. The bathroom was much larger than she'd anticipated, with a huge round bathtub and sink shaped like scalloped shells.

The tub was already full of steaming water. Hettie stripped eagerly, excited to sink into a tub large enough for her round frame. The water was heavenly, just the perfect temperature. It was a little awkward that the construct hovered nearby, folding her clothing and laying out new garments for her, but she got over that quickly as it seemed to be politely ignoring her. It was hard to mind when the hot water had her feeling boneless. She hadn't had a bath so nice in... probably ever. The amenities in her lodging above the magic shop were nice enough, but a bath just wasn't as relaxing as it should be with your love handles squeezed by cold porcelain and your knees poking up into the chilly air.

When she'd had a chance to soap and soak the amount she desired, she stood in the tub, windy water cascading down her brown skin. The construct held out a towel for her, and as she secured it under her armpits, it took a wide-toothed comb and gently separated her abundance of curls. It was completely unnecessary, as she was more than capable of doing it herself, but she wasn't complaining. She had a lot of hair, and taking care of it was always so much work. She didn't have any of her usual hair products, so it was likely to dry a little wild regardless of the way it was cared for wet.

After that, the construct shook out the dress it had brought and held it out to her. It was a simple wrap dress, with a tie on the inside and outside. Likely it was the easiest way to ensure she had something that fit her without knowing her measurements. It wasn't her usual style, but the fabric was lovely and soft, and the blush color looked quite pretty against her brown skin.

Overall she was feeling quite relaxed and pampered, but that faded instantly when she stepped back into the bedroom.

Posted up in the doorway to the hall was a familiar dark-haired, four-horned man.

"I supposed this confirms the identity of my rescuer," Hettie remarked blandly. She could feel her shoulders tightening back up. "Or should I say abductor?"

The stranger's golden eyes flashed, "Are you done freaking out now?"

"Are you done assaulting me?" she quipped back, folding her arms. Her temper was flaring, and with it she could feel the buzz of magic start to burn.

The stranger looked at her for a long moment before he shook his head and said, "I apologize. I handled that situation at the shop poorly. I didn't mean to frighten you."

Her next retort died in her throat. Hettie was a little surprised he capitulated so easily, but she supposed she shouldn't have been. She didn't even know this man, after all.

"What did you mean to do?" Hettie asked levelly. She wouldn't give him any credit until he earned it. He had, after all, still pinned her against the table against her will.

"Stop you from running." He shrugged. "I was afraid you were going to hurt someone if you got away."

I would have, she thought to herself grimly. She'd never felt so out of control. She'd also never transformed an item when she was panicked before, only destroyed them.

"Did that broom actually turn into a snake? It wasn't just an illusion, or a hallucination?"

"Yes, it did," the stranger confirmed simply.

Hettie bit down on one knuckle absently, anxiously. That sort of magic was – *should have been* – impossible. Transmuting one substance or object to another of the same type was difficult, changing an organic item to a non-organic one even harder, but both were in the realm of the possible. A non-living item into a live creature? Unheard of.

"Who even are you?" Hettie noticed her fingertips were

numb when she dug her fingers into her arms. Her palms stung and itched with wild energy.

"Yes, I suppose a formal introduction is rather overdo, isn't it? My name is Gylharen, and I'm the Golden Dragon of Death's Maw." He flashed her a fluid wink. "But if you like me, you can call me Gyl."

"Gylharen," she rolled the name over in her mouth, testing it. It was rather regal sounding, especially compared to hers. The second part of what he said came to slow awareness in her brain. Fear opened the sluice of her magic a little more, and it pooled in her belly like lava. "Wait, we're up in the *Maw*?"

Easily the most dangerous mountain range in Cilirien, Hettie had heard all kinds of stories about the creatures that lurked in the peaks that shadowed the horizon of her home city, Serpent's Bay.

"Easy, now," Gyl's voice was a low, smoky hum, "I'm the most dangerous thing on the mountain. There'll be no rocs or manticores slipping into your bedroom at night. Your name?"

"I'm Hettie, junior apprentice at *Pollimer's Potions* and chronic danger to herself and others, apparently." She tried not to sound too bitter about that, or to let her voice shake too much.

"Hettie," a syrupy-slow smile revealed wickedly sharp canines, "I like it. It's sweet."

Why did that send a burst of fluttering butterflies straight to her belly? It sent the scorching magic sunk there swirling, for certain.

"What am I doing here?" Hettie swallowed hard, her mouth suddenly dry.

Gyl raked one hand through his silver hair, "I brought you here."

"That much I gathered," Hettie shoved her glasses up her nose impatiently.

"You were like a bomb, Hettie. If I'd left you to your own devices once I'd startled you, you might have blown up your shop's entire inventory. I brought you here to keep you contained."

"That was very kind of you," Hettie told him uncertainly, "but I'm sure Crystal must be worried sick. I left such a mess behind. I'm responsible for cleaning it up. It's the least I can do when I have an episode."

"They'll have to manage on their own." Gyl's golden-scaled tail whisked behind him.

Those words set Hettie's teeth on edge. Something that was not entirely anxiety swirled in her belly. "What do you mean?"

"I can't let you go back there," his voice was a low rumble.

"You can't just keep me here against my will," Hettie backed up a step and collided with the cold, hard chest of the construct exiting the bathroom behind her. It braced her to keep her from overcorrecting, and kept its hands on her shoulders. It was likely just assisting her, but it felt like it was pinning her, trapping her.

"I have to, Hettie," Gyl prowled forward. The closer he got, the clearer their height difference became. He towered over her, likely somewhere in the neighborhood of seven feet, peering down his nose at her. His black shirt was incredibly low cut, almost down to his navel, and as he walked it gaped open. She could see the hard shadows outlining the planes of his chest.

"Why?" she demanded with a gulp, dragging her eyes back up to his face. That wave of magic in her belly rose like the tide.

"You're a danger to yourself and others." He mimicked her words from earlier, speaking in soft tones that didn't quite work to soothe her, "We have to keep you contained."

"So, what," Hettie clenched her fists to keep her hands from shaking, "I'm just your prisoner now?" Beside them, the curtains on the bed started to flutter as if in a breeze.

"Calm down, Hettie," Gyl urged as the movement caught his eye, "It's only temporary."

"Until when?" Behind her, back in the bathroom, she heard jars rattling on shelves.

"Until you have better control." He held his hands out placatingly.

"So, indefinitely," Hettie hissed. She shrugged off the construct and stepped towards the bed, the curtains whipping like they were caught in a maelstrom now. Her control had only been slipping, no matter what she tried lately. There had been no improvement. If he was keeping her here until she could handle her magic again, she'd never get to leave.

"You need to trust me, Hettie. I can help you." He waved the construct out of the room. It's robe twisted wildly around its legs, nearly tripping it as it hurried to obey.

"Trust you?" She huffed a humorless laugh, "What have you done thus far that would lead me to trust you?"

"Hettie-" he began, but she was tired of stuffing down her temper to keep her magic contained. She whirled on him.

"First you chase me through the shop, then you pin me to the work table and hold me until I pass out. No introduction or explanation of who you are!" She unleashed her voice, shouting at him now. In the bathroom, a chorus of shattering glass tore the air. The panes in the windows behind her rattled. "Then, while I'm unconscious, you abduct me, drag me to the top of the most dangerous mountains in Cilirien, and now you tell me you won't allow me to leave! Did I miss the part where you did something trustworthy?"

"Settle down, witch," Gyl growled the warning, lip lifting in a snarl.

"Or what," Hettie snapped, "you'll lock me in my room? Send me to the dungeon?" Sparks dripped from her fingertips, flames licked at her lips. She could taste the bitter tang of sulfur and bile, her magic truly out of control.

"Or you might not like what I have to do." Gyl took a step towards her.

Hettie gulped, her anger swamped for a second by trepidation. It was a vague statement with ominous consequences, but she'd sent the boulder of her ire rolling down the hill already, her magic rushing like a river in its wake, and there was no stopping it now.

"Try me," she snarled right back, "I won't bow to my jailer."

Gyl moved so quickly that Hettie was caught off guard. He took two quick steps into her space and snapped one hand up. Hettie flinched, expecting a strike that never came. Instead, he laid the length of it on her chest, along her collarbones, the dip in her throat just above the crease where his thumb met his palm. His touch was firm, but not violent. He pushed her roughly into the post of the bed, pinning her back to it with that unyielding hand.

"If I wanted you to bow, witch, I have much better methods

at my disposal," he growled. "This is about your *safety*, you stubborn thing."

Stunned, Hettie didn't even resist, her hands limp at her sides. Everything stopped all at once: the rattling, the whipping fabric, the sparks. It was like his touch had trapped the magic inside her, and she could feel it swirling and buzzing in her chest, against his palm.

The two of them stood in silence, panting heavily. A stream of smoke puffed from his angular nose when he let out a heavy exhale.

"I would never put my hands on you in anger," his voice was soft now, velvety, "please be assured of that. I would not have done so at all without your permission, not again, except I noticed in the shop that my touch quiets the magic." His eyes were glued to where his hand touched her. His skin was hot but dry, warm against the uppermost swells of her breasts. He bent his elbow so he could close the distance between their bodies.

"It does," she agreed, swallowing hard. "Sort of." She wasn't about to argue that it wasn't quiet, just contained, not with him in her space like this. He was so close that her heavy breaths stirred the sable curtain of hair that fell over his shoulder. His scent washed over her, charcoal and smoke and cinnamon.

Goddess, but he was attractive. Hettie had always liked a partner that could take charge and follow through, and despite her whirlwind of emotions, her body was reacting to his touch and proximity. Her nipples pebbled against her stays, and she could feel her pussy grow wet. She hadn't been given underwear, so her arousal quickly slicked her thighs as she fidgeted in his hold.

How good was a dragon's sense of smell? Judging by the

way his nostrils flared, and his eyes flicked down her body, Gyl noticed her arousal. A smirk flickered at the corner of his mouth.

"Take a deep breath," he told her gently, his thumb swirling circles against her collarbone, "Try to calm your emotions. We don't want you passing out again. You were out for nearly ten hours the last time."

"How am I supposed to calm down," her tongue flicked over her bottom lip, "when all I can think about is your hand on my throat?" She felt her face burn as soon as the words left her mouth. Had she really said that? That should have been an *inside* thought, Hettie. This man was a stranger! She didn't need to be handing him her kinks on a silver platter.

Another curl of smoke escaped Gyl's mouth and his slit pupils blew wide until they were almost circular. "Do you want me to put my hand on your throat, little witch?"

He slid his hand smoothly up the column of her throat until his fingers and thumb rested on either side. She was sure he could feel the pounding of her pulse. A rush of magic swirled under his hand with the movement, and she squeezed her eyes shut, struggling to breathe around it.

"It's too much," she wheezed, "I can't control it."

"Don't fight the magic, Hettie," goddess the way he said her name was like a sultry, gentle promise, "let it come to me."

"I don't know how," she choked, tears leaking from beneath her closed lids.

"Look at me, little witch," that hand pressed gently, tilting her head back. When she opened her eyes, his gold ones caught hers and held them captive. "You can do this. Say it."

"Say what?" The magic was making her mind fuzzy.

"*I can do this*. Repeat it." His voice was gentle, but it was not a request.

"I can do this." It was a release to obey, to let him steer her, to let herself trust what he was saying.

"Good girl. Now, this isn't your everyday witchery. This is chaos magic. The tighter you grip it, the wilder it gets. It wants to come to me, so just... let it go."

Easier said than done, she thought bitterly. She started to look away from him, to hide her doubt, but a gentle squeeze to her throat brought her eyes snapping back to his.

She took in a deep, struggling breath, eyes unfocused on the gold coins of his gaze, and imagined loosening her hold on her magic, like a hand releasing a ball finger by finger.

"Just relax."

"Working on it," she huffed.

"You're tensing up," he told her drily.

"I'm *trying*."

"Well try something different," he crooned, still keeping his cool despite the fact that Hettie had a hurricane brewing under her skin at the moment. The edges of her vision were going black again.

So, Hettie did, try something different, that is. She thought of the way all her muscles loosened in that bath. She pictured instead that sensation, but the thing her magic was sinking into was Gyl instead of a bathtub.

And it *worked*.

There was a release, like when your ears pop in a high-pressure system, and all the magic threatening to overwhelm her whooshed out of her. It swirled around Gyl's arm in streaks of flashing blue and green and sunk in through his skin. Gyl finally broke their eye contact, throwing his head back and groaning in something akin to ecstasy.

As if Hettie needed more fuel for her still-flaming libido.

"Marvelous, Hettie," he praised her with a gasping breath, "I knew you could do it. Now next time let's see if we can release it before it builds up so much." He dropped his hand from her throat, and Hettie was surprised to note she was almost disappointed when their contact was broken.

"It's going to take me a while to get used to," Hettie groused, "I've spent my whole life practicing and perfecting rigid control."

"No wonder your magic is rebelling if you've been keeping it in a chokehold," he said thoughtfully, his breathing returning to normal.

Hettie wasn't sure why she bristled at that, "It's how all my magic tutors taught me, and it's what they expect at the university."

"Yes," he agreed amiably, "for *normal* magicians, one of which you are not."

"I didn't know that," she grumbled, glaring at the stone between their feet.

"How could you?" He lifted her chin so she was forced to meet his gaze, to see his softening smile, "I'm sure your magic manifested just the same as everyone else's for a long while, correct?"

"Yes." Why did his touch light such a fire in her? It was innocent enough at the moment, and yet her core was absolutely quivering. At the barest mention of sex she'd sit up and beg like a dog. What was wrong with her?

"So you had no way of knowing. But do you see now why I need you to stay here?" He dropped his hand.

Hettie nodded reluctantly. As much as she hated feeling confined, he could keep her contained during her episodes. Even if he agreed to go back to town with her and stay nearby, if he didn't catch her in time someone could still get hurt. As far as she knew, there was nobody else here.

"Good girl," he purred at her before squatting down. He angled his head, peering under the bed. "You can come out now, little bird."

Hettie gasped, hand flying to her mouth, "Cordelia! Oh, I am so sorry, Didi! Are you okay?"

The speckled chicken waddled out from under the bed, settling her ruffled feathers. She gave Hettie a judgmental cluck, but she allowed being picked up and fussed over without a single peck.

"I'd be interested in hearing how that happened," Gyl inclined his head toward Didi.

"You know...? T-that she's..." Hettie was stunned.

"Not actually a chicken? Yes." He gave her a fanged smile. "So spill it."

Hettie let out a long-suffering sigh, "It's a complicated story." Not to mention embarrassing.

"Let's hear it. We're not going anywhere anytime soon. We've got nothing but time."

Hettie eyed him for a long moment, though she could feel herself begrudgingly folding to his whim. She wanted to hate him, wanted to maintain the flames of anger at him for whisking her away from everything she knew and loved in her old life, but she found it hard to pin him with the blame when her old life had been slowly crumbling away for the past two years. Piece by piece, everything she loved, everything that brought her joy or even peace, had been methodically taken from her in an effort to help her keep her magic under control. If anything, Gyl was offering her a chance to get it all back.

Besides, it was hard to hold a grudge against a man who'd managed to completely arouse her with just a hand on her throat. Her cunt still ached with unsatisfied desire.

Reluctantly, Hettie began, "Well, it started at Oros's Festival, almost exactly two years ago..."

5

Gyl sat across from Hettie on the bed, gaping at her in stunned disbelief.

"You're telling me you'd never had a climax before Cordelia?"

"I-well..." Hettie fidgeted, said chicken in her lap, "I thought I had? I guess they just weren't very good ones."

A growl rumbled up in his chest, "They've done you a disservice then." He'd never have allowed her to leave a coupling so unsatisfied, had he had the lucky privilege of being her bedfellow.

"Probably," she shrugged, shoving her glasses up her nose, "but their incompetence saved them from me, in the end."

Gyl glanced down at Didi. He may have been imagining it, but he could have sworn that chicken looked smug.

He refused to be jealous of a chicken.

He wanted the witch, badly. The smell of her arousal during their confrontation had nearly overwhelmed him. He likely could have taken her then and there and she would have allowed it, but he needed to take his time. She was in an incredibly compromised position here. She was stuck in proximity to him for the safety of herself and others. He may be out of touch, but even he knew that it would be unfair for him to pursue her as aggressively as he wanted to. He needed to give her some time - and space, but he was unlikely to be able to tolerate that one.

She soothed that bizarre longing, searching feeling burrowed in his chest. He gave her some space for the duration of the night while she was unconscious and as long as he could tolerate in the morning, but even being as far as the other side of the castle resumed that aching, tugging sensation in his chest. Now that he was by her side again, he was finally getting some relief.

Not to mention that burst of magic he'd absorbed from her felt incredible. The very blood in his veins was still thrumming with the last threads of that power. He hadn't felt this energized in a long time.

"So, you know something about what's happening to me?" Her voice was small but hopeful.

"I know *what* it is but I don't know *why*." He reached out and snagged her left hand, giving it a gentle squeeze. "Once we get your magic under control, we can visit one of my elders and see if they have any ideas."

"I was supposed to be seen by the university soon." Hettie glanced over at the window, stroking Didi's head absently.

Gyl had had dealings with the Arcane University in the past.

In fact, one of the senior mages there had enchanted several of his constructs. He doubted they'd be able to do more than observe her.

"Fie on the university," he huffed, a curl of smoke escaping from his nose, "This magic is ancient. There's not a mage among them old enough to recognize it."

"How old are *you*?" She frowned at him, the glare on her glasses partially obscuring her expression.

"Hmm," he considered her question. He hadn't paid attention to the passing of the years for some time. It occurred to him he didn't actually know how old he was anymore. "What year was the fall of Ozark the Conquerer?"

"Gylharen!" She snatched her hand away, gaping at him.

"What?" His eyes widened in genuine confusion.

"That's over two hundred years ago!"

"Was it? Well, I was born fifty years before that."

"*Two-hundred and fifty?*"

"There are dragons much older than that," he chuckled, "By dragon standards I'm still a youngster."

"How long do dragons live?"

"A very long time." He shrugged. He'd never heard of a dragon dying of old age. Usually they died in battle, or were killed, or ended things themselves when life became too much to bear – he'd probably been on the road to that ending for a while, and maybe would have already done so if he still had access to his beast form. It was with a spark of gratitude that he realized that wasn't his reality anymore. At least for the short term, he had a purpose and a reason to participate in the world again.

"And we're going to see one of these very old dragons at some point?"

"Yes," he agreed, though it occurred to him that was going to be difficult in his current state. They couldn't exactly take a carriage to any of the elders' dens, particularly not the one he thought would be most helpful, his uncle's. How could he possibly explain that to her?

"Can I at least send word to my bosses, so they don't worry about me?" Hettie chewed her lip thoughtfully.

Gyl considered his response carefully. The last thing he wanted was to rip her away from everything familiar. He wasn't actually trying to be her jailer, after all. He did, however, have some genuine concerns. He needed her to see things his way, rather than trying to make demands of her.

"I won't stop you if that's what you want to do," he told her slowly, "but any word you send them will make you easier to trace. If they care about you, and from the way you talk about them I can tell that they do, they'll do everything in their power to find you, and that could be dangerous for them."

"You're right," Hettie groaned. She pushed her glasses up to rub her eyes. "I just don't want to cause them any grief."

"Because you care about them too." Gyl was not unsympathetic. She was in a tough position.

"They've been good to me," she sniffed, her eyes red rimmed when she lowered her hand.

Oh, no. Please don't cry, he thought desperately. He didn't think he could handle it. How did one manage tears? He was clueless. He'd been so angry on her behalf at the shop when she looked like she'd been crying. There was no one to blame here, no easy solution to the problem that was upsetting her, and that made him feel like the earth had fallen out from under his feet.

"Come," he held out his hand, scrambling for something to distract her, "would you like to see the rest of the castle?"

"*Castle?*" That seemed to have done the trick, her incredulity overriding her grief.

"Did I forget to mention?" He flashed her one of his cheeky, smoldering smirks, and she rolled her eyes, not quite hiding the blush in her cheeks.

Fucking precious.

"I was just kidding about the dungeon thing," she huffed, "I didn't know you actually lived in a castle."

"Come see. Come, come." He stood, beckoning her to follow him with both hands, holding them out to her. With only a little reluctance, she took them, and Gyl took her out into the heart of his home.

Gyl had shown her the kitchen, the dining room, the ballroom, the sitting room, the library, the indoor pool, the observatory, and six empty bedrooms, each decorated in a different color scheme. From the sheer size of this place, she didn't think that was even the half of it.

She'd expected it to be impressive, and it certainly was that. What she hadn't expected was for it to be so *sad*.

It was all so... empty. Their footsteps echoed as they walked, their voices bouncing back to them from all around. There truly was nobody else in the entire castle, just more metal constructs like the one that had tended to her that morning. It was pristine from floor to ceiling, but it looked completely un-lived in. Even the kitchen, which must be used regularly, was sparse and bare, with nary a dirty pan in sight.

The place was practically silent. Hettie didn't realize just how used to noise she'd become until she'd experienced a complete lack of it. Where was the ambient, incessant street noise? The periodic clamor of the shop bells? The shrill screeching of the senior apprentices bickering over nonsense? This place was devoid of all signs of life, except for the ones they made as they moved from room to room.

"So then, all that's left is... Well, you probably wouldn't want to see," Gyl rumbled thoughtfully.

"What is it?" Hettie peered up at him as they walked, hands thrust deep in the pockets she had joyfully discovered in the dress shortly after donning it.

"No, I don't think so. It's a mess in there," Gyl hedged.

"*Where*?" Hettie cried, exasperated. She didn't miss the little flicker of amusement across Gyl's face.

"It's my workshop," Gyl chuckled, then looked uncertain again, "but it's messy. I've not been taking very good care of it."

Curiosity was eating Hettie alive. She was dying to know what the spaces this man actually *lived* in looked like. Surely they wouldn't all be cold and lifeless.

"I don't mind," she assured him, "but if it bothers you..."

"No, it's fine." He shook his head. "I don't want to keep things hidden from you."

Hettie stopped in her tracks, stunned at the sudden

sweetness of that sentiment. She didn't think she'd ever had anyone be so candidly sincere with her, and she didn't even know him.

"What is it?" he asked, brow furrowed, when he realized she'd fallen behind.

"N-nothing," Hettie tucked her chin, adjusting her glasses to hide her expression.

"Come along, then." He held out his hand expectantly. Confused and uncertain what else he might want, Hettie laid her hand in his. He grasped it tightly and tugged her along, his palm hot against her skin. If he were anyone else, she'd worry he had a fever.

"Is that a dragon thing?" she mused aloud, scrambling to add, "The heat, I mean."

He swiveled his head to peer at her, that constant, simmering smirk on his face, "The heat between us?"

Hettie's face flamed. "Your *body* heat," she choked.

"So you think I'm hot?"

"*Gylharen*," she laughed.

"Sorry," he chuckled, "I didn't mean to embarrass you."

"Yes, you did," Hettie grumbled, though she couldn't quite keep from smiling. Gyl just grinned and pulled her into his side as they walked. If she'd thought his hand was hot then being pressed into him, beneath his arm, was like sitting beside a furnace.

He took her down a flight of stairs and to a set of double doors – two sets, rather, set across the hall from each other. Without preamble, he pushed through the doors on the right, holding them open for Hettie to follow.

Inside was, well, a mess. He hadn't been lying about that.

It took Hettie a moment to sort out all the visual noise in the room. There were several work surfaces, all of them cluttered with bits and bobs: spools of wire, gears, a collection of tools with unknown purposes, flat metal pieces, and dozens of partially constructed contraptions. The floor was cluttered with larger parts, frames holding wire armatures, and chests filled with more tools and pieces. The room was fairly dim, lit with strings of fairy lights that flickered to life as they stepped into the room. Some of the magic-brightened bulbs shone through filigreed shells, casting light through them like sunlight scattered through leaves of a tree.

In the corner, hidden behind a table until she'd stepped far enough inside, was a nest-like pile of cushions and blankets. Hung by hooks from the ceiling was a tented drape that covered the edges of the nest, open at the front like a cave. Hettie looked at Gyl quizzically.

"I've been sleeping in here," he told her almost sheepishly. "It started when I crashed in here once or twice after working late into the night, and after a while it just became habit, I suppose. Though I haven't even touched any of my projects lately." He rubbed the back of his neck and shrugged.

Hettie walked over to the mouth of the little nest. It was larger than it looked from the outside, roughly circular and large enough that Gyl could have laid down at any angle and fit. There was enough room in there for her to join him, even.

Not that that was on her mind.

When she stepped closer, that cinnamon and smoke smell intensified. Would it be nice to fall asleep wrapped in that scent?

There was no sense of order to the pile, just cushions and

blankets tossed in there pell-mell. She caught sight of several shiny things that looked like metal tools, what looked like the hose from a hookah pipe, discarded articles of clothing, a red rubber ball, and... gross. She bent down and picked up a cup that was nestled between two long pillows, face crinkling when the dregs at the bottom didn't move when she tipped it.

Gyl cleared his throat and tugged the cup from her hand. "I did say it was a mess in here."

She thought she'd feel better after finding somewhere in the castle that seemed lived in, but this room had the feeling of being lost, of someone set on a path they could not see the end of.

She thought of that summer that Nastia had been dumped by the jeweler on the next street over. She'd spent weeks holed up in her room, alone, and every time they checked in on her, every surface was covered with old food, crumpled letters, spilled cosmetics, and empty alcohol bottles. It had accumulated, so she had said, because she hadn't had the energy to take care of herself, let alone the room. It was more than just being sad. She'd been paralyzed by the dark feelings, like a weight on her chest pinning her down. The mess had bothered her, she told them, but it had just been another shitty thing to make her feel bad at the time. If it weren't for his constructs, Hettie thought Gyl's entire workshop would look just the same.

"How long have you been alone, Gylharen?" Hettie asked softly as she turned from the mouth of the nest. She ran her fingers over the edge of a table, finding all the scratches and nicks from his work.

She heard his slow intake of breath, but he didn't answer her question.

Hettie turned to look at him, her curls bouncing over her shoulder, "Has it been that long?"

He looked so sunk in on himself, almost vulnerable. Gone was the cold, haughty façade he'd worn the day she'd first seen him in the shop. Gone, too, was the self-assured master of sexual prowess he'd been trying to be the past hour or so, so easily clutching her by the throat and mercilessly flirting with her during the entire tour. In its place was an open, injured expression, like she'd just pried open some secret part of him, and he expected her to cut into it. Or maybe more like a little boy preparing to be scolded for something that wasn't his fault.

Hettie couldn't stand to see him look at her that way. Compassion melted the last remnants of her anger and resentment. There was something about him that made her want to comfort him. Before she even realized she'd done it, she darted forward and wrapped her arms around his waist. She pressed her cheek to the hard muscles of his chest, feeling his deep rumble against her skin. He wrapped his arms around her, their heat banding her to him.

"Was it that obvious?" His voice was wry but a little choked, and when she didn't reply he just tightened his hold on her.

Even if it was the only thing she could offer, at least for the duration of her stay here, Hettie could be sure he'd never be alone. If he could fix her she'd be indebted, despite his little snatch and grab operation, and she'd owe him at least that much. She had no way of knowing if she could even help him in return, but she couldn't bear to leave him here alone after seeing what little she'd already seen.

It was while she was in the circle of his embrace that it actually registered what was on Gyl's tables. She spotted a metal arm first, flayed open down the middle with its inner workings on display. Propped against the same table was the framework for a torso, and on the stool was a foot with an ankle attached.

"Oh!" She exclaimed, leaning back to better see, though she didn't let Gyl go. "The constructs, do you make them yourself?"

"I do. The body of them, that is. I can't enchant them myself." He loosened his arms so he could turn her by the shoulders and steer her closer to the table, "Though as I said, I haven't worked on them for some time."

Hettie leaned over the arm on the table, gently manipulating the joints. They were incredibly smooth, gliding far better than her own right hand. Gyl tapped the witchlight over the table and pointed the shade so the halo of light illuminated the arm. Hettie gasped, unable to hide her enchantment.

In the better light, she could now see that the metal plates on the arm were etched with delicate images of leafy plants – just ordinary kitchen herbs, but ones she recognized nonetheless.

"An upgrade for one of my cooking constructs," Gyl offered by way of explanation.

"It's stunning," she told him breathlessly. "Absolutely impeccable work."

"I could make one for you," Gyl murmured the offer in her ear, his breath puffing over her cheek.

"I couldn't ask that of you," Hettie hedged, but seeing his work, it was suddenly her deepest desire to wear one of his pieces. Each façade piece was like a work of art, each inner working just as thoroughly tended. Sketches lined the walls above the tables, scraps of paper pinned to cork that gave her a glimpse into this man's true creative potential. Her mouth practically watered at the idea of owning an arm like that.

"Nonsense," he snorted, "It's no trouble."

"Even so..." she trailed off, hands lingering over the delicate details on each joint of the fingers.

"I can tell how much you want it, Hettie," he said, voice full of smoke. "You can't hide your covetous desires from a dragon."

She was all heat from the shoulders up. "Wanting it and deserving it are two different things. What would a nobody like me do with a piece like that? These are fit for a lady, a king even."

Gyl was frowning at her, his face tight. "These are my pieces. I decide who earns them. Anybody can wear them." She shook her head, and Gyl clucked his tongue against his teeth. "I decide who wears them, witch, not you. If I want to make you one, you'll wear it like a good girl, won't you?"

Hettie stared at him, mouth agape. How could he just whip that imperial tone out of nowhere and talk to her like that?

And why did she like it so much?

"I'll make you a deal." Gyl spoke when she didn't answer him. He cleared the stool and sat, drawing Hettie to stand between his knees.

"I'm listening," she told him as she tried not to think about how nice his thighs felt under her hand as she rested both of them just above his knees.

"I'll make the piece for you, and when you can enchant it yourself, we'll know you're ready to go home. Then the piece is half your artistry, and you don't have to worry about your ridiculous notion of 'deserving' it."

"That's complicated magic," Hettie bit her lip. She'd never been able to perform the animation spell that constructs used, not even the simpler version used to weld smaller pieces to living folk.

"You can do it."

"I've never managed it before." Her lack of ability with more complex magic was how she'd ended up at a potion shop and not pursuing further education with the Arcane University.

"You've never understood your magic before. Things will be different going forward." He sounded so sure.

"You don't know that."

"Yes, I do," he insisted stubbornly.

Hettie eyed him doubtfully, "How? You've barely known me a day."

"You've transformed a living girl into a chicken," he gestured above them, vaguely in the direction of the bedroom where they'd left Didi, "and, even more difficult, you've transformed a non-living broom into a perfectly alive snake. You can't tell me the construct animation is more difficult than that. Am I wrong?"

"No," Hettie admitted begrudgingly.

"If you can do all that by accident, just imagine what you're capable of once you've gained equilibrium. You can do this, Hettie. I am going to help you. Do we have a deal?"

She eyed him for a moment. He'd pulled another switch on her, that moment of vulnerability swapped out for the self-assured version of Gyl again.

She had no reason to trust him, except he could have done great harm to her and had only shown her kindness, despite their rough start. He'd offered her a glimpse into the vulnerable depths of his spirit, and she had already decided she was invested in keeping him afloat from those. Not to mention he'd been right about her magic every step of the way thus far. She had to believe he was right this time too.

"We have a deal," she agreed, fingers tightening ever so slightly on his thighs.

He got that sly look in his eyes again. "What if I told you dragons sealed their deals with a kiss?"

"I'd say you were a liar," Hettie chuckled.

"Maybe that's just me, then," he grinned at her, pointed fangs poking out.

"That sounds more like the truth." Hettie leaned forward, face tilted upward.

Something akin to panic flashed over his face. "I was teasing, Hettie. You don't have to."

"Oh." Hettie felt like a fool. He'd just been teasing her. She lifted her hands from his legs. Before she could step back from him, he snatched both her hands in his.

"Do not mistake me," his voice was a soft thunder, hanging in the air between them, "if I had no sense I'd pin you to this table and plunder your body for every sweet treasure it had to offer me." His eyes flashed as his pupils stretched wide. Hettie held her breath. "But I am not unaware that you're in a rather... *delicate* position here. I just want to be careful of your feelings."

"My *feelings* are not delicate," she quipped, though she didn't pull back against his grip. "I'm a big girl who's been making big girl choices for some time now."

"And scant hours ago we had a fight about whether or not you were technically a prisoner here," his wry tone was not lost on her, "pardon me if I'm being a little overly cautious so you don't feel like you have no option but to entertain my every whim."

He was worried about *pressuring* her? How... endearingly sweet that was. Though rather misguided. She'd not had a romantic encounter in two years, and being so close and flirty with this charming dragon had left her *hungry*.

"Less than a day ago," Hettie murmured huskily, "I thought I was destined to live a touch-starved, miserable existence. Suddenly, I find myself faced not only with an incredibly attractive male," his lip twitched at the compliment, "but one who is not only unharmed by my episodes, but seems nourished by them." Hettie could feel a little of the magic stirring with her agitation, but she was still too spent for it to rise to the surface, "Forgive me if I'm overly eager to acquiesce when it seems like he is perhaps a little interested in me."

The low growl that burst from him almost startled her, "More than a little, witch."

"Then quit fighting it and kiss me, *dragon*," she leaned forward again, heartened that she had not mistaken his interest before for a friendly tease.

He didn't hesitate this time, bringing his mouth down against hers. It was a soft kiss, sweet but not exploring, though he teased her with a gentle nip of her bottom lip as they split.

"Now, little witch, there is just one more thing left for you to see," he told her as he finally released her hands.

"What's that?"

"My hoard."

6

Every dragon had a hoard, though not all of them contained just the usual precious metals and gems. One of his elders, his uncle, had a hoard composed almost entirely of books. His own mother collected intricate textile and needlework pieces, from tiny hoop embroideries to massive tapestries. A dragon's hoard was personal to each dragon, and they lived long enough to amass incredible stashes of wealth in addition to each of their special collections.

Gyl collected a myriad of things, though some of his favorites were the gadgets he found along the way, things that wouldn't fit in a construct but still fascinated him with their construction. There was also, of course, the gold and gems and things he'd gained when he was still interested in trading his constructs for money.

Hettie's eyes as they crossed the threshold were round as saucers. Her mouth went slack as she scanned the large room.

"This is all yours?" Her voice was breathy and quiet, full of awe.

"All mine," he confirmed. He preened, proud that he'd managed to impress her. "This is the room I needed the trap for. Come see."

Gyl took her to the side of the room with the hidden problem. He drew the tapestry aside, revealing the hole that the rat and his lady had shown him – gods had that really only been the day before?

"The thief slipped in through here, and I had a feeling he'd come back a second time. I was more interested in catching him than actually figuring out how he got in." Gyl shrugged.

"You didn't eat him, did you?" She glanced up at him, her expression wary.

Gyl laughed, "No, I let him go."

"Really? I thought dragons were sensitive about their hoards?" She perked up, curious.

"Usually, but I've never really been much bothered by all this." He toed a loose pile of coins with one foot. "I was more interested in meeting the man who had the balls to break in here twice. I thought it would be more fun that way."

"Like a literal cat and mouse," Hettie laughed and shook her head as she leaned over the hole, peering down into the twisting depths, "What's glowing down there?"

"Paint." Gyl didn't need to look over her shoulder to know. That detail had been included in the recounting of events he'd gotten from the rat. He did it anyway. It was an easy excuse to snake his arm around Hettie's middle, pressing into her soft belly like he was preventing her from pitching forward. "He marked his handholds on his first trip up so he would have an easier time of it the second time."

"Clever," she remarked wryly as the metal fingers of her right hand came to rest on his forearm. The cool touch sent a chill racing along his nerves. "How do you plan to close this thing up?"

"I haven't gotten that far yet," Gyl sighed. "It was only yesterday that I discovered them in here."

"That happened *yesterday*?" Hettie sounded incredulous. "Then that must have been just before you..."

"Yes, it was." He didn't need her to finish her sentence. He knew what she was saying. It was wild to him as well that that erotic wake-up-call had been bare hours before he'd found his witch out of control in that shop. He didn't like to think about what may have happened if things had occurred on a different timeline.

He tugged Hettie back from the precipice, letting the heavy fabric fall back over the hole. He didn't have an excuse to hang on to her anymore, but he didn't let her go, instead dropping his nose to her hair and taking a long inhale, the smell of cloves and sage mixing with the more floral scents in the shampoo and bath oils she'd used earlier. She leaned back into his hold, evidently just as content as he was to bask in their little moment.

He wasn't taking things slow like he'd intended, but she wasn't exactly letting him. At every turn, when he teased her, not intending to press but to make his interest known, she was eager and responsive. It was not helping him bank the fiery desire that was smoldering low in his belly, stirring his long-still loins.

He shouldn't be thinking about that right now. There was no reason he should be fantasizing about dragging her back across the hall, throwing her down in his nest, and doing all sorts of terrible, wonderful things to her. He definitely shouldn't let his rapidly hardening erection press into her lower back.

But he did it anyway.

He felt her soft inhale against his forearm when she noticed. She didn't pull away. If anything, she leaned into him harder. Her hands slid along his arm, tightening as she let out a little whimpering sound.

Oh. *Oh.* He was slow on the uptake this time, distracted by the smell of her arousal and the rush of blood to his groin. The magic inside her was awake again, swirling against him where their bodies were touching. She was not clinging to him eagerly, not anymore, but out of fear.

"It's alright, Hettie," he soothed, murmuring in her ear, "We've done this once already. Just remember how it felt to let the magic sink into me."

"It's not that easy," she bit out through gritted teeth. She smacked his arm with her palm. "Let me go."

He did so, but she didn't get three steps away before the gold coins around her feet started glowing cherry red, bubbling and puddling dangerously close to her bare toes. The hem of her dress started smoking.

"Shit," she spat, thrusting a hand back out to Gyl, who clasped it immediately and tugged her gently back from the hot metal puddles. They immediately stopped melting as his touch contained her magic.

Hettie squeezed her eyes closed, breaths coming in short pants as she tried to focus.

"Relax," he reminded her gently, "the harder you try to hang onto control-"

"I *know*," she snapped, "I remember. Shut up for a second."

"Take deeper breaths. Make yourself slow down," he couldn't help but offer the advice. She was about to start hyperventilating at the rate she was breathing.

"Gylharen," she growled.

"Sorry," he grimaced. It was hard to watch her struggle and not say anything, but his advice was clearly not helping matters. He worried his bottom lip with his fangs, gratified when her chest expanded with one massive, slow breath. After a few more, the energy rushed into him once more.

He let his head fall back as it washed over him. The sensation as it sank through his skin was akin to orgasmic bliss, though it did not have the same, er, *emissions*. It left him feeling flushed and loose, and he muffled a satisfied groan as it settled within him.

"I got nervous," Hettie dropped his hand and folded her arms, glancing sideways at the puddle of gold on the floor, "I guess I'm a little off-kilter still when it comes to..."

"Sex?" Gyl filled in bluntly. There was no point dancing around it. They'd been flirting heavily in his workshop, and things between them a moment ago had quickly been turning steamy.

"I didn't think I would be," she continued quickly, "I mean I never was before. I quite miss it, in fact. And I want it, *goddess* do I want it, but after Cordelia..."

"I understand," Gyl offered. He wished he knew how to soothe her, but the two of them were still basically strangers, and he was wildly out of practice.

It seemed that despite their chemistry, they would need to hold off on getting too physical too quickly. Their first task was to get her used to funneling the overflow of magic into him when it threatened to overwhelm her. That would have to be the first step to achieving their ultimate goal – which was *not* for her to control her magic, no matter what he'd already said. It was for her to reach equilibrium with it, so she wouldn't *need* to control it.

"I am sorry about the coins," she grimaced down at them, "You showed me your horde, and I damaged it."

"You didn't do it on purpose." Gyl shrugged. When he first started collecting as a dragonling, he'd likely have been fuming over it. As he aged, he quickly became less possessive, even of his favorite things in his horde. He was an anomaly for his kind, even before he became despondent and shut in and lost his ability to shift entirely. As it was, she'd damaged one of the things he cared the least about, the money, and in a way that hadn't really diminished its value by much. "The coins are inconsequential. I'd have been much more upset if it had happened over there, with my gizmos." He gestured over to the part of the room where most of the favored part of his collection lie in the shelves and shelves of inventions and mechanical toys he'd collected.

He squatted down beside the puddle, no longer glowing though the air still bore the tang of hot metal. He reached out and tentatively touched the edge, and found it was still malleable enough to peel up off the stone, but cool enough to come up in one piece.

"Isn't that *hot*?" Hettie squawked indignantly.

Gyl spared her a wry glance. "Very."

"It's not burning you." She squatted beside him, eyes behind her glasses wide with rapt fascination.

"I'm a dragon," he told her flatly, "It would have to be much hotter." He flipped the flat piece to see the back, where one half had taken the imprint of the flagstones and the other had collected half-melted coins that were now all stuck together in a cluster.

"I wouldn't think your more dragonesque traits would transfer to this form."

"Most of them do." He shrugged again. Normally he would be preening under her fascination, but this was a sensitive subject at the moment.

"I've seen you blow smoke, but can you breathe fire?"

"Yes." He was amused now. She was absolutely enraptured. He could really see the scholar in her poking through. He imagined her with a little pad and paper, frantically scribbling notes.

He just hoped she wouldn't ask for a demonstration. He hadn't spat fire in all the years he'd been alone. He wasn't sure he still could. Though perhaps since his internal fire was being kindled again...

"How big is your dragon form?" She pressed her glasses higher up her nose.

Gyl flinched. He hoped she didn't notice. "Large, though not too large to fit in here." He didn't actually know. If he couldn't take his true form, would it grow at the rate it should? Would his scaled form be fifty years or more stunted?

"How strong are you in this form? Like, is it proportional to your other one?" She eyed his arms, apparently, thankfully, missing his discomfort from her previous question.

"It is lessened somewhat, but I am still much stronger than most creatures my size would be. I can carry you easily."

"You cannot," Hettie scoffed.

Gyl tossed the gold blob onto a pile and scooped Hettie up, one hand under her knees, the other behind her back, much like he'd carried her back in the magic shop. She squealed and kicked but he straightened up with nary a wobble or a grunt.

"Okay, fine, I believe you!" She swatted him anywhere she could reach. "Put me down!"

He did, and she fixed her dress indignantly, though he could see the hint of a smile tug at her cheeks.

"Well, that's the entire tour, excitement and all." Gyl gestured to the room at large. "You've seen everything there is to see."

"There was certainly a lot of it," she remarked.

"I know there will be things you'll need that I don't have, things you'll like to eat, things for your hair and whatnot. If you make a list, I can send the constructs to town. I have an arrangement already set up with the grocer. I am sure for a little extra coin he'd be happy to help me procure whatever else you may need."

"Sure," Hettie nodded, "though I wish you could have someone fetch my things from the shop."

He shook his head, "That wouldn't be-"

"Safe," Hettie interrupted, flashing him a sad smile, "I know." She seemed resigned, like this place really was her prison. That chafed him a little, even if he knew she was justified.

"It's not forever," he reminded her.

"Sure," she didn't seem convinced.

A gurgle sounded from somewhere in the vicinity of her

belly. She pressed a hand to her abdomen and he could see a rosy cast rise in her brown cheeks.

"Are you alright?" He cocked an eyebrow at her.

"I'm hungry again," she told him meekly.

"Now there's a problem with an easy solution." He gestured towards the door. "After you."

After lunch made by the constructs and served at the awkwardly large dining table, Gyl brought her to the linen closet and gave her free reign to choose new curtains, bedding, towels, anything she could find in there for her rooms.

This "closet" was big enough to walk into and turn a circle with her arms straight out, and tall enough that she'd need a step-ladder to reach the upper shelves. There were fabrics in every color and texture stacked up to the ceiling.

"If there's something you can't find in here we can just add it to the list," Gyl told her, hovering in the doorway.

"I think I could find East Romancia in here," she laughed.

Gyl frowned at her. "That's not a real place." He looked embarrassed when Hettie flashed him a look, "Oh, that was a joke."

"A joke, yes," she agreed genially. It was both off-putting and strangely adorable how he could go from suave to clueless in the span of a breath. That wasn't the first joke she'd made since the start of their tour that he'd missed. Particularly quips that referenced more modern historical events or popular culture went right over his head – understandably, now that she had an idea of how he'd been living for a while.

"I like that green color." She pointed to a stack of dark, forest-y colored fabrics on an upper shelf. "Though I can't quite..." Hettie strained up on her tippy toes, the bottom of the shelf just out of reach.

She yelped with surprise when something solid connected with the back of her thighs and she was hauled upward. Gyl had hoisted her up to sit on one of his shoulders, his sure grip searing but secure on her thigh.

"I'm not a parrot," she huffed with exasperation. "Why do you keep picking me up?"

"Would you rather wait while I hunted down a stool?" The points of his horns brushed her side as he turned his head to look up at her.

"I'm already up here," she sniffed. She could pretend to be miffed, but there was something to be said for being thrown about as if she weighed nothing. She'd never been dainty or delicate, certainly not with her metal limb. She couldn't miss what she'd never known, and yet being thrown around as if she were a weightless slip of a thing made her feel small and treasured. He took such care with her that it didn't feel like he was doing it just to brag on his strength, but like he liked holding her.

She tried not to think about that too much.

Her face burned as she dug through the pile of green fabric and found a duvet cover with a favorable texture – soft but not slick – and a couple of pillow covers to match.

"I think I'll keep the white curtains on the bed and windows, but what about this color for an accent?" She pointed to a stack of bronze-colored linens.

"I'd prefer gold, personally, but it's your space." Gyl told her, shifting her closer to what she needed.

Hettie glanced down at his gold-coin eyes and smirked, "I'd bet you would, but I'm going for woodsy here. You don't really see gold much in the forest." She tugged down several shiny decorative pillow shams, a russet-colored knit blanket, and some other accent items that were almost orange.

"I think that's all." She struggled to hold all her finds at once. Gyl let her slide carefully to the ground. "Thank you," she told him, mollified.

"What does it need now?" Gyl asked her a short while later, gazing at her room with its new linens.

"I'm not sure," Hettie fidgeted, gazing around. It was better, but it was still missing... something. Likely it was the lack of any decoration or personal touches that was throwing her off. She stroked Didi's head absently as she glanced around the room.

"Well, you'll have all night to meditate on it. I won't send my construct to town until tomorrow," Gyl told her, clearly trying to be helpful.

"Right." All night. Alone in this room. Floors away from the one thing keeping her from turning into a bomb. "Will you be sleeping in your workshop?"

Gyl perched on the edge of her bed, hands dangling loosely over his knees, "I usually do."

"Do you have another bedroom to stay in?" she asked. Her heart pounded. She hadn't been nervous about sleeping in a strange place since she was a child, and yet here she was attempting to wheedle this man into sleeping closer in case she had a nighttime incident.

"Do you have something you want to ask me, little witch?" Gyl rumbled, a little curl of smoke escaping from his nose.

She twisted her hair around her fingers, "What if something happens during the night?"

"I told you, you're safe here." He gestured to himself. "Dragon, remember?"

"It's not that," Hettie made a slashing motion with her hand to cut him off, "What if something happens with *me* in the night?" *And you're not here to help*, was the silent end of that sentence. Hettie could see he understood when he straightened slowly.

"I can stay with you, if you're worried," he offered softly.

"I wouldn't want to inconvenience you." She felt silly all of a sudden, like she was worried over nothing. She'd been sleeping at night with no incidents for months. What was different now?

She'd started to let go of her control, that's what was different. Even now she could feel the slip and slide of her magic beneath her skin as her nerves ebbed and flowed.

"All you have to do is ask," he told her mildly.

Her face burned. "Just forget it." She turned to the window to hide her embarrassment, eyes scanning the stone spires around them.

"Hettie."

"I was just being silly."

"*Hettie.*"

"It's really not necessary-"

A hand reached over her shoulder and grasped her chin in

delicate fingers. Gyl turned her with a gentle touch until she was looking up into his vaguely amused but unmistakably kind expression.

"Ask me your question, Hettie." The instruction was soft, but unyielding. It left no room for refusal. She finally felt free to give in to that impulse she'd almost brushed off as too silly.

"Will you stay with me tonight?"

"Of course I will." His thumb brushed a hot streak across her cheek. "Do you want me to share the bed with you, or sleep elsewhere?"

Hettie wrinkled her nose. As if the answer to that question wasn't obvious.

"With me. No funny business," she followed up quickly, to cover her embarrassment. "You're here to prevent incidents, not start one."

He laughed, a deep, melodic sound that made her belly squeeze.

"I'll behave," he promised, shoulders still shaking.

"Right, good," she wiped her sweaty palms on her skirt. Why was she so nervous? "Now let's see if you have anything good in that library."

Gyl normally crawled into bed in whatever he'd bothered to wear for the day, which was often not more than a loincloth. Keeping Hettie's comfort in mind, he'd opted for a pair of soft white trousers that tied around his ankles. The clothing would encourage him to mind his manners, and would hopefully hide the inevitable erection he was going to be sporting all night lying beside her.

He lay on her green bedding now, hands laced behind his head, waiting for her to finish up in the bathroom. He'd offered her a selection of nightwear, hoping something would fit her. Now that he had her measurements, he could have some things brought up from town for her. She'd made a list of pieces she'd need, and he'd added a few surprises of his own to it.

The door opened a crack, and a sliver of Hettie's face appeared, "Gylharen?"

"Mm?"

"I'm coming out, but you have to promise not to laugh."

"Why would I laugh?" He cocked an eyebrow at her.

"I look ridiculous."

Impossible.

"I'm sure you look fine. We're going to sleep, anyway." He hadn't given her anything silly in her options, not that he'd thought anyway.

She stepped out of the bathroom, steps short and stiff as she shuffled forward to stand by the edge of the bed.

She'd donned the white option he'd brought for her, a short cotton nightgown tiered with flowy stacks of ruffles from bust to hem.

"You look fine." An understatement. She looked adorable, though he didn't think that the style quite suited her.

"I look like a cupcake," she groused as she crawled on the bed. She unfurled a ribbon from her hand and reached back to braid her hair away from her face.

"I'd eat you up," he teased.

"Shut it, you," she huffed as she plopped down on the bed. "Where did all this clothing come from anyway?"

Gyl fell quiet, much of the amusement falling away from him.

She glanced over at him, face pinched with concern, "You don't have to tell me."

He shook his head. "I just made this place and stocked it thinking it would be... fuller." He'd had some wild idea that if dragons didn't like to den in groups, then perhaps he could find a way to surround himself with other creatures. He'd had some unsteady dream that he'd throw wild balls and parties and keep this place full, but by the time the construction was finished, he'd been alone too long already, and it was harder to push off the darkness long enough to take care of himself, let alone to make social connections.

"Full of friends or family?" she asked softly.

"Anyone," he answered frankly.

Hettie turned from him, digging her hands into her hair. He watched her flinch as she raked her fingers through her curls, attempting to separate them into three strands.

"Do you want some help with that?" he asked, shaking off the gloom that had started to gather in his thoughts again.

"I'll manage. I washed my hair without any of my products and now it's being unruly," she let out a frustrated growl, "I normally tie it up in a silk scarf for bed, but I don't have one."

"What about your work scarf? Won't that suit?" He gestured to where it lay on the nightstand.

She shook her head, "It's too small to contain all this mess."

She huffed and threw her hands down into her lap, "I'm about to give up on it."

"Here, before you get all worked up." He could already smell the tang of chaos magic from her frustration. He carefully scooted up behind her, gently continuing the work she'd started and splitting her hair into three segments. He wove them into a plait down the middle of her back, loose enough not to cause her discomfort, but tight enough to keep it out of her face.

"Interesting to see how much longer it is when it's not curled," he mused, tickling her with the little tail of the braid.

"Stop that," she snipped, tugging her hair away from him.

Smiling softly to himself, Gyl finally lit upon why he liked it so much when she was grouchy with him.

"I'm not complaining, believe me, but how come you're not more scared of me?"

"Why should I be?" she scoffed. "Because you're a scary, fire-breathing dragon?"

"Essentially," he agreed wryly, laying back on the mattress and gazing up at her. She ran her hands down her braid, one over the other, staring off into the middle distance as she considered his question.

"I don't know," was her soft reply, "I was at first, back in the shop, but I think..." She bit her lip and glanced down at him shyly.

"What do you think?" he prompted.

"I think there's something in you that calls out to me – or maybe the other way around." She averted her eyes, like what she was saying embarrassed her. "I lost my fear pretty much instantly after that first transfer of power. Not to mention it's hard to be afraid of you when you're parading me around the castle and being an all-around shameless flirt."

Gyl grinned and walked his hand over Hettie's leg to squeeze her thigh.

"And here I thought maybe it was because you thought I was pathetic." His tone was jovial, but he'd worried about that when she'd taken one look around his workshop and caught a glimpse into his bared soul. It was equal parts unsettling and a relief for her to have a hint of the darker nature of his solitude.

"Maybe a little." She leaned over him, tickling him under the chin with the end of her braid. He captured her easily with one arm, hauling her down beside him and peppering her neck and shoulder with playful bites.

"Careful, my glasses!" Hettie squealed, but her words were punctuated with laughter.

He plucked them off her face and folded them gently with one hand, reaching over her to place them on the side table. With his other arm, he kept her pressed to his chest. When he lay flat again he loosened his hold on her, but she made no move to get away. No, instead she settled onto his chest, resting her cheek on the softest part of his pectoral muscle.

"Goodnight, Hettie," he told her with a grin, reaching over to douse the witchlight.

"Goodnight, Gylharen," she murmured. Her breath across his skin sent goose flesh prickling along its path.

He circled his fingers gently against the skin on her arm. A soft warmth diffused him, separate from the constant burning heat of his body.

"Hettie?" he murmured after a moment.

"Hm?"

"Can you kiss me goodnight?"

It felt like a silly, boyish request. A need for one last scrap of attention before they dropped off to slumber. However, he wouldn't take it back. The affection she'd already given him was like a drop of water in a parched desert. It had only intensified his thirst for it.

Even so, despite how silly he felt for asking, Hettie lifted her head instantly and tipped her face towards him.

Gyl captured her mouth, reveling in the feel of her plush lips against his. They let this kiss linger rather longer than necessary, and when they parted Gyl caught the swirl of magic in Hettie's eyes.

"You alright?" he asked her guiltily.

She squeezed her eyes shut, pressed her hand to his chest, and passed him a small rush of her power. Gyl gasped, his nipples tightening as electric sensation zinged over his torso before settling into his body.

"A little warning would be nice," he panted.

"Sorry," she huffed.

"You're getting the hang of that." He tried to keep his voice pleasantly neutral and free of the smoky desire now rushing through him. This transfer of magic had been only enough to set him on edge this time, rather than give him a feeling of release.

He couldn't, however, hide the goose flesh on his chest or the hard points of his nipples. Her eyes traveled down his chest. She cleared her throat.

"I am. It's easier when you're not reminding me to relax."

"Sorry." The tension was growing slowly between them. He should tell her goodnight again, should encourage her to lay down and go to sleep, but her hand hovered over his chest as if she wanted to touch him again and it was all he wanted in that moment. If he opened his mouth he'd beg her to, so he stuck his tongue firmly to the roof of it.

She finally trailed her fingertips over his skin, and his magic-lit nerves fired into overdrive. His cock throbbed to aching life below. Gyl swallowed hard, trying not to moan.

"What does it feel like?" she asked softly, "When I transfer it to you?"

"Ecstasy." He couldn't quite keep the tremor out of his voice. Sensation rippled out over his body from beneath her hands.

"Oh, no," she gasped, and when he glanced at her she was staring guiltily at where his cock was lifting the front of his trousers. "I'm so sorry."

"Don't be," he hummed, laying his hand over hers. "I'm not."

"Is..." she swallowed visibly. "Is that thing supposed to *fit*?"

Surprised, Gyl chuckled, "Oh, it'll fit."

"It's just so..." Hettie bit her lip, her cheeks heating.

"So what?"

Hettie shook her head, clearly intimidated by the outline of his cock. Gyl reached up and pinched her chin between thumb and forefinger.

"There's no need to worry, Hettie. We're going to go as slow as you need to, but I assure you, it *will* fit. We may need to condition you a little before you can take the knot, but the shaft-"

"A *knot*?" Hettie squeaked, clearly perturbed.

Gyl bit his lip to hold back his mirth. It wouldn't do to

laugh at her embarrassment, but she was just so cute. He didn't expect everyone to be familiar with dragon anatomy, given their generally reclusive nature, but knots were not that uncommon of a feature.

"Have you ever seen one? Lycans have them, and some canid fae. Sometimes those with demon blood in them as well, though not often."

"My bedfellows have been decidedly human," she murmured, leaning into his hold on her face.

"And incompetent," Gyl snorted, a ring of smoke escaping from his nose, "Perhaps their human nature was part of the problem."

A crooked little smile hooked one of her cheeks. "Perhaps."

"Come, let's sleep," he urged her.

"But you... your..." she glanced down at his groin.

"Will be fine," he told her patiently.

"Won't you be in pain? I could help you, since it's my fault."

Gyl felt a momentary twinge of annoyance at whatever man – or men – had taught her that their arousal was her problem to solve. If he was uncomfortable enough, he'd solve the problem himself after she fell asleep.

"It's neither your fault nor your responsibility, Hettie," he told her gently, schooling the annoyance from his tone. "You need rest."

He tugged her back down beside him, tugging the sheets up over them. He didn't bother with the duvet. He threw off heat like a furnace. She wouldn't need anything heavier.

"Sleep," he ordered her.

"Goodnight, Gyl." This time she nuzzled into his neck, her breath puffing over his throat.

"Goodnight, Hettie," he told her fondly, nuzzling against the top of her head. He curled his tail behind her knee, tugging her leg over his hip.

"Ouch! *Goodnight, Didi*," she said with sleepy exasperation after a flutter of feathers by the foot of the bed.

He'd almost forgotten about the fucking chicken.

7

Hettie woke with the morning sun streaming through the windows. She was pleasantly toasty, almost too warm, as Gyl was pressed right up against her back, one arm and one leg draped over her.

She smiled into her pillow. He was such a strange mixture, this dragon. In some ways he was completely estranged from modern society, and in others he was proficient in it. He hadn't known how to confront her at the shop, or how to give her advice for channeling magic that wasn't annoying, but as far as soothing her fears about intimacy, he was practically professional.

She also found him reaching out to touch her constantly. Like feelers on a vine reach out for support. She wasn't even sure he knew he was doing it, but he'd taken every excuse he could to touch her the day before, and now seemingly in his sleep he'd wrapped himself around her. It was incredibly endearing.

She shifted a little, looking to get comfortable and just enjoy the early-morning cuddle, and that's when she felt it. He had a hard-on. It pressed firmly against her ass as she moved, her nightgown rucked up so the only thing between them was his thin sleep pants.

It felt huge.

It made sense, the man towered over her, after all, but that didn't mean it didn't light her body up with desire that was laced with just a touch of fear. On the one hand, pain with intimacy was not necessarily her thing. On the other, her sex clenched at the image of him stretching her wide up to his knot and then forcing her to take it.

Despite the warmth enveloping her, she shivered. As her arousal spiked, so, too, could she feel the magic swirling.

The movement roused Gyl, who sucked in a deep breath and tugged Hettie more firmly to his chest. The movement ground his cock firmly against the seam of her ass.

"Good morning," he rumbled in her ear, his voice rough and gravelly with sleep. He took another deep breath, this one deliberate, and hummed, "You smell fantastic. What's got you all worked up this morning?"

Hettie was mortified at this confirmation that he could, in fact, smell her arousal.

"It's nothing," she peeped, "but I do think I'm going to need to make a transfer here soon."

"Thanks for the warning this time," he chuckled. "Whenever you're ready."

It was getting easier to do, this funneling of her power

between them. She was grateful for that much at least. It made her feel as if she was, at least a tiny bit, in control still.

She passed it to him now, an emptying rush with her arm over his forearm, and felt Gyl stiffen and arch behind her. The motion pressed his cock into her ass with a long, rocking stroke. Gyl let out a strangled grunt seconds before something hot and damp pressed into her back.

Both of them froze, Gyl still breathing heavily.

"Did you just...?"

"Yep," he bit out, "If you'll excuse me."

He slid off the bed, quickly trotting into the bathroom and closing the door.

Hettie was still stunned. Her magic and a little grinding had been enough to...? Truly?

She sat up, retrieved her glasses, and glanced down at the foot of the bed, where Didi sat with her beak tilted up, glaring at her beadily. For a chicken, she had a piercing judgmental stare.

"Don't look at me like that," she murmured. "It's not like I did it on purpose."

Didi clucked resentfully and turned her back on Hettie. Guilt pooled low in her belly. She'd been fooling around with Gyl while Cordelia was in the room, trapped in this little feathered body.

"I'm sorry, Didi. I didn't think about how all this would make you feel."

If a chicken could roll her eyes, Hettie swore she did. Didi strolled up the bed and climbed in her lap, giving her fingers a gentle nibble, for once not looking for blood.

"Is that your way of telling me you're not mad about it?"

she asked shyly. Didi blinked up at her slowly. Hettie was fairly certain if that were a no she'd have received a peck.

If she was going to pursue things with Gyl, she was going to need a way to give Didi a little privacy. It was the least she could do. While she was under no illusions that she harbored romantic feelings for her still, Cordelia had been her lover for a night. It was insensitive to pursue Gyl in front of her, when her pursuit of Cordelia was what had damned her to life as a chicken in the first place.

"I'm going to make sure Gyl is alright." She displaced Didi gently and slid off the bed.

She could feel her arousal slicking her thighs as she walked. She'd emptied the welling magic within her, but the desire was still a powerful ache in her core.

She knocked on the bathroom door and called out, "Gyl-haren?"

"I'll be out in a moment." He sounded almost angry.

"You don't need to be embarrassed." No response. "Can I come in?"

She was about to turn away when he called out, "You can."

Hettie stepped through the door, closing it behind her.

Gyl stood at the sink, leaning on the counter with a towel around his hips. His sleep pants lay on the floor, kicked into the corner. The man himself was the picture of forced nonchalance, arms folded over his chest, ankles crossed, shoulders relaxed but jaw tense.

"That doesn't usually happen," he told her, not quite looking at her.

"I imagine it doesn't," she told him gently. Poor thing. His ego was clearly bruised.

"I'm fully capable of satisfying a partner before I-"

"*Gyl*," she interrupted, holding back an exasperated chuckle, "it's alright. I know you're embarrassed, but there's no need. You've been alone and without partners for some time. Not to mention the magic on top of it. It's a lot to handle all at once."

She stepped up to him and leaned against his knees until he parted them for her, framing her hips with his thighs. She reached up and cradled his cheeks in her hands, turning his head to look at her.

"It's alright," she repeated. "Can't you smell me still?"

His nostrils flared, his slit pupils dilating. He let out his indrawn breath on a growl. His hands traced up the outside of her thighs, lifting her nightgown to dig into her hips.

"I can." He tipped his head forward, bumping their foreheads together. He lifted his head after a second, cocking an eyebrow at her. "Wait, did you call me *Gyl* a moment ago?"

Hettie smiled at him, "Well you said that's what I should call you if I liked you."

Gyl grinned at her in response, his fangs poking out, "I know what I *said*, but you weren't actually doing it."

"Well, *Gyl*, now I am," she stated simply.

"And you're not upset about... what just happened?"

"No." She shook her head. "I'm glad you enjoyed it. I like that it feels good for you when we transfer."

He tucked a stray curl behind her ear. "To say I enjoyed it is an understatement. You're a treasure, Hettie."

"High praise from a dragon," she teased.

"It's deserved."

She slid her hands down his chest, his skin heating her palm.

"Hm. Maybe you ought to reward me?" She almost couldn't believe she was being so bold, except she was aching with need.

"You think so?" His voice was soft as velvet, his eyes heavy-lidded. She almost jumped when something touched her leg, but quickly realized by the heat and the scaly texture that it was his tail twining around the back of her knee.

"If you're feeling up to it," she amended. She didn't want to push him if his embarrassment had him completely out of the mood.

"I think I can manage," he chuckled.

He spun them around, pressing her back against the counter so it bumped her rear. He penned her in with his hands braced on either side of her, smoke curling out of his nose as he considered her with heated eyes.

"Hop up, treasure." He patted the counter beside her, eyes sparkling. She did so, Gyl lifting her a little when she couldn't quite get high enough. Her metal hand clicked against the stone as she caught her balance.

He took a step back from her once she was planted. He locked eyes with her and reached down to tug the towel from his hips, letting it dangle from one hand.

Hettie couldn't keep eye contact, not once he'd bared himself to her.

Gods but he was beautiful. He looked like someone had cast him in bronze, from a master mold sculpted in every loving detail by an artisan. There was nothing soft about him, all hard planes and edges, and that was becoming true for the monster that hung between his legs too.

Even half-hard it was impressive. It was a ruddier color than his skin everywhere else, and had a triangular tip that was almost flat. Segments ran down its length in V-shapes, all the way to two swells in his shaft near the base on either side of it – the knot in question.

"Do you like what you see?"

Gyl made it twitch as she watched, the bounce of it making her core clench with need.

"Mm, I can tell you do," he growled. "I'd offer to let you explore me, but if the smell of you gets any more delicious I just might go a little feral. Grab that towel ring for me, will you?"

Half hypnotized still, Hettie reached up and curled her fingers around the empty ring where the hand towel hung earlier. Before she realized what he was doing, Gyl had twisted that towel around her wrists and tied it to the ring.

"What's this for?" she huffed, tugging at the tie. It was snug, but she could pull free if she really wanted to. He watched her test the knot, and he gave her a questioning look. The message was clear. *Are you willing to pretend and play the game?* She definitely was. Not having use of her hands meant giving up control, and he'd already proved to her she liked that immensely. She adjusted her hands so her left wrist wouldn't pinch the right and waited for him to answer her question.

"I'm guessing you'll need to make a transfer while we're doing this. Sex seems to wind up your magic more than most other things. The last couple times you've been using your hands. I want you to do it without them, to practice directing it."

She rolled her eyes. Trust him to turn this steamy encounter into a lesson. "How am I supposed to do that if I'm not touching you?"

"Don't worry, *I'll* be touching *you*." He shot her a wild, fanged grin as he sunk to his knees. He kissed up her thighs as he pressed them open, tugging her just a little so her ass was perched just a fraction over the edge of the counter. It felt a little precarious for a second, but once Gyl settled his shoulders under her thighs that solved that problem.

He dug his fingers into the outsides of her thighs, taking great big handfuls of her and really digging in. He traced his nose over her mons, the curves of his horns brushing her belly over her nightgown.

He took in a deep breath, growling on the exhale.

"You really do smell divine, treasure. I could bottle this." He ran the flat of his tongue along her slit, tasting her. "I hope you weren't particularly attached to this." She felt the pinch of his fangs digging into the fabric to start a tear a split second before he gripped it with his hands and tore her nightgown up the front, baring her body to the air and to his eyes. Hettie could do nothing but gasp and cling to the towel as he tossed the shredded remains across the bathroom. The position of her arms thrust her breasts outward, and his eyes were molten as he cast them down her body.

He wasted no time getting down to business, tugging her knees wider as he dove right into her pussy, licking her sex in long strokes. His tongue was hot, smoke curling from him in a constant stream now, and the searing heat of it combined with the cooler rush of air anytime he pulled back was both torturous and divine.

Hettie clung to that towel for dear life as he learned every inch of her with that wicked tongue, circling her opening and clit in a figure eight.

When he delved his tongue into her, it felt somehow like

it just kept *going*. She could feel the sharp prick of those fangs pressing into her flesh as he opened his mouth wider to plunge it deeper. Though it hadn't seemed any larger than a normal man's tongue, what pulsed within her at that moment felt just as long and girthy as some men she'd had sex with, though it was wonderfully more agile. She rolled her hips against him as he curled that dexterous muscle against her perfect spot, her legs shaking on either side of his head as he hit it over and over.

He was right about one thing. It was definitely more than an orgasm building within her, though that was thundering closer like a herd of wild stallions. When he withdrew his tongue to pull his head back, Hettie whimpered before he replaced it with two fingers, stimulating her with slow strokes as he leaned back to look up at her.

"When you come, my treasure, you're going to transfer the magic to me at the same time." It wasn't a question. He was telling her what she was going to do, and she was desperate to obey if he'd just put his mouth back on her.

She nodded, whimpering her assent and digging her heels into his back to urge him to put his tongue back to its task.

He chuckled and leaned back into her. His hand left a wet trail on the outside of her thigh as he traced it around her limb, placing it on her lower belly so he could slip his thumb above his mouth and circle her clit with it. As his tongue slid back in she was certain this time that the organ in question was nowhere near human, and as it curled and stroked her the addition of his thumb was enough to have her clutching at the towel and keening out his name. Her toes curled and her cunt clenched around his tongue. Her thighs clamped closed around his ears, and she'd have worried she was suffocating him if it weren't for the constant stream of smoke that escaped him as he kept on stimulating her through her peak.

And laced with it, somehow entwined with it, was the chaos, the magic, out of her control and yet not dragging her down into unconsciousness. It flooded her veins with heat, carried with it the same ecstasy that pulsed in her core until every joint and muscle in her body could feel it. It threatened to flood her, to overwhelm her, before Hettie remembered what she was supposed to do with it.

She imagined Gyl taking it through his mouth, pictured that clever tongue lapping up each and every drop that spilled over the brim until she was empty of it once again.

There was the same release and rush as the energy flowed through her, but this time, between Gyl still mercilessly tonguing her and the magic flowing directly down her pussy as a channel, she came again, harder this time. She arched her back, as well as she could without losing the knot around her wrists, and screamed wordlessly, her entire lower half trembling as the last of the magic left her.

Gyl was panting heavily when he finally pulled back from her, the press of her thighs not enough to keep him contained. His cheeks were flushed when he gazed up at her, his eyes glazed and his mouth shiny from her release.

"Did it get you again?" she asked raggedly, mouth twitching.

"Fuck yes it did," he growled. "I haven't come like that in… I don't think I've ever come like that."

The double powerful climaxes were making her feel sex-drunk, "If you thought that was good, just wait until I do a transfer though your cock."

Gyl growled abruptly, a wave of golden scales appearing

over his shoulders and then disappearing again as he stood. He undid the towel knot and gently massaged her wrist where the terrycloth and rubbing against her prosthetic had started to irritate it.

"Come on," he told her huskily, "As delicious as you are, treasure, I need breakfast if I'm going to survive you."

"Will there be fruit?" she asked brightly. Fruit sounded incredible. She was suddenly ravenous. She'd kill for a strawberry.

"Do you want fruit?" He cocked an eyebrow, she nodded. "Then there will be fruit."

8

"You're trying too hard."

Hettie let out a very Gyl-sounding growl, gnashing her teeth in frustration.

"Your advice is *not helpful*, old man," she snarled.

Gyl hid his smile behind the hand that propped up his chin. She'd picked up that name in the past half-hour as her frustration bloomed heavy and sought an outlet. He was, indeed, much older than her, but by dragon standards he'd barely lived at all.

That would also not be helpful to point out in that moment, so he kept his mouth shut.

They sat in a room Hettie had chosen for practice, one that they emptied of everything except a heavy wooden table, two chairs, and the curtains on the windows. No need to invite accidents, Hettie had told him. She'd been practicing all

92

morning, and her temper was growing shorter and shorter, like a lit fuse.

The table around them was littered with puddles of hard white wax and scorch marks. She sat in front of one of the last candles from the pack she'd been working with, still unlit, though with a shiny melted spot about halfway down its tapered length.

It had been a few days since Hettie's arrival, and even if she felt she were making no progress, Gyl could already tell she was getting the hang of handling her magic. Their transfers had been getting easier and easier, to the point where sometimes while he feasted on her she'd just pass him her magic in a continuous stream the entire time. It was woefully, blissfully distracting, but he enjoyed it immensely.

He'd yet to let her touch him, despite her begging and pleading in the throes of pleasure. He had a few reasons for that, one being despite his bravado about being able to fit inside her, he was actually quite large if she was only used to human men, and he didn't want to hurt her. Another reason being he wanted to build up a tolerance to her magic before he let her anywhere near his cock.

He couldn't have anticipated the effect she would have on his body. It responded to her of its own volition, reacting in ways that surprised him. The *early arrivals* for example. The first one had caught him by surprise, the second he'd expected, and since then he'd been more focused on delaying his climax. He was doing much better, particularly as she got better at controlling the flow of the transfer. It was easier to do when he received it as a stream rather than a torrent dumped into him all at once.

Not to mention there were other changes her magic encouraged his body to make. He was still trapped in his human form, but pieces of himself could shift again, particularly when he was near or touching her. His tongue, for example, was able to change to its more bestial length. All the better to devour her with. Scales were another common shift, though he couldn't hold them, passing over his skin like ripples in a pond. Once he'd unintentionally shifted his hands. His claws had dug into the soft flesh of her thighs, leaving behind little red nicks. He still felt bad for that one, even though she assured him she hadn't even felt them.

"You know why you can't light it?" he asked finally, knowing he was about to piss her off royally.

"Please, enlighten me," she huffed, petulantly knocking the unlit candle over.

"Now, now," he chuckled. He stood from his chair, circling to lean over her shoulder and brace his hands on the table on either side of her. He tucked his mouth against the shell of her ear and whispered, "You can't light it because you don't think you can."

"Excuse me?" She bristled below him.

"You doubt yourself and it shows. If you had faith in your ability, the task would be much easier."

"I'll show you, old man," she huffed. She righted the candle.

Gyl straightened and folded his arms, "Do it then. Light it." He took a step to one side to better watch her.

Hettie narrowed her eyes, glaring at the candle. Gyl really bit down on the instinctive *relax* that bubbled up from his belly. She was still trying too hard. She needed to let it come more naturally, rather than trying to ham-fist round magic into a square hole. She was too tense, too focused, too...

Ah, there it was. A subtle shift in her posture. A leaning back in her chair. The loosening of the tightness around her eyes. She let slack some of that rigid control, took in a deep breath, and on the exhale a steady flame flickered to life on the end of the wick.

She turned and gave him a smug look, though it fell away when she caught the triumphant grin on his face.

"Oh, fuck you."

"But it worked," he snickered. "You don't like when I offer advice. I had to think of another way to get you out of your own head."

"It felt different that time," Hettie said, his little trick seemingly already forgotten. She absently passed her metal fingers through the candle flame.

"You're getting the hang of it." He threw himself down into his chair, arranging his long legs under the table so his feet rested next to hers.

"You think so?" The look she flashed him was so full of fragile hope, his heart ached at the sight of it.

"I know so. I know this seems like small progress, but this is just the beginning." He reached over the table, over the wasteland of all her failed attempts, and patted her hand before reaching up to snuff the flame out with his fingers. She gasped with outrage, her mouth gaping, but he just grinned at her.

"Now do it again."

They practiced small magic for most of the afternoon, lighting that candle until it burned down to a useless nub. Gyl hunted down another box, and they kept going until Hettie could light three at once without incident.

She grinned at him, pressing her glasses up her nose.

"Good work, treasure," he praised her. When he leaned into her space, she tipped her head back expectantly. His heart squeezed, and he couldn't squash his silly grin. He plucked the glasses from her face and tucked them into his pocket. He'd discovered over the past couple days that if he kissed her with them on, they got terribly smudged and dug into her nose and cheeks.

He cradled her face in his hands, drawing her mouth up to his and claiming it with soft, slow strokes of his tongue.

The perfume of her arousal bloomed immediately as her body responded. Her hands slipped around his back, her prosthetic cold against his skin for a second before the fire within him warmed it.

When he released her mouth a moment later, she gazed up at him with soft, unfocused heat. He slid her glasses back on, smirking as an idea occurred to him.

"Come with me, treasure. I think you've earned a reward for all your hard work and progress today."

"Where are we going?"

"You'll see."

Hettie sat on her bed and waited. On Gyl's insistence, she'd taken Didi to the room several doors down that they'd set up as her own space away from them while they were exploring each other. Everything in there was on the floor or ramped for her access, and Hettie always left the door open. She wanted to make it clear this wasn't a punishment or a time-out. If Didi would rather explore then she was welcome to, but Hettie always found her curled up on a pillow when she went to fetch her later.

Hettie flopped backwards onto the bed, her belly fluttering. Asking her to put Didi in the other room meant that whatever Gyl had in mind, it was likely filthy. It meant that with every second that passed she was wound tighter with nervous anticipation. She stretched her limbs out, trying to relax, but the ache in her core was driving her to distraction.

Maybe she could just...

She tugged her skirt up, one made of lovely, soft cotton that the constructs had brought back from the city. She traced her hands up her thighs as she went, trailing them over the fabric-covered lips of her sex. She could already feel the gusset of her panties growing damp. She shoved them down her legs, getting an inkling that if she didn't Gyl would rip them from her body. Again. He seemed to have a fondness for it, and promised to buy her a thousand pairs if he could keep doing it, so she let him. Besides, she liked it too. It was carnal, heated, feral, but she rather liked this pair and wanted to save them from his primal urge to tear things from her body.

She bent her knees as her panties fell to the floor, bracing her feet on the bed to give her better access to her slick core. She dragged the fingers of her left hand through her folds, groaning at the immediate spark of pleasure that flared between her legs. She whimpered, circling her sensitive clit with the pads of two fingers.

"Well, isn't this a pretty sight."

When Hettie looked up, Gyl stood in the doorway. He leaned against the frame, two wooden boxes under one arm, smoke curling from his nostrils as he watched her.

"Don't stop on my account," he told her when she paused her ministrations. "I like to watch."

She kept touching herself. She even spread her legs wider so he could see better. She watched his eyes flash as he moved into the room.

"Gorgeous. You smell so good," Gyl groaned. "I could practically taste your arousal from down the hall."

Hettie slipped those two fingers into her channel and watched the front of his trousers grow tight.

"You don't have to just watch," she panted, stroking her fingers into her own soft flesh. She loved the way his body moved towards her, slinky and fluid like a predator stalking a rabbit.

He *was* a predator, she reminded herself. What bigger predator was there than a dragon? Somehow the danger made that hungry look he cast her even hotter, and she whimpered as the press of those digits was suddenly not enough to satisfy her.

"Please," she pleaded. He'd kept his cock from her so far. She'd been able to admire it, but he hadn't let her touch it. She wanted it. Badly. It hung heavy and twitching between his legs as he divested himself of boxes and clothing. She could practically feel the drool pooling in the back of her throat.

"Please, what, treasure?" he murmured, voice all smoke and sin as he walked up to the edge of the bed, eyes fixed to her fingers still pumping into her cunt.

"Please, I need your cock," she cried desperately. "It's not enough."

He gave her a wicked grin. "So my tongue isn't good enough for you now? Does it not fill you well enough, treasure?"

"I need more," she huffed, "I want to be full of you until I can't take it, and then I want you to make me take your knot."

A growl burst from Gyl's throat. Judging from the look on his face, he wanted that too.

"You know what you're asking for?" His voice was soft, almost a purr. He tugged on her wrist, slipping her fingers from her pussy and bringing them up to his mouth to lick them clean with that agile tongue.

"Tell me."

"When you ask this, you are giving up your control to me. You take what I give you, when I give it to you. You let me own this sweet body and use it as I please. Knotting is primal, instinctive, and those are the things *my* body craves when I'm preparing to do it. Can you do that? Can you let go for me?"

Hettie's breath caught in her throat, and she nodded eagerly. She trusted him, a decision only compounded by his treatment of her over the past few days, and the idea of shutting off her brain and letting someone else make all the decisions, do all the worrying, sounded divine.

"Please," she repeated, her voice sounding pitiful even to herself.

"You're so pretty when you beg," Gyl hummed with appreciation, kissing the back of her captured hand before releasing it. He stepped back from her, over to the bedside table where he'd set the boxes. Hettie took advantage of his turned back to admire the taut, muscular planes of his shoulders and ass.

The valley of muscle where his tail merged with his back was splashed with golden scales that faded into his skin tone and caught the light as he moved.

Gyl turned to her with the smaller of the two boxes in one hand. He sprawled belly-down on the bed beside her, placing the box between them.

"What's this?" Hettie sat up, her dress falling back around her hips.

"Your reward," Gyl told her. His lip quirked in the corner as she reached out and lifted the lid.

She frowned in confusion at the contents of the box. Rings, bracelets, and chains of all sorts filled the interior, each piece of jewelry studded with gems of various hues. They were beautiful, but they were much too large for her.

"I don't get it," she told him blankly, "what's this for?"

"This," Gyl curled his fingers over the edge of the box, "is so you can decorate your necklace for tonight."

Heat flushed Hettie, as if she could be any more on edge. She had a flash of memory, a quick image of her submission to Gyl that first day with his hand on her throat.

"Oh, absolutely," she breathed.

"Get to it then," he grinned. He stretched out his arm so it lay flat beside the box, his hand loose and relaxed.

Hettie picked through the treasures, plucking out bits and bobs when they struck her fancy. She held his hand as she slid the rings on and off his fingers, swapping them out until she found a combination that pleased her, all in gold to match his eyes.

On his middle finger went an intricate filigreed piece with a hinge in it that went over his knuckle. It was decorated with dangling chains that looped around his wrist. On his ring finger went a ring with the band shaped like dragon wings and set with a ruby the width of her thumb. The rest of his fingers got slim bands with matching patterns and smaller gemstones, made in various sizes to sit between his higher knuckles as well as at the base of his fingers.

"Finished?" He smirked at her, eyes molten.

"Finished," she confirmed.

"You have good taste," he told her, wiggling his fingers and tilting his head as he admired her selections. He sat up and set the box back on the night stand, swapping it for the slightly larger one. "Are you ready, my treasure?"

A thrill raced up her spine, "I'm ready."

"Then if you like your new clothes, you should take them off. Otherwise they'll end up in ribbons on the floor." Casually, he palmed his cock, a shining pearl of his arousal beaded on the tip.

Hettie was on her feet in a breath, enraptured by his liquid gaze as she unlaced her clothing.

"Are you going to give your body to me, treasure?" he hummed, tracking the fall of each garment to the floor. "I know how much you like being told what to do." Pure mischief tugged at the corners of his mouth.

Hettie's cheeks burned, "This is different, and you know it."

"I do," he conceded, "but I need to know if you're going to submit to my instructions or fight me like you do when we practice magic. I'm happy to do either, but they're very different types of play."

"I don't want to fight you." Hettie tucked her chin and folded her arms as her last piece of clothing fell to the ground.

She wanted him to do as he pleased with her, to use her like a toy until he was satisfied. She had no intentions of being a brat.

Not this time anyway.

"Come here, Hettie."

She stepped between his legs as he shifted to the edge of the bed. He pulled her close, pressing his hardness into her belly. He caught her chin with one hand and held her face pointed at his. The other gripped her hip with possessive strength, his fingers digging into her flesh.

"Is there anything you don't want me to do? Or don't want me to touch?"

Her mouth twitched. "I thought you wanted to take control."

He growled, low in his throat, "Oh, I intend to, but it's just as much about your pleasure as mine. I don't want to frighten you, or hurt you, unless that's what you want."

Hettie bit her lip, considering his question. "I have some experience, but it's all been rather... tame. If your tastes border on the wilder side, I'm just going to have to tell you if I like it as we go."

"Fair," Gyl chuckled. He released her chin to rub both his hands up and down her body. "Well, we know you don't mind being handled by the throat. What about restraints, if I tie you up so you can't move and have no choice but to take what I give you?"

A fresh ache flooded her groin. Gyl was smirking before she even said, "I like the sound of that."

"What if it's in an awkward position? Like tying your wrists to your ankles?"

"I'd try it," Hettie shrugged. She trailed her fingers over his chest.

"And what if I gagged you so you couldn't beg?" Gyl watched her face carefully.

"I'd try it," she repeated, her breath catching.

"And if I wanted to pinch or slap or spank you?" He dug his fingers into her ass, his voice soft as velvet.

"I don't want it to hurt too much," she bit her lip, "but I'd let you."

"But you'd be okay with just a little?"

She nodded. That day he'd lost himself and dug his claws into her she'd been surprised how much she liked it. She hadn't thought herself one for pain, and truly she still wasn't, but those little snags in her skin had only heightened her enjoyment of his tongue deep in her cunt.

"Mm," he hummed appreciatively, "and if I wanted to put something back here?" He spread the globes of her ass, pressing the pad of one finger to her puckered muscle.

She jumped, startled, and said, "I've never tried that before."

"Would you?" He circled that finger, putting gentle pressure but not trying to enter her. It felt different, but she didn't want him to stop. She shivered.

"Yes."

"What a pliant little thing you are," he murmured. He claimed her mouth in a quick, rough kiss before he stood and tossed her down on the bed. He dragged that second box to where he could better reach it, and drew from within a coiled length of golden rope chain.

"Hold your legs just so," he told her, bending her knees so they were folded as far as her plump thighs would allow, with her feet flat on the bed. He started to wind the chain around one ankle, then paused and set it aside. He crawled over her, once more grasping her chin and making her look at him.

"I'm going to bind your legs with this chain," he told her, "but I want you to tell me if it's uncomfortable – pins and needles, pain, anything. And most importantly, do not ever let anyone bind you with something they cannot sever in seconds. It is not safe." To prove his point he snagged the end of the chain, wrapped the first few inches around his fingers, and snapped off a short piece. He handed it to her, the girth of the woven links made the chain nearly as wide as her finger. She knew at a glance she could not have broken this same piece herself, yet he'd done it like it was made of matchwood.

"I understand."

"Good." He kissed her and sank back, coiling the cold chain around her calf once again. "Tell me stop at any point and I'll take them off."

He looped the chain around her thigh and lower leg, twisting and knitting it so the knot rested against the crease where her calf pressed into the back of her thigh. He repeated the steps until there was a ladder of knots, her leg bound into the folded position.

She could already feel herself starting to float. There was a mild discomfort from the chain digging into her leg, but being unable to move it was already removing a facet of her control, releasing her.

He moved on to her second leg, repeating the treatment until both her legs were folded and bound.

"You doing alright?" he asked with a soft hum, strumming the knots on either side.

"Mhm," she confirmed. Her legs were weighed by the chains so they fell open, exposing her core to him.

"Can I do your arms now, treasure?" He bent and pressed a line of kisses from knee to inner thigh on each side.

"Yes," she groaned.

"Mm, I will then. In just a moment." He nuzzled the curls on her mons and dragged his tongue along her slit.

Hettie whimpered. She could feel her legs twitching against her restraints, but they were held captive by the chains.

While he teased her, almost without looking, he reached for one of her arms, taking another length of chain and looping it around her upper thigh, and then her wrist, effectively pinning her arm at her side. He again repeated this on the other side, with her metal arm, until Hettie was unable to move at all. She was now thoroughly under Gyl's control, and the only thing that would make her completely powerless was a gag.

When he lifted his head, she glanced over at the box expectantly. Gyl chuckled, nipping at her inner thigh.

"Eager are we? What else was it you were wanting?"

Hettie flushed, "You mentioned a gag."

He smirked and gave her hip a pat. "Not while you're on your back. They make you drool, and it's hard to swallow."

"Lovely," she remarked. "You've used them before?"

"Watched others use them. It was what inspired me to start my collection. You couldn't even imagine the kinds of toys I have down there in the vault," his grin was wicked, his eyes smoky. Gyl chuckled again, the soft sound sending a pulse of heat through her, "Gags can be messy, but sometimes you can't know if you like something until you try it. But you're getting me off topic." He teased her with the brush of his fingertips over her entrance. "I have something else that might be fun for us this time."

He reached into the box again, drawing out yet more gold chain. This was an implement with a handle, from which hung dozens of strands of fine gold chain.

"Do you know what this is?" He asked her. He tickled her knees with the ends of the chains, and she twitched against her bonds.

"No."

"It's a flogger."

Hettie wasn't sure if that shiver was of fear or anticipation.

"I don't intend to flog you, not tonight, but I thought it might be fun for a little sensation play." He danced the ends of the flogger over her breasts. The cold metal made her nipples bead up. He kept going, tracing those strands over her, tickling her, occasionally giving the whole implement a little spin and letting all the strands thud gently against her skin.

Hettie was on fire. Not only was her pussy soaked and aching, but the cold metal played off her heated flesh, and her magic swirled and thundered within her. Strangely, she didn't feel out of control, like somehow submitting to Gyl had contained it in a different way.

"Please, Gyl," she was back to begging, pulling a little against the bonds that held her still.

"Just one more thing, and I'll give you some relief," he promised, setting the flogger aside.

He reached into the box and pulled out one more length of gold chain, this one dripping with gems, with ruby-encrusted clamps on each side.

"Those look painful," she commented, wary of those clamps.

"Not unless you want them to be." She could tell he was trying not to be amused. "They're for your nipples. They'll only go as tight as I make them. Can we try?"

Suddenly her breasts felt achingly untouched, despite the almost overstimulation from the flogger a moment ago.

"Please," she whispered.

"My treasure," he hummed. He closed his mouth around each brown peak, suckling them until they were prominent enough that he could tighten a ruby clamp on them. The chain hung between them, the weight adding pressure to the not-quite-painful squeeze.

"Oh, gods," Hettie moaned, her head falling back. Stimulation everywhere, except the one place she really wanted it. Her cunt was still achingly, weepingly empty.

"I promised you relief," Gyl growled, "but if you keep making sounds like that I'm going to skip right to the rutting."

"Please," Hettie gasped desperately. She needed to be filled.

"No," Gyl huffed, "you first."

He sealed his mouth on her clit, slipping finger after finger into her channel and curling them against her front wall. All she could do was squirm and clutch what bedding was beneath her hands. She cried out as her climax thundered through her, her legs shaking as the urge to extend them made her strain against her bindings.

Gyl sat up, licking his lips as he crawled over her. She whimpered as he dragged his monster down her slit, those V-shaped ridges stimulating her sensitive clit.

"Still alright, treasure? How are your legs?"

"*Please,* stop stalling," she near-sobbed. She might combust if he didn't just fuck her.

Gyl clucked his tongue, "And here I thought I was the one in control."

His hand curled around her throat, the bands of his rings hard and warm against her skin. He held her firmly, pinning her down to the mattress. Hettie went completely lax, gazing up at him foggily as he tightened his fingers ever so slightly.

"There she is," Gyl purred, "Sweet treasure. Don't worry. You'll get what you're craving, even if you weren't patient."

He shifted, and that broad, flat head pressed at her entrance. She couldn't see what he was doing, not pinned like she was, but he was digging in the box again. A moment later, something cool and slick splashed where their sexes pressed together.

"Just something to make this a little easier for you, treasure," he told her when she twitched, startled. She'd assumed it was, but was grateful for the explanation regardless.

Now well lubricated, that throbbing monster pressed into her. She could already feel the ache as he stretched her, but she wanted more.

He was gentle, moving in slow, pressing thrusts. He gripped her hip, held her throat, eyes focused downward on where his cock disappeared within her.

It wasn't long before she felt the swell of his knot pressing at her entrance. Gyl let out a shaky breath, his fingers twitching against her pulse.

"You're taking me so well, treasure." His voice was ragged, his face strained. "Look at you, stretched wide and ready to take my knot. Do you want it?"

"Yes!" Hettie keened. The edge of discomfort was creeping

into her legs, her nipples were starting to throb with a dull ache, and her cunt was burning from the stretch of him. She felt like if she took any more she was going to fly to pieces, and yet that was all she wanted.

"Hold on tight," he teased. Before Hettie could ask, *to what*, he was already moving, filling her, *fucking* her, in long, rolling strokes that had her feeling every ridged inch of him. With every thrust her breasts bounced, jostling the chain that tugged on her nipples and awakening an ache in them.

This was so much better than any prior experience she'd had with men. Gyl had spent so much time devoted solely to her pleasure – and truly still was, given the way he moved those hips. Everything he did added to the song her body played for him, and she was ready for the crescendo. She could already feel another climax approaching.

Then, Gyl gripped her throat a fraction harder, and black spots swam in her vision. She floated fully, carried away in a wash of sensation.

Hettie came with a wordless cry, every muscle begging to be let free and spasming against her bindings. Gyl released her throat, tugging the clamps free from her nipples. Sharp pain flared as the blood rushed back to the pinched flesh, fading quickly into a dull, aching throb that mirrored the one in her cunt. Her sex pulsed around Gyl's cock, trying to squeeze, but the stretch was too tight.

He shivered and let out a strangled groan, "*Hettie.*" He pressed himself hard against her entrance, and she felt the moment she gave way to his knot.

She took in a sharp breath. She felt so *so* full, bordering on pain, but the magic within her swirled and danced as the sensation extended her own peak.

She hadn't needed to release any magic at all, she realized. She was brimming full of it, but it was almost like since she hadn't been able to focus on anything but Gyl's ministrations, she hadn't been able to stress over it, and thus it wasn't stirred into causing mayhem.

Hettie could feel his cock pulsing, heat filling her as his seed painted her from within. Before he was even finished rocking that knot into her, he was already reaching down to her bindings, snapping them with a series of metallic pops.

"Don't break them," she protested weakly. How would he bind her next time if he did that?

"I have more," he panted, tossing away the broken pieces. He rubbed her legs, one at a time, encouraging the blood back into them as she extended them. "How are you feeling?

"A little stiff, but no worse for wear," she reported, squeezing him with her knees. The movement jostled them, and they both hissed as his knot pulled against her entrance.

Gyl wrapped his arms around her, rolling them carefully so she lay on his chest.

"How long will we stay locked together?" She asked, resting her cheek on her forearm. Those swirling eddies of magic were settling back in, leaving her feeling warm more than just physically.

"It depends," Gyl murmured sleepily.

"On what?" Hettie prodded. She ground down on him experimentally, feeling the fullness of his swollen knot truly trapped within her sex, the swell of it pressing against her pubic bone.

Gyl's drooped eyelids flew open, and his fingers dug into the supple flesh of her hips, holding her still. He growled, an almost animal sound low in his chest that she could feel rumbling beneath her.

"On how still you are," he ground out finally.

"Oh." Hettie had half a mind to cause mischief, but she was actually starting to feel sore. She lay flat on his chest and sighed as he toyed idly with one of her curls, wrapping the strand around his fingers and pressing it tenderly to his lips.

"You did very well today, treasure."

"On which thing?"

"All of it," he chuckled. "Practicing your magic, submitting to me, taking my cock – you did well with everything we tried today."

"I live to please," she huffed, half-laughing. Truly, she did feel accomplished. She was making positive progress, she'd just had the best sex of her life, and nobody new was a chicken at the end of the day. She'd accept it as a win.

A short while later, when his knot finally eased, she sat up and slid his cock free and an absolute torrent of his spend began pouring from her. Gyl shifted quickly, snaking one hand between them and covering her slit with it, trapping his release within.

"I like the idea of you full of my seed," he growled thoughtfully, "of you swollen with my dragonets."

Hettie's belly flipped. There was something faraway about him like this. Something feral, like the smooth Gyl she knew had temporarily taken a backseat to the one who was alone for years on end. His eyes were distant and sharp, trained vaguely on his hand on her cunt. She wasn't afraid of him, but there was something unsettling about him, something inhuman, bestial.

She combed her fingers though his hair, the strands like fine black silk. She kept doing it, petting him and grooming him, until his gaze softened and he finally looked her in the eyes, looking a little less wild.

"It's too soon to talk about babies, Gyl," she told him gently. She didn't even know how long she'd be staying here. She had a life in Serpent's Bay, and as lovely as her stay here had become, she missed her old life terribly. She had a job and coworkers she cared for, and once she got control of her magic again she might even have friends. She didn't want to spend the rest of her life locked in a castle, having babies. Besides, didn't dragons lay eggs? She didn't think her body could do that.

He blinked, like he'd only just realized what he'd said, "No, you're right. I don't know what came over me."

"I'm marked, so I can't get pregnant," she told him, turning her left arm so the faint scar-like lines on her wrist were visible. He lifted his free hand and circled her forearm with it, stroking those lines with his thumb. The way he traced his thumbnail over it gave her a vivid image of him breaking the skin with one dragon claw and dispelling the charm. She hated that that didn't repulse her.

"You know," Hettie continued thoughtfully, "as long as my mark is unbroken, I wouldn't mind if you wanted to pretend."

"Pretend?" His brow creased.

"If breeding me is something that lights your fire, as they say, I wouldn't mind if you wanted to pretend you were putting babies in me."

"Dragonets," he corrected.

"But I'm not a dragon," she laughed.

"It doesn't matter. Dragon blood isn't dilutable. A drop of dragon blood makes it a dragon."

Hettie couldn't possibly see how that would work, but she didn't want to break down the biology of dragon babies while he held her cunt full of his spend, so she said, "I see. Well, either way, if you want to pretend, you have my permission."

Gyl's pupils blew wide and he cleared his throat. "I think the urge was triggered by knotting you. I've honestly never thought about it before."

"Now that you know you can do it whenever you want, will you let me go so I can clean up?" She tried pulling back, but his hand followed her.

"I don't really want to," he admitted sheepishly.

She laid her hand on his forearm. She knew she couldn't push him away, she didn't have the strength, but there was clearly something instinctual going on here that she needed to disrupt. Gyl was obviously not used to fighting his urges, so denying whatever signal his brain was firing telling him to keep her full of seed was going to be difficult for him. If she was here to learn to do hard things, then he could do it too – with some help from her.

She leaned forward until their foreheads touched, the curl of his horns pressing into her skin. Nuzzling their noses, she whispered to him, "Don't you want to come shower with me and watch your seed drip from my pussy? Don't you want to witness the result of how truly well you mastered my body?"

Gyl shuddered, a needy little gasp puffing across her cheek.

"I do, I want that."

"Then you have to release me," she teased.

Gyl let out a whine, eerily similar to several begging dogs she'd heard, and said, "Fine, but you keep your hand here while I ready the shower."

She slipped her hand under his, and he let her replace him over her entrance. Immediately, she felt the hot, wet press of his seed pool in her palm. She pressed a little more firmly as she rolled off of him.

He scampered into the bathroom, throwing her little glances as he walked. His tail twitched agitatedly as he disappeared around the doorframe.

Needy thing. It was a little cute, Hettie admitted to herself. She felt she should be more alarmed by this behavior, but it amused her more than anything. She wasn't sure what that said about her.

In the shower he made her stand with one leg propped up on the ledge while she spread her sex wide with her fingers. He knelt on the ground with his hands on her thighs as the water pelted them, watching his release trickle from her. When she squeezed her lower belly and sent a spurt sliding down her thigh, he shuddered, and a pulsing wave of scales traveled over his body.

"Thank you for this," he told her, reaching for a cloth and some of her new soap.

"For what?" She hummed with contentment as he started swiping that cloth over her from his position on the floor, starting with her sex before he rinsed and soaped it and began moving up from her feet.

"For easing me out of... whatever that was."

"You've already helped me immensely. I don't mind returning the favor."

He gently pulled her leg down from the ledge and cleaned that one too. "Still."

The hiss of water spraying over them was the only sound for a moment as Hettie enjoyed Gyl's care. He kissed her soft belly before standing and continuing his work.

"I'll probably attempt to make some healing balm to-morrow." At his alarmed glance, she assured him, "I'm just sore. You've got a monster between your legs, did you forget? If you'd like to enjoy that activity with any sort of frequency, I'll need a faster way to recover."

Some of that familiar smoothness returned to Gyl, and he flashed her a smug look. "So you enjoyed it? Everything?"

"No," she said tartly, "I came so hard my eyes swam because I hated it so much."

He laughed and drew her into his arms, the water and soap making their skin slick where their bodies pressed together.

"Will you lie with me tonight?" Her lips skimmed his collar as she spoke.

"You always ask, and I always do."

"I don't want to assume." What if he wanted to go work in his shop and sleep in that cozy little nest?

"Assume away, because I'd rather eat my own tail than be apart from you."

Her heart squeezed. Unsure how to respond to that, she reached for the cloth still dangling in his hand.

"Gimme. It's your turn to be pampered." She could do that much for him, at least.

The next day she almost could have fooled herself into thinking she was back in the shop, making a restock of healing balm for the shelves. Once they were both certain she wasn't about to blow anything up, Gyl slipped away to tidy his work-shop, and it was just Hettie and Didi in her work room – a dedicated room separate from the practice room, stocked with things she needed for spell weaving and potion brewing.

She'd brought her chicken companion down for the day, feeling a little like she'd been neglecting her. It was unintentional, but Gyl and Hettie had been all over each other, which means that Didi was left alone in her own space fairly often. Hettie couldn't shake the guilt over that, but she doubted she ever would, at least not until she managed to change her back into her beautiful red-headed self.

So she chattered idly to Didi as she worked, petting her feathered head any time she put down her tools.

"I'm not trying to get wrapped up in this dragon, you know," she confessed to Cordelia. "He's just so..." She trailed off, focused on the herbs she was crushing for a moment. "He needs me. He's been alone too long, and I guess I sort of relate."

If chickens could give exasperated looks, Cordelia certainly did.

"I know, I know, it's ridiculous," Hettie told her, her face burning, "but I can't help but feel like he was meant to find me that day, you know? Do you believe in fate? Is that a real thing?"

Cordelia tilted her speckled head to and fro, like she was considering it. Finally she tipped her beak in a nod.

"Do you think *us* meeting was fate? Ow!" She'd received a sharp peck in response to her question, the first she'd gotten in quite a while. "Okay, okay, I get it! I'm not trying to shift blame for what happened. I just think it might comfort both of us if it was always supposed to be this way. Temporarily!"

She added the last part frantically as she yanked her hand away from Didi's striking beak. She wasn't quite fast enough. "Goddess, have you been sharpening that thing? Why does it hurt so much more than I remember?"

Cordelia rustled her wings and tipped up her beak, gloating.

At least the blood she drew gave Hettie something to test her balm on once she'd finished making it. The punctures closed easily, and Hettie smiled. She was doing real magic again, and nothing was blowing up in her face. It was both a tremendous relief and a point of pride.

Not to mention she could use it to soothe her tired, aching pussy. She hoped she'd get used to the size of that knot soon, because it had felt incredible, but she'd definitely been walking bowlegged all that morning.

Sobering from that thought, she also realized this meant she was one step closer to fixing Didi. In mere days she'd made more progress figuring out her magic issues than in a year at the magic shop. She loved the ladies who owned *Pollimer's Potions* dearly, but they had not been equipped for this. Whether or not Hettie and Cordelia crossing paths was fate, Gyl finding her most certainly was.

"I'll change you back, Cordelia. I swear I will," she promised. She lifted the bird into her arms and rubbed her cheek over the top of her head. She was spared the peck she expected, Didi instead making soft little coos at her. "I won't rest until I do."

9

Hettie was making remarkable progress. She had no problem making her balm the day after her first successes, and after that day if she needed to make a transfer it was for her comfort, not her safety. Every other potion she'd tried so far was a success, though her spells were not quite as successful.

She still struggled with more complex magics, particularly anything that wasn't channeled through ingredients like potions, but her failures were mostly theatrical, not dangerous. Bright lights and smoke were the bulk of the consequences so far, but she'd also not tried any magic where a partial result would be devastating – like changing Cordelia back.

Despite her progress, she was getting restless. She'd begun asking him questions he didn't have answers for, and when he admitted to having no clue, she moved on to things he *wouldn't* answer.

"Where do you think this magic came from?"

"But how does it work?"

"Surely I wouldn't be capable of that, would I?"

"Can I see your dragon form?"

"When are we going to see your elder?"

He thought these questions stemmed mostly from boredom, and so when she started delving into things he didn't want to talk about, he turned to distracting her with his body.

She took his cock much better than he ever could have dreamed, pliant and supple and so, so willing.

Though he kept his knot to himself after that first time. The deep-rooted, primordial instincts that welled up in the aftermath... They had scared him. He had never been particularly possessive, but suddenly he was absolutely rabid to claim her. He had wanted to pin her to that bed, rake through her mark with his claws, and knot her until she was round with his eggs.

Had wanted to, but he still had enough control that he'd never do that to her. Not unless she asked him. Could she even bear his eggs? As she had pointed out, she was not a dragon. He knew dragons had mated with other creatures in the past, but he had no knowledge of how dragonets from those pairings were formed.

It had been nearly a week since he'd first tied her. The last thing they needed was for both of them to be out of control, because he still had no willful mastery of his beast form. Nearly all those little partial transformations were completely random, not anything he'd done with intention.

But Hettie was relentless, and he was nearing the end of his patience. As his temper swelled, so too did his knot.

"I just want some answers," she huffed at Gyl after a particularly stressful practice session. She'd had her spells blow up in her face every time, one even starting a fire that climbed the curtains of her practice room before he contained it, and she was clearly feeling dejected.

"We're finding your answers," he told her with as much patience as he could muster. They'd been around in circles on this one already that day, but she was not giving it up this time. They were both sporting tempers that were worn thin, and he was struggling to dodge her questions with kindness.

"We're sitting on our thumbs," she groused, "C'mon, Gyl, I'm not a walking bomb anymore. Take me to see your elder. You said you would."

"Not yet." Gyl had been trying to push this off for a few days now. He was clearly running out of time.

She was ready. He could admit that to himself. *He*, on the other hand, was not. The only way to reach any of the elders' dens, particularly his uncle, the one he thought most likely to help them, was to fly. He could not do that in his current state.

He had not told her this.

What was stopping him? It wasn't like she wouldn't understand. If there was anyone who would sympathize with his body being out of his control, it would be her.

It was shame, primarily. What use was a dragon that couldn't *be* a dragon? A part of him worried, however irrationally, that if she found out just how broken he was, she wouldn't trust him to help her fix her own problems, and she'd leave.

He couldn't handle that. Not now. Later, after she'd gained

more mastery over her magic, if she wanted to go... he'd do his best to allow it. He'd assured her she wasn't a prisoner, and that was still true. He couldn't keep her here after she mastered her ability, not in good conscience.

"You keep saying that," she growled, pushing off the table she leaned against to stalk towards him, "*Not now, Hettie. I don't want to talk about this right now, Hettie.* I'm tired of it. I thought you were going to help me?" She folded her arms, eyes flashing with temper.

"I *am* helping you," he ground through gritted teeth. Smoke curled from his nostrils in a constant stream. At least his internal fire was still alight. It was brighter and hotter than he could ever remember it being, and it felt pleasantly sizzly in his chest.

"Then help me get answers. I just have this feeling that once I know where this magic came from, I'll be able to manage it better."

She was ever the scholar. Only an academic would think they needed to see the root of a problem before the fruit could be harvested properly.

"I can't take you yet." He folded his arms too, and the two of them posed in a stand-off.

"Can't, or won't?" she finally asked after a few seconds of tense silence.

"*Can't.*"

Eyes narrowed, she scanned his face thoroughly. "Are you going to tell me why?"

Gyl couldn't look at her. He said nothing, eyes on the space just over her shoulder.

Hettie sighed, "Then I need to go back to town."

"No." His response was immediate, flung from his mouth by a wave of panic.

"Yes," she quipped, "I need answers. I want to see if the university has contacted the shop yet."

Did his face betray how wildly his heart was beating? It felt like a wild thing, caught and caged, beating against the bars and bludgeoning itself in a desperate bid for freedom.

"You can't go," he clasped her wrist. "It's not safe."

"It'll be fine, Gyl." She turned her hand and clasped his forearm. "I just won't use magic while I'm there. I've not lost control completely in days."

"Yes, but a few short days is not proof of control," he clung to that reasonable excuse desperately. "You've been in a relaxed environment, without many stressors or bystanders. You don't know how you'll manage under pressure."

How was he supposed to tell her that the idea of her being that far from him was frightening beyond measure? Anything could happen – to her or because of her – in the city. And his going with her was out of the question. With the way he was feeling right now he'd roast alive the first person to look at her with an ounce of interest.

He had never before felt the sharp ring that tightened around his heart, but he recognized the feeling all the same. Possessiveness. Jealousy. A fierce protective instinct.

Dragons were hoarders by nature, greedy creatures with selective special interests. When one of his kind found their treasure trove threatened, their instinct to protect what was theirs often overrode all good sense. As a dragonet, his mild-mannered mother had once pinned him to the ground when he'd flamed a little too close to one of her textile pieces. He'd been unhurt, and she'd apologized profusely, but the message and the memory were both burned clear – no matter who you are, don't fuck with another dragon's hoard.

Gyl had always thought he'd escaped this particular dragon behavior, that he'd been a singular idiosyncrasy in the hundreds of thousands of years of dragon history, a dragon who loved his hoard but lacked that aggressive protective streak.

Clearly, he was wrong.

He'd dubbed her "treasure," but it was far more than just a cutesy pet name. He wanted to keep her, to cherish her, to make it known to her each day that she was precious and beautiful, and most of all keep her safe and away from any and everything that wasn't him.

But Hettie was a person, not one of his constructs. He couldn't just lock her away. Eventually he'd have to concede. He'd have to let her do as she pleased, or she'd feel like a prisoner again. He couldn't abide by that.

But he didn't have to let her go just yet. He had more excuses left yet.

She fisted her hands on her hips, "What's your problem?"

"I don't have a problem," he lied.

"Yes, you do. Why don't you want me to meet the dragon elder?"

"Of course I want you to meet him." He pinched the bridge of his nose. He was tired, and being repeatedly on the brink of humiliation was only making him grouchier. He needed to be done with this conversation, and soon.

A flicker of something like hurt flashed across Hettie's face, "Are you ashamed of me or something?"

"What?" Anger sparked in his belly. How could she possibly have arrived at that conclusion? "Of course not."

"Then why-"

Gyl growled with frustration, taking a quick step into her space. His hand snapped up to the back of her head, his fingers gathering up her hair and gripping it tightly. He tugged her head back, baring her throat. She fell silent with a ragged gasp, her eyes fluttering.

"I have answered all the questions I have patience for today," his voice rumbled low in his throat. "If you say one more thing about leaving this castle I'm going to gag you and fuck you into silence. Is that clear?"

A shiver traveled up the length of her body and into his hand, but not one of fear. The perfume of her arousal bloomed, heady and sweet. He inhaled until his ribs hurt, taking in as much of that sweet scent as his lungs could hold.

That little pink tongue flicked out over her bottom lip, "You're going to have to gag me, because I'm not giving this up."

"If you insist," he purred. He released her hair and clasped the neck of her dress with both hands, making sure he had all the layers of her clothes. With a sharp tug, he ripped them down the center of her body. Her bare breasts fell, and as he dropped her ruined garment he lifted his hands to cup them.

"You're lucky those were singed, or I'd be a little annoyed by that," she said, but the words didn't match her breathy tone, or the surging flood of arousal in the air.

"Hush," he told her, claiming her mouth with a rough kiss. He tugged her firmly into his body, luxuriating in the way her soft curves molded to him, contrasted sharply by the hard bite of her prosthetic into his shoulder as she clung to him, and the rims of her glasses into his cheeks.

When he'd kissed her so thoroughly that he started to feel some of that stubborn tension melt from her, he walked her back toward the table. She gave a little squeak of protest as he lifted her, settling her so she was seated on the scorched surface.

"I'm going to fetch your gag," he barely broke their kiss to speak, his lips feathering over hers, "and some other things, and you are going to stay right here, exactly where you are."

"I'm going to touch myself while you're gone."

A feral sound burst from his chest. "There will be consequences for you if you do." Normally he liked watching her please herself, but today he wanted to be the only one with that privilege.

A devilish little smirk creased her cheek.

Well, if that was how she wanted to play...

He swept her ruined garments up with the tip of his tail, passing them into his hands so he could rip them into strips. With a few deft movements, and after catching her squirming limbs as she giggled, he bound her with her feet together, her wrists behind her back. He left her sitting up, but she could easily lay on her side if that was more comfortable for her.

His ran his thumb across her lip and told her gruffly, "Be still, treasure. I'll be right back."

The room she had chosen for practice was only a few floors away from his vault, so it was a quick trip down to fetch the things he needed. He would be back in a matter of minutes. He would not leave her alone trussed up like that for long.

Despite his more laid-back nature when it came to his hoard, and the sheer chaotic state of the room, he still knew where every item was. It only took him a moment to collect his implements and return to the practice room, a chorus of tinkling metal draped over one arm.

"Took you long enough," she grumbled when he walked in.

She'd really sharpened her tongue, hadn't she?

"Tough talk for a woman tied up on a table," he told her with a low laugh. She just harrumphed in response. "First thing's first, open wide."

He separated the gag out from his other tools, setting them aside on the table. It was a simple one, a gold ring on a leather strap, charmed to be easier on her teeth. He showed it to her and watched the eager heat spread across her face. The moment she realized what it was, she popped her mouth open. He settled the ring behind her teeth and fastened the buckle behind her head.

"How's the fit? Not too uncomfortable?" He was grateful when she shook her head, because the sight of her mouth stretched wide, unable to speak, with a gold glint from the gag shining inside, was absolutely magnetic. A pulse of blood flooded his cock, and it throbbed – as if he wasn't already achingly hard for her.

That smug look on her face told him she knew exactly the effect she'd had on him.

He grasped her by the chin, tracing her bottom lip with his thumb. The metal ring was already growing hot from her body, and it was so easy to just slide his thumb into her mouth, pressing down on her tongue with the pad of it. She squirmed, a helpless sound gurgling up from her throat.

Oh, how tempting it was to just knock her flat and take her like this, but he'd brought other toys he wanted to try.

"Since you can't speak, we need to give you another way to alert me, yes?" Gyl removed his hand from her face and snagged his next tool from the pile. He held it in front of her, a palm-sized filigree ball – gold, naturally – with a smaller ball on the inside. He shook it, and a musical chime sounded from it. "I'm going to give you this bell, and if anything feels off, or too much, or if you just want the gag out, you shake it. Clear?"

She gave him a slow nod. He grinned and kissed the tip of her nose as he reached around her to press the bell into one hand. He went ahead and claimed her glasses, setting them out of the way so they wouldn't get broken.

The next thing he grabbed was a pole with four cuffs attached. He reached down and freed her ankles, gesturing to the table. "On your knees, treasure."

She obeyed. Slowly, because her hands still bound made her balance awkward, but he let her do it on her own. Once she was up on her knees, he knocked her legs apart, baring her glistening pussy for his eyes. He rested the bar on his shoulder, leather cuffs swinging into his chest. With his other hand he traced up her thigh, trailing his fingertips over her sex.

"Can I assume you've never seen one of these before?" he asked as he circled her clit.

She shivered and nodded, a soft little moan escaping her.

He continued, "Can you guess what it's for?"

Another nod. He could already see the shine of saliva pooling in her mouth.

"And you don't mind being strapped to it?"

Hettie made an annoyed sound, her eyes narrowing. She rocked her pelvis against his hand as if to say, *get on with it.*

Gyl chuckled, "Turn this way then." He directed her so she

was facing down the length of the table. He guided her top half down to the surface, supporting her so she didn't hit her face since her hands were still behind her back.

He lay the bar between her legs, spreading them a little more so he could buckle each of her ankles into the padded leather cuffs hooked onto each end with metal rings. Already she was a pretty sight, bound tight and dripping from two holes, but there were still two cuffs left to fill. He climbed up on the table behind her.

Though before he adjusted her any further, he braced both hands on the backs of her thighs, spreading the lips of her sex with his thumbs so he could taste her honey, dragging his tongue along her slit. She made a strangled sound, pressing backward into his seeking mouth. When he pressed his tongue into her, letting it take on its beast length, he felt her sex pulse and squeeze it, and the helpless sounds she made were like music to his ears, the squeal the grand finale.

"Did you come, treasure?"

She nodded, eyes glazed.

He reached up and undid her wrists, "Tuck your hands under your body, reach as close to your ankles as you can." Slowly, she did so, her cheek squashed flat to the table as she tucked her arms beneath her. He caressed them as he lifted the last two cuffs, each attached by a short chain further in the from the ends of the bar. He secured her wrists and rocked the bar, pleased with the little movement she still had.

"Show me you can still ring your bell," he told her, tracing his fangs over the swell of her ass. A chime sounded from below her. "Good girl," he praised.

He lined himself up behind her, shoving his pants down

around his thighs and freeing his cock. It fell forward and lay in the valley between her ass cheeks, nestled perfectly against the soft brown globes. He rocked against her, letting out a groan of his own as the friction stimulated his already sensitive knot.

He leaned forward, stroking a stay curl back from her face. "Do you want my cock, sweet treasure?" He knew she did, but she got impatient when she was needy, and he lived for that peevish little huff and side eye. He grinned and reached for the glass bottle, one of the last remaining items on the table. He pulled back so his cock was out of the way, then dribbled the heavy, clear liquid from high up, so it hit her anus in a cold, thin stream and dripped down over her cunt.

She jumped, turning her head as best she could to glare at him, though that look of irritation faded into one of foggy pleasure the moment he started rubbing that lubricant into her channel with two of his fingers.

That's right, he thought to himself, *why would you ever need to leave, when I can take care of your every desire, satiate your every need?*

He took a moment to run that slick hand over his cock before he pressed the tip to her entrance. The head slipped in easily, but as always he met a little resistance beyond that, where the thickness and ridges made it less of an easy glide.

But, *oh*, how he loved the way her cunt fluttered and pulsed around him, almost sucking him deeper. He pressed further into her in slow, pulsing thrusts, until his knot was flush to her entrance. He reached down and wrapped his fingers around the bulge if it, the flesh softer there than the rest of his cock – at least until he climaxed, when it stiffened and swelled to lock inside.

Before he could indulge those thoughts too much, he started moving, stroking his cock in and out of her. Beneath him, Hettie squealed and grunted, sounds that would normally have been words, no doubt, but were now just incoherent exclamations of pleasure.

He leaned over her, still stroking into her heat, and pressed a toothy kiss to her shoulder. Her face was faraway and flushed. Her tongue poked through the ring in her mouth ever so slightly, a little puddle of drool pooling on the table.

How pretty she was.

He reached down and slid two fingers into her mouth, hooking them gently into her cheek. She blinked in surprise, alert for a moment, but quickly fell back into her pleasure-fogged state, her tongue lolling softly against his knuckles.

She was so pliant like this, willing to do pretty much any-thing as long as he'd fuck her. The amount of trust she must have in him, to let him render her helpless and have his way with her, was deeper than he could comprehend with his own mind pleasure-fogged. Every press of his knot against her en-trance blanked his mind of everything except the need to bury it deep within her.

He wanted to. So badly. His composure was thin as spider silk. His body craved it, craved her, particularly when she gifted him the upper hand like this.

Because it was a gift. If at any point she'd seemed uncertain or unhappy, bell ringing or not he'd stop immediately, and she knew that. She was too precious for him to tolerate any unruly behavior towards her, even from himself.

A chime from below made him stutter, thrusts that were quickly going erratic as his climax built coming to a halt as he pulled out of her. He leaned over her, checking her face and stroking her cheek. She didn't seem upset, in fact she still seemed pretty content.

"Do you want the gag out?" he guessed. She nodded. He reached up and undid the buckle, carefully displacing the ring from behind her teeth.

Before she'd even closed her mouth all the way, she was already gasping, "Knot. Please, Gyl, I need your knot."

It was hard to see his expression tied up as she was. She twisted as best she could, trying to get a look at him.

"Please," she whimpered again. Her mouth ached a little from being stretched open, but she found she liked the reminder that he'd been there.

"If I knot you down here," he growled, "we'll be stuck lying on this hard table for as long as we're tied."

"I don't care," she was near tears, desperately craving that intense stretch and heat of that first, and only, knot he'd given her almost two weeks ago. She knew he was embarrassed of the way he behaved afterward, but she also knew he'd never hurt her, instincts or no.

"You're sure?" He was already lining his cock back up with her entrance.

"*Yes*," she gasped with relief as he sank back into her,

resuming the slow, pulsing strokes that had been steadily building her climax.

She heard the clink of metal and felt the tug on her ankles and wrists as he picked up the bar between her legs, using it as leverage as he picked up speed. She felt the stretching press of his knot at her entrance with each thrust, and it had her panting with need.

Despite the fact that the gag was gone, she was still a wordless, panting mess. Her lower cheek was streaked with drool she couldn't wipe away, the table beneath it also wet from her saliva. Drooling unhindered had been a little humiliating, but it added to the fact that she was powerless to do anything but let him use her as he pleased.

She'd liked that. Liked it a lot. Wanted to repeat the experience, in fact, and it wasn't even over yet.

"Please," she whimpered, on the brink of a powerful orgasm and desperate for release.

With a wordless growl and a stuttering thrust, Gyl pressed his knot firmly to her entrance. There was, as last time, a moment of burning resistance before the flesh gave way, his knot sliding within her until his hips were pressed firmly to her rump, his cock pulsing inside her as he released a flood of his seed to fill her, gasping and groaning.

Hettie's climax followed, released by the tremendous stretch of that knot pulsing within her, filling her beyond capacity. She cried out, rocking back into him as best she could. Gyl grunted, and she felt him twitch within her as she wrung a fresh spurt of release from him. Then they were both still, locked together.

Panting, he reached for one of the shredded rags from her dress to clean her face and the table. "Are you alright, treasure?"

"Good," she murmured floatily, though she was quickly becoming aware of an ache in her knees where they pressed into the table.

"Let me see what we can do about these," he told her, twisting so he could reach beneath her. As he turned, his knot pulled at her entrance, and they both let out twin cries of agonized pleasure.

"I think I've got it," she told him quickly.

"How do you think you'll manage that?" He asked wryly.

"My magic always behaves better freshly fucked," she told him by way of simple explanation. She smothered a little grin when she felt his cock pulse within her in response.

She encouraged a little of her magic to gather, flicked her fingers, releasing the bell to roll away, and felt the buckles on her wrists and ankles flap open. She carefully drew her arms up in front of her and lifted them above her head.

"Impressive," Gyl kissed her shoulder, "Now hold still."

He curled his arms under her and shifted the both of them so she was sitting on his lap, knees bent under so she was straddling him backwards, him holding her with his arms around her and his knot still firmly implanted. He leaned back against the wall, trailing his hands up and down her thighs. One hand dipped down between them, his fingers stretching wide to feel where his knot swelled at her opening.

"You did it again, treasure. You took me so well," he groaned.

She wanted to preen with his praise, but the reason he'd gagged and fucked her came bleeding slowly back through her sex-hazed consciousness.

"I know what you're doing, you know," she told him gently. She felt him stiffen beneath and behind her.

"I don't know what you mean." She smelled more than saw the agitated puff of smoke that wafted from him.

"Don't lie, old man." It felt weird to call him that with his cock buried in her, but it was his name for when she was annoyed with him. "You've been distracting me with sex for days." And then afterwards, if she tried to bring it up again, he'd either scurry into the bathroom and take an inordinately long time cleaning up, or he'd dive back into pleasuring her again until either way she was too tired to focus.

This incident had been no different. She'd enjoyed herself immensely, but a pleasant side effect of getting what she wanted was that Gyl was trapped, forced to at least listen to her. She just wished he'd knotted her facing him, so she could at least see his expressions.

She reached back and tugged his arms around her midriff. He tightened them, leaning forward to rest his chin on her shoulder.

"You're right," he admitted softly, tilting his head so his temple pressed to hers.

"I know I am," she told him primly. "That's manipulation, Gyl. I don't like it." Well, the sex part she did, more than liked it, in fact.

"I..." he trailed off. His breathing was erratic, and she could feel his heart pounding against her back.

When he didn't speak, she pressed forward, "I need answers, Gyl. If we can't get them from your elders, I need to visit the university."

"No." His voice dropped into a low register, rumbling in his chest. "You can't." His fingers, morphed into sharp claws, dug into her sides.

"You could come with me," she told him gently. She wasn't trying to run from him. In fact, it hadn't even occurred to her to stay in Serpent's Bay. While she had much better control of her magic again, it was not perfect. She wasn't ready to go home, but she'd at least like to assure everyone she wasn't dead.

A growl burst from him, "I couldn't."

"Why not?"

"It's complicated."

Hettie tamped down her frustration. She had to remember he'd been all alone for decades. His social skills were still improving, healing. She realized, like a dip in a cold pool, what one of the things that must be worrying him was, and eased her fingers into those claws, loosening his near-painful hold on her flesh.

"I'll come back," she told him, turning her head to whisper against his cheek, "Even if you stayed behind, you wouldn't be alone for long."

He shivered against her. "Please, Hettie. No more. I know you are ready for this, but I am not. I need more time."

Hettie settled back against his chest, resigned. She'd been afraid of this, that he still wouldn't relent.

"Will you at least tell me why? Even a hint?" It was a desperate plea. She was seeking any thread to grasp, any way to understand.

"Since I've been alone," he hummed, rocking the two of them gently as if seeking comfort, "my bestial nature has been... strange, unpredictable. I fear what I'll do if you go to Serpent's Bay, with or without me."

"Okay," she told him, squeezing his hands.

"That's it? You'll drop it now?" He sounded so relieved, she almost hated to burst his bubble.

"I didn't say that."

"Hettie," he growled.

"But I'm done provoking you for now." Her time was almost up anyway. She could feel his knot sliding within her, nearly soft enough to pull free.

She let him hold her, coddle her, and carry her upstairs and into the shower once they were separated. All the while the wheels in her head turned, spinning thin, wispy thoughts into the threads of a better-laid plan.

She couldn't wait for Gyl to be ready for this. Her progress was stalling, and she just had this feeling that if she knew more about the source, a better understanding would be not just helpful but essential to her continued improvement.

She lay in bed beside him that night, many hours later, mind still churning madly, making plans.

10

It took a day or so before Hettie could act on her plans.

It started with magic practice. She'd found that Gyl didn't know the difference no matter what she was making when brewing potions, so if she happened to brew a batch of extra strength sleeping drops instead of headache tincture, there was no way for him to know.

And if those sleeping drops happened to end up in his wine the next night, he didn't notice that either.

When he dropped into sleep after dinner, it was a heavy, stone-like slumber. Even shaking him didn't wake him. The steady rise and fall of his chest was the only sign that she hadn't accidentally killed him.

With any luck, he'd sleep until she returned, and he'd never know she had gone. She would make amends later, after she returned, hopefully with something resembling answers. Even if he woke before she returned, how mad could he be if she returned successful? He'd pushed her to this, after all. It may not have been intentional for him to let whatever bestial instincts he was struggling with overwhelm him, but they were fucking with her recovery. She wasn't going to keep sitting here while her progress was stagnating.

Transport to town was the easy part. A few days into her stay, Gyl had instructed his constructs to follow her orders as well as his. All she had to do was ask for the carriage to be readied, and they hopped to it. She wouldn't have made it down the mountain otherwise. Despite Gyl's many assurances that she was safe, she had, on occasion, heard the screeching cry of something large and predatory in the distance. It would not be safe for her in her current condition, perhaps not even at her full strength.

Didi eyed her beadily as she prepared to leave, watching as she stuffed her pockets with anything she thought might be useful.

"Don't look at me like that," she told the hen sternly, "I had to. I'll be back before he even knows I'm gone. He won't even have a chance to panic." And he'd likely be furious anyway, as he was sure to figure it out, but at least then they'd circumvent any questionable actions he might take. She would already be back, after all. Didi continued to give her that judgmental look, head slightly tilted, until finally Hettie huffed, "I'm doing this partially for you, you know. Do you want to be a chicken forever? No? Then quiet your eyes. I don't like this any better than you."

She turned her back on both the bird and the sleeping figure in the bed, heading at a steady clip through the castle, toward the front door.

In a handful of hours, the coach was rolling to a stop in front of *Pollimer's Potions.* Hettie's gut churned when she remembered the state she left the shop in. If she showed her face there, would they even speak to her?

She had to try. She needed to know if the university had ever contacted them. They'd been waiting to hear from them when Gyl had abducted her. If she just showed up at the university, they may not even see her unless they were expecting her.

The familiar chime of the bell above the door rattled her nerves. The shop within was as it was before the incident, with little remaining evidence besides a scorch mark here and there on the shelves.

"Be right with you!" called a familiar voice from the back room. Nastia. Hettie was a little disappointed. It was a typical slow period, just before closing, so she was likely manning the store alone. She had hoped it would be Crystal or Poppy. Preferably the latter, since she was likely to be the most compassionate about the whole incident.

Nastia came waltzing up from the back room. "How can I help... you. *You.*" Her eyes widened, her mouth narrowed.

"I can't imagine what this looks like. I know the state this place was in when I was forced to leave." Hettie wrung her hands, hesitant to approach the senior apprentice.

"Nobody forced you to leave," Nastia approached the counter, leaning against it.

"Well..." Hettie fidgeted, opening and closing the hand on her prosthetic and listening to the clicking of her joints. "That's not quite true."

"I find that hard to believe," Nastia folded her arms.

"It's true. Crystal didn't want me to tell you, but I was having trouble controlling my magic. I had an incident, and the man who caused it took me for my own safety – and everyone else's."

Nastia frowned and examined Hettie for a moment before folding, "Why don't you come in the back and tell me the whole story? I'll make some tea."

As Hettie told the story, Nastia's eyes got wider and wider. Her tea was soon forgotten, her slender fingers curled loosely around the cup.

"You're serious? This is all true?"

"Every word," Hettie grimaced. She took a sip of tea, trying to hide a flinch at the bitter taste. Nastia never had been any good at brewing tea, but she'd gone through the trouble, and Hettie wasn't in good enough graces to risk snubbing her. She swallowed again. Was there mint or something in there? Her throat almost felt numbed. If there was, the taste of the herb was overpowered by the bitter bite from being over-steeped.

"That's... awful. I'm so sorry."

"No, it's alright, really. Like I said, things have been going well," Hettie reassured her. She pushed the cup of tea aside. Her stomach was starting to hurt.

"With the man who kidnapped you?" Nastia asked, clear judgement in her eyes.

"It's not as weird as it sounds," Hettie laughed awkwardly. "Look, I won't take much more of your time. I just came to see if the university had contacted Crystal or Poppy yet?" She cleared her throat to try and get rid of the weird, lingering numbness.

"They've been here." Nastia's hands tightened on her cup. "I'm sorry, Hettie."

Hettie blinked back the slight headache that was forming, giving the lights halos. "What for now?"

"I didn't know you weren't volatile anymore."

Hettie realized her tongue wasn't just numb, it was getting clumsy. "What did you do?"

"They told us if you came back you'd likely be dangerous, that we should stall as long as we could until they could arrive with a team. They gave us a panic charm. I activated it when you came in."

The halos around the witchlights were stretching and turning colors. Hettie glanced down at the tea, fairly certain the sheen on the surface was real and not a hallucination.

"The tea?" She went to grasp the handle of her teacup and found her fingers would not obey her. The bell in the shop chimed.

"Drugged. I'm so sorry, Hettie."

Hettie managed a dry, humorless laugh. "The irony is killing me." Only hours prior she'd done the same thing to Gyl, likely even with a similar concoction. Though she'd like to think hers didn't have as many unpleasant side effects.

Darkness swam in restless spots on the edge of her vision. The work room thundered with footsteps. Before she knew it, there were several people grasping her arms and shoulders. Before she could react, something was sprayed in her face with a puff of air, and as she breathed it in, that hesitant darkness surged forward and swallowed her whole.

11

Gyl's tongue felt glued to the roof of his mouth when he woke. His whole body was stiff, and his joints creaked as he sat up.

How long had he been asleep?

A profound sense of *wrong* pervaded his body. It wasn't until he swept his hand over the bed and found only cold, empty sheets that he realized where it came from.

Where was Hettie?

He tried to resist the instant spike of panic. She could just be in the kitchen, or the work room. There was no need to worry yet.

But he knew that wasn't true. That thread that had bound them, which had only been spun thicker and stronger with their prolonged exposure to each other, was drawn taut and stretched to a thin wisp. She was not in the castle.

A hot rage boiled in his belly, and his extremities started tingling. The idea of Hettie alone somewhere without him made him want to spit fire.

Yet he wasn't mad *at* her. Somewhere in the back of his mind was the knowledge that she must have done this to him. She gave him something to make him sleep and left the castle, but his rage was not centered on her. It was a wild thing, almost separate from him, and it coursed through his veins like acid.

He stumbled out of bed, staggering to the door. When he caught himself on the frame, his fingers left deep gouges in the wood. His hands had transformed, deep black claws at the tips of his fingers that faded into gold scales up his wrists.

Shit. He hadn't done that, and he couldn't change them back. He couldn't control anything.

He stormed along the halls, bracing himself on the walls when the remnants of the drug in his system made the floor tilt.

The carriage house was empty. He had a feeling it would be.

Upon his reentry, he spotted one of his maid constructs sweeping the entry hall.

An accomplice for his treasure and a target for his rage.

He knocked the broom out of its hand and grabbed it by the arm. The pieces beneath squeaked and snapped as he curled his fingers too hard. Instant regret cooled his temper enough to keep him from yanking it forward and taking the lower part of its arm off. His creations were perhaps the only thing he cared about other than Hettie. They'd taken care of him when he was deep in his own mind, even if it was only because they were told to.

The construct tipped its blank face up towards him, waiting patiently for his command, completely unaffected by the damage to its limb. His mind filled in the sight of Hettie standing in front of him while his talons dug deep into her prosthetic limb, and he released the construct, recoiling back from it. He took deep breaths, trying to regain his control.

"Did Hettie take the carriage to town?" Could it even answer questions? He didn't know that he'd ever asked one.

The construct nodded.

Gyl growled, a spit of flame escaping from between his teeth. The construct didn't jump, didn't move, didn't do anything except wait for him to tell it something. It was not alive. It could not offer him anything. It could not help him.

Gyl turned away from it as a wave of flame rushed through his body. He could feel his skin rippling with scales, burbling on his back where his wings were bursting through.

He was transforming.

It was completely out of his control. He dropped onto all fours as his limbs lengthened and his form grew. The change didn't hurt, but it *burned*, racing through him like magma in an underground vein. He could feel himself stretching, pins and needles racing through his body as the hall shrank around him.

The growing and prickling ceased, but the fire and rage remained.

Later he'd be thankful he was not a bigger dragon, and that he'd built the front doors to accommodate his scaly size.

Now his only concern was getting outside so he had room to spread his leathery wings. He rammed the front doors with his shoulder, pressing them wide, and scrabbled out onto the gravel that flattened the area in front of his castle. His claws raked into ground as he launched, dirt and scree clattering against his home as his feet left the ground. His wings caught great billows of air, thrusting his golden body forward through the sky.

It wouldn't take him long to reach the city, and when he did, anyone standing between him and his treasure would be sorry.

12

"I'm telling you," Hettie told them through gritted teeth, "that this isn't necessary."

The salt-and-pepper-haired man she'd been dealing with all afternoon adjusted his monocle as he paced the perimeter of the round room. "It's just a precaution, I assure you."

Hettie glared at the translucent purple dodecahedron that domed over her head. "If you've shielded me, then why bother with the binding?" She tugged at the ropes on her wrists where they were tied behind the wooden chair she sat in. They buzzed against her skin, clearly something more than just hemp. Not only was the position uncomfortable and the chair unforgiving, but it was not built for her frame, and the arms of it bit into her hips and thighs. She was getting quite stiff, as she'd been sitting here since she woke, and was starting to feel a pressing need in her bladder.

"The ropes are threaded with strands of spellsilver wire. Additional precautions only, nothing personal."

Hettie blew a strand of hair out of her face, resisting the urge to roll her eyes. She'd already, quite patiently, explained that the information they were working with was out of date, and that she hadn't had an incident in some days. As long as she didn't try to use her magic, she was unlikely to be dangerous, though she hadn't had any bouts of stress or strong emotion to test that theory in a while.

Though if the rope was really twisted with spellsilver, she shouldn't have felt her magic stir at all. The metal was extremely rare and well known for its ability to dampen a person's access to their internal well of magic. She could feel it against her skin, but it didn't seem to do anything to whatever kind of chaos magic she possessed. That was a curiosity she was sure they'd like to know but she kept to herself out of spite. They weren't listening to her anyway.

She'd managed fairly well, so far. Despite the perceived danger of the situation, she had been doing a fine job of staying collected. There had been a stirring within her when she'd first woke, uncomfortable and unable to move, but rather than fight to stuff it down as she might have before, she let the feeling run its course. Her magic had bristled along with the emotion, but it settled under her skin instead of bursting free, thrumming along the natural pathways her body's systems created.

In addition to her hours of practice, it also helped that the monocled figure peering at her from the other side of the wards was a familiar one. Matthias Swallowtail was one of the senior advisors in the university's magic theory program, though he hadn't been Hettie's. Even so, he was well-known on campus for his ego, expertise, and ill-timed flare for the dramatic. He'd recently been named as one of the people responsible for dispatching a monster in the capital city of Avarel, and she hadn't even been able to read his interview in the local newspaper without rolling her eyes at things his pompous ego made him say.

"*I'm* not taking it personally, professor, but I'm telling you-"

Matthias interrupted like he hadn't been listening, "It's rather curious how this condition didn't emerge until your mid-twenties, wouldn't you say? Generally, if students are going to crack under pressure, it happens during their schooling."

Hettie bristled a little at the implication that she was cracking, but there was a more pressing matter at hand. "Yes, very strange, but-"

"We need to run some tests before we can let you free. I'm sure you understand. Public safety and whatnot." He gestured to a group of his peers hovering around a table in her periphery. "Sit tight a moment longer."

Swallowtail's assistant stepped close to the barrier as the man himself joined his colleagues. She was rather short and pale, with a round, freckled face and coppery, chin-length hair. The tips of her pointed ears poked through the strands.

"I told him this was not the way to handle this, but that man listens to nothing except his own ego and his unreliable visions."

Hettie grunted. She had no response for that. "*Not the way to handle it,*" was an understatement at best.

"And for the record, I am sorry," the assistant told her, walking away without waiting for another response.

"You will be," Hettie murmured darkly to herself.

She sighed, her chin sagging toward her chest. No matter how hard she tried, they weren't listening. Based on context clues, she'd been knocked out for the entire evening and most of the next day. She'd given Gyl enough sleeping drops to knock out a horse for a week, but Gyl was a *dragon*. She had no doubt he'd be awake soon, if he wasn't already, and he was not going to be happy. She'd seen his instinctual side intrude upon his good sense more than once when it was just the two of them. It would have been bad enough for him to find her their willing guest. If that possessive streak reared its head while she was tied up like this? She feared what he'd do if he found her compromised this way.

It seemed like this idea had been a bust anyway. Gyl had been right. They had no clue about the origin of her power. That much had been clear from the start. One of the first things they'd done once she'd shaken the fog of the concoction she'd been slipped was interrogate her on the nature of her magic. After she'd finished describing how it had manifested in the beginning, they'd lost interest in listening to her. She'd tried to explain how it had changed since, tried to explain *who* had helped her change it, but they were all as self-absorbed as Professor Swallowtail. Anything that might indicate she could possibly know better than they did was promptly disregarded.

She'd forgotten how infuriating the Master-Tier mages were. It was why she'd declined furthering her education with the university in the first place.

What was additionally frustrating was the knowledge that one of these people *knew* Gyl. He told her he had his constructs enchanted here. Several of these master mages were skilled in animation magic. If they would just listen to her, they'd know the danger they were in.

Though they'd find out soon enough.

As she glared at the backs of their heads, the crowd of mages shifted and parted, gifting her a glance at the table they surrounded. She couldn't have named anything she spotted in that brief handful of seconds, but the glint of a row of metal implements was enough to set her heart pounding again. She felt the hot acid burn of her magic rise up in response to her fear.

She squeezed her eyes closed, sucking in a long breath through her nose. She could hear the sparks popping at her fingertips. She tried letting the fear run its course, to let it wash through her like she had earlier, but she couldn't help but imagine all the terrible things those implements were intended for. She'd heard stories once of what they'd done to a novel creature they'd found mutated from a local source of natural magic. There were conflicting stories on if they'd euthanized the creature first or not. At the time she'd told herself those stories of cutting things apart while they were alive were just tall tales to scare the freshmen, but it was hard to keep that mindset when she was trapped and nobody would tell her what was going on.

The thing to stop her blowup wasn't something she should have taken comfort in, and yet the sound of it ceased every flare of her wayward magic before the echoes even faded away.

An inhuman shriek tore the air, loud enough to rattle the glass in the windowpanes and send ripples across the faceted barrier over her head.

The mages across the room all stilled.

"Shit," Hettie hissed. Her relief was short-lived. They were out of time. She'd never heard that sound before, and yet somehow she knew exactly what the source was.

"What is this?" One of the mages finally deigned to address her, "What's happening?"

"I tried to tell you," Hettie told them weakly, "You weren't listening."

Matthias approached the purple barrier, taking off his monocle and plucking a cloth from his pocket to polish it with. "You mentioned a man who took you from the shop that day. What was his name?"

The gray pallor to his face, tinted lavender from the ward, told her he already knew, but she said anyway, "Gylharen."

"The Golden Dragon of Death's Maw?" His voice was carefully neutral as he replaced the circular lens over his eye. It seemed she'd identified Gyl's contact.

"The very same."

"Well, why didn't you say so?" he huffed. He spun away from her before she could answer, not that she had more than a flabbergasted look to give him. He called to his colleagues, "I've had dealings with this creature before. I suggest the rest of you go, and I'll-"

He didn't have time to say what he'd do before the bay of windows exploded inward in a cloud of fire. Massive claws raked at the wall, dislodging stones in great chunks until there was enough room for the top half of a hulking golden body to intrude into the room.

Massive eyes, shining gold irises with slit pupils that nearly filled the sockets, locked instantly onto Hettie's. His nostril's flared as he took in a breath, a deep rumble splicing the air on the exhale. She watched that body shudder and the space between his teeth glow for an instant before he opened his maw and let loose a rush of flame paired with a fury-filled roar.

Hettie flinched as the flames rushed toward her, but the shield protected her from the worst of the heat. As he bit off the tail of the flame, the spell began to break down, crumbling and dissipating as if it had been burned to ash. Across the room, half a dozen hands glowed behind their own ethereal shields. There was a hard line between the scorched wooden floors and what lay behind their magic protection.

Without the shining barrier in the way, Hettie was able to admire Gyl fully in his dragon form. Those four black horns he wore in his other shape were present here too, curling backward and giving the impression of a flared fringe. His claws where they dug into the wooden floorboards were a deep black, that color fading into burnished gold as it traveled up his limbs. All over he was a patinated gold, the color darkening anywhere his body bent or creased. He bristled with spines along his tail and back that curved up into his shoulders and even across the joints of his dark, leathery wings.

And the *size* of him. With his legs extended she thought she might draw level with his armpit, though it was hard to tell with only half his body in the room, the other half visible in quick glances through the hole in the wall. He looked built like a panther in the body, with a long, elegant neck that moved like a snake as he looked her up and down.

He looked *angry.* His eyes narrowed, his lip quivered in a snarl, and flames licked up from his nose and between his sharp, deadly teeth.

And though he was looking at her, she knew, intuitively, the thing stoking his fury. She was bound to a chair, seemingly against her will, in a room full of strangers. This would look far more dire to him than it felt to her, despite her momentary spike of fear, and as that massive, wedge-shaped head swiveled back to the crowd of mages, she knew she had seconds to act.

He took a step forward into the room, putting his head past her. His chest expanded like a bellows, a hiss and a burst of something acrid and sharp billowing from him a second before the cloud of fire that followed. She could see the glint and glimmer of shields beyond the rush of flames, but the question was could they hold them longer than Gyl could spit flame?

Hettie closed her eyes to help her focus. That magic that lived under her skin was easier to access than ever. It came to her call like a living thing, swooping down into her hands eagerly. She needed the ropes gone, needed to be free. She'd done something similar to what she was about to attempt that day Gyl found her in the shop.

Now she was going to see if she could do it on purpose.

Ropes. She focused on those. She imagined them squirming around her hands, changing texture, morphing...

The snake fell to the ground with a leathery hiss. Her hands free, she flung her arms forward and propelled herself out of the chair, sending it clattering to the ground as it clung to her hips when she stood.

Gyl bit off the stream of flame at the noise, one eye rolling to face her.

"I'm free now, Gyl," she soothed, holding one hand out to him, "you can stop now."

A growl rumbled from his open mouth. His eye flicked to the chair on the ground and the unmarred patch of floor that had been under the wards.

"I was never in danger," she stepped closer to him, her voice low and soothing, "they would have let me go once I proved I had everything under control." She didn't know any of that for certain, but Gyl didn't need to hear that.

"Miss, stay back! It's not safe!" Matthias hissed, still behind his own shield, which was noticeably more sparkly than the rest of them.

Gyl, who had been tracking her slow approach with his head tilted towards her, snapped his attention back to the mages, growling louder. The spaces between his teeth began to glow.

Hettie hurried to close the gap between them, lifting her hand to press it to the side of his muzzle, angling her body so he could not breathe fire without danger to her.

"No need for any more of that," she told him gently. She kept her voice low, her posture relaxed. "I'm not hurt, and now I know you're right. They can't help me."

Gyl's curled lip flattened, and the flames in his mouth sputtered and went out with a rush of gray smoke. His eyes fluttered closed as she started stroking her hand slowly along the ridges of his face.

Carefully, Hettie turned to the watching mages, who eyed the two of them with expressions ranging from horror to fascination. "I think our business here is concluded."

"I should say so," Matthias agreed, with a tone of one suggesting that that had been his idea all along. He made a gesture with his hands, as if to say, *"Get him out of here."*

"Let's go, Gyl," she told him with a barely restrained eye roll, "Take me home." She was a little surprised that when she said home she meant that the castle *was* her home. It felt more familiar to her now than the potion shop or this university.

That was a strange realization that left her stomach with an odd twist.

Gyl opened his eye and nudged her with the side of his head towards his shoulder. He bent his front leg so she could use it as a ladder, and she found there was a gap in the spiked ridges right in front of his wings the perfect size for her to sit. He was considerably bigger than a horse, and without any sort of saddle she could feel every liquid muscle move beneath her widely stretched legs. He maneuvered in the small space so he was facing the opening. Behind them she could hear the sound of things breaking and outraged exclamations from those still gathered inside as his tail swept the room.

Hettie gulped as she looked down into the city. They were in one of the university's many towers, and she could see the top of nearly every building for miles. She gripped the spikes in front of her so tightly her hands ached.

"You won't let me fall, will you, Gyl?" she asked, a tremble in her voice.

Gyl turned his head and peered back at her with one eye. He gave her a slow blink, a second, clear membrane closing slowly over his golden eye.

Then he bent his legs, and leaped.

13

Hettie's thighs ached from holding on. She had to keep her head tucked behind the ridges on his neck or the whip of wind against her face would snatch her breath away. Every bunch and glide of muscle felt like it was going to unseat her, every turn a dangerous tilt no matter how slight. She didn't actually think Gyl would let anything happen to her, but she also wasn't certain how clearly he was thinking right now, given his near-murderous rampage in the university. She was nervous but not fearful, and that meant her magic was just buzzing under her skin instead of boiling to be released.

She'd tried pleading with Gyl to slow down, or give her a break, but received no response from him. He hadn't spoken to her at all, in fact. She was fairly certain he could, he was just ignoring her.

Fair enough. She probably deserved that.

She lifted her head as she felt the tearing of the wind lessen.

The view was breathtaking – and also terrifying. From up here, the spikes of the Maw really looked like their namesake. They were sharp, spiky peaks that looked like jagged teeth that would impale her if she fell. She clutched at Gyl's neck with her knees, though she knew he'd never let her plummet to her death, regardless of how angry he was with her.

The castle's gray stone walls loomed closer as Gyl snapped his wings out to slow their descent. She could see the front door yawning open, a dark mouth in the stone façade. Her teeth rattled at the force of his landing, and her glasses slid down perilously close to the tip of her nose. She kept her head ducked down behind his head, waiting for him to stop moving. She could hear his claws scraping over dirt, the sound changing as he crossed the threshold. Darkness closed in on them as the hall swallowed them.

Gyl crouched, a clear indicator he wanted her to get down. She forced her tired legs to obey her and dismounted with considerable difficulty. At least his scales weren't slick. Though they were hard and keratinous, they had a subtle texture that kept her from slipping.

She stood beside his head for a long moment, stroking the ridges above his eye. That golden iris was bigger than her hand, and the slit pupil in the center slowly tracked over her. She was reluctant to back away from him. He cut a stunning figure in his more human shape, but his true form was downright regal. She just wanted to bask in every fleck of light that glinted off his scales, but the guilt pooling in her belly also made her want to hide.

"I'm sorry," she murmured softly, "I understand if you don't want to speak to me anymore." The idea of missing out on his particular brand of snark and sass was like a dart to the chest, but she couldn't begrudge him that. Drugging him had been an act of betrayal, and she'd understand if he wanted to actually send her to the dungeon after this. She had hoped that it would be fruitful enough to make up for the heinous nature of what she'd done, but she accomplished nothing.

He snarled and lifted his head high above her as he arched his neck. He stretched and twisted in a way that almost looked like he was writhing in pain before his body started to change. His form shrank, and his upper half morphed into more human proportions until he was bipedal once more, but by the time he was stalking across the floor towards her he hadn't lost any of his dragon features. It was like the gods had taken his dragon form's wings, head, and lower half; bonded them to his more human torso and neck, and wrapped the whole package in golden scales. He had not a stitch of clothing on, and there was a stripe of darker scales from his neck down to his groin, where the scales split in a seam where his cock would usually hang.

He was larger than the form she was used to, and he towered over her as he stalked forward. She found herself backing away, yet somehow also transfixed by his intensity. A tendril of fear low in her belly coiled tightly with rapidly blooming desire. She squeaked as her back collided with the wall.

Gyl's tail lashed the stone floor, his wings snapping up and filling her vision a split second before one dark, clawed hand slammed against the wall beside her head.

"You're sorry?" His voice was low and raspy, his tongue hissing against his razor-sharp teeth. "You send me spiraling into madness, and you're *sorry?*"

"Yes." Her voice was a bare whisper, "Things didn't go as planned."

He huffed a laugh, a puff of smoke curling into her face. "You don't say? Ideally, how would drugging me and sneaking off to town have gone?"

Hettie's face grew hot. "I was supposed to be back before it wore off. I didn't know they were waiting for me."

He snarled, his lip curling and baring those wicked, pointy teeth. With excruciating gentleness, despite the clear and hot fury pulsing through him, he wrapped the fingers of his other hand around her throat. She could feel the delicate prick of those razor sharp claws against her pulse. She was instantly both soothed and elated, and those emotions were shook up in a bottle at his next words.

"Did they hurt you?" His thumb slowly stroked the column of her neck.

"No. They wouldn't have." Her eyes went heavy as she relaxed under his hand. He could snap her neck with a twist of his fingers. She had no idea if the University would have harmed her, but she knew Gyl wouldn't.

"Really? Then explain the stench of your fear I smelled when I split that tower like firewood?" Smoke coiled from between his teeth as he spoke, but Hettie couldn't bring herself to be afraid of him when he still handled her so gently despite his clear rage. She relaxed into the wall, her eyelids drooping. Gyl let out a frustrated snort at her reaction. "Really, woman, do you have any sense of self-preservation? Answer the question." He gave her a little shake.

"They were debating which tests to run. Stories about the tests the university runs are not always... favorable," Hettie admitted. "I think they were afraid of me too. They bound me with spellsilver. It wasn't working as it was supposed to."

He gave a soft, pleased rumble, "They couldn't hold you, could they?"

"No," she agreed, though without his help she wasn't sure she could have broken that shield.

"*I* am the only one who can bind you, treasure." He leaned in close and flicked his tongue against the shell of her ear. His hand tightened on her throat possessively. "If they had harmed you, I swear, I would have ripped the spine from every body in that room."

Hettie shivered. She wouldn't have wanted that, but she had no doubt he would deliver on that vow.

A strange tremor wracked his body, "Promise me you won't run again."

"I won't." There was no point now. Where would she go? She didn't actually want to leave him in the first place. She'd only snuck out in the first place because he hadn't allowed her to go on her own. But he'd been right, and she'd hurt him for nothing.

"There will be consequences for this stunt, I assure you," the liquid heat of his voice told her exactly what kind of *consequence* he intended for her, "but I think perhaps I've earned one as well." He dropped his arms, wings climbing as he staggered back from her with a groan.

"Gyl?" She reached out, though there was nothing she could do if his massive body took a fall.

"No, stay there. It's safer." He held up a claw. His chest was heaving. "I have a confession to make, treasure, and I'm running out of time."

"Okay?" Hettie urged him uncertainly.

"I haven't had control over my shapeshifting for some time now. I've been stuck in that mortal shape until today. When I saw you gone, my body snapped into my true form. Even now my body is screaming to return to that shape."

He'd been stuck? Her heart was in her throat as she said, "Then let it. Don't torture yourself on my account."

He shook his head sharply. "Not until I've had a chance to explain. I can't speak common in that form, our mouths aren't shaped for it."

So he hadn't been giving her the silent treatment after all. And if he'd been stuck human-shaped... then he hadn't been putting off taking her to his elder for no good reason. He literally *couldn't* if they had to fly there. "Why didn't you tell me?"

"I was embarrassed," he grunted, "ashamed. I was worried if you knew you wouldn't want my help any more... that you would leave."

"Why would I leave?" She frowned at him, stepping forward despite his warning hand. She flinched when she realized she *had* left, even if she'd had every intention to come back. She'd blundered right into his greatest fear, and now she ached to comfort him. "You've been a great teacher."

"How am I supposed to instill confidence in your own magic when I can't control mine?" He gestured to his body. "Look at me."

"That's silly." She stepped into his space, pressing her hands against his chest. The heat of him was almost too much.

"Hettie, stay back. I don't want you hurt," He put his hands on her shoulders like he was going to push her away.

"Hush." She brushed off his hands. "You won't hurt me."

She slid her arms around his middle, as far as she could, anyway. "Let it go."

"Treasure-"

"Change," she urged him. She pressed a soft kiss to his scales.

She felt the moment he let go. She was holding his trunk one moment, and the next she found his neck under hands, his head tucked around her back so when the sheer size of him pushed her backward, she was supported even as her feet slid across the floor. When they were still again, she grinned up at him.

"I told you."

His eye roll was almost impressive given it was the size of a dinner plate. He bumped her with his nose, urging her back to his crouched forearm.

"Wait, one second, please," she begged, shoving at his immovable jaw.

He snorted at her and lifted his head, tilting it as if to say, "What now?"

Hettie fidgeted, an almost forgotten need now pressing her urgently.

"I'll go wherever you like, I promise, I just-"

Gyl hummed impatiently. Hettie shoved his head again, skittering around him towards the nearest hallway.

"I really have to pee."

14

Gyl tried not to revel in the terrified squawk Hettie released when he launched into the air, but he could not deny it was gratifying to know she felt a fraction of the fear she'd instilled in him. It was vindictive, and certainly a little mean, but she had earned that.

He could not shake that all-consuming fury. It still burned in his belly, heavy and hot.

He'd wanted desperately to claim her on that stone floor, to soothe some of that inner furnace with her body, but he was terrified of losing his hold on that half-form mid-coitus. If his cock had stretched her before, in its true size it would split her in half.

He was gentler on this flight, at least he was after the take-off. He'd been blinded a bit by his need to see her safe, and had not thought about her comfort as much as he should. He could have burned that university to the ground. Happily would have, had they harmed her. He may have felt a modicum of regret for it later, but that wouldn't change that he'd still have done it. He'd let that tightly spooled aggression bleed out a little into his speed on that flight home. Her pleas to slow down had fallen on deaf ears before, but now he set a gentle, sweeping pace, even though he wanted to get to his uncle's as fast as possible. The sooner he spoke to the old lizard, the sooner he could get on the path to controlling his shifting again.

He should be more furious with her, but he couldn't bring himself to blame her completely for her actions when he'd been so immobile in the first place. If she'd tried to leave without drugging him, he would have dragged her back. It wasn't kind or rational, but where she was concerned he went all big lizard brain, and big lizard brain was a possessive asshole right now. It was wildly out of character for him, but he couldn't seem to help himself.

The press of her knees into his neck was the solid comfort he needed to stay calm. She was with him and safe, and that settled his mind better than anything. His anger pooled low in his belly like magma, cooling into a hard lump of guilt.

He was taking her to see his elder, finally, as he had promised. They both needed advice, and he only knew one dragon who may be able to provide it – his great uncle Wendamyr. He knew no dragon wiser or older than Wendamyr. His den was in another peak higher up in the Maw. The flight from his castle to his uncle's den was about the same distance as the flight from his castle to the town.

They encountered no other creatures, dragon or otherwise, on their journey. Once he heard the rustle of wings nearby, and Hettie must have spotted something, because she made a squeaky little whimper and tightened her knees on his neck. Whatever it was, it did not approach them. Gyl had not been posturing when he told her predators knew better than to mess with him. He wished he could remind her of that, or at least reach back and comfort her. He had longed to return to this shape, and yet now that he had it, he wanted to go back.

Gyl was grateful when the jagged mouth of Wendamyr's den came into view. It meant they were one step closer to answers – for both of them. The cool darkness swallowed them as he tucked his wings. The landing was a little sticky due to his lack of practice, and Hettie yelped as she was jostled. He gave her an apologetic glance over his shoulder.

He called out to Wendamyr in dragon-tongue, the language they spoke in their true forms. Because of the way their mouths were formed, it was mostly guttural noises and hissing. He felt Hettie freeze with apprehension on his back, and he felt a sudden stab of regret that he couldn't translate for her what he was saying.

The old dragon's response came from deep within the cave, his dragon-tongue almost raspy with age.

"Gylharen? Is that you?"

"It's me," he responded, *"I have come with a guest... and questions."*

"I love questions," came his wheezy reply. *"Come in, come in. No need to keep your guest out there in the draft."*

Gyl ducked further into the cave, an easy feat since it had been carved wider for the passage of the older dragon, who was at least half a wing wider and taller than Gyl himself. Wendamyr's cave was shaped like a loose, climbing spiral and took up much of the interior of the peak, with his hoard in the uppermost section and several smaller chambers studding the spiraling hallway along the way.

He found his uncle in his hoard room, the biggest room and the one where he spent most of his time. It was, inarguably, the most impressive hoard room he'd yet seen.

Wendamyr always said he hoarded history as an explanation for why he had such a variety of items – unlike Gyl who was just indecisive. The room was built like a spiral on the outside, matching the rest of the cave, with an inclining ledge that was wide enough for Wendamyr's large frame. The walls were lined with shelves stuffed with books and scrolls and artifacts of all kinds, organized by some wild system known only in the depths of his uncle's mind.

A glance upward showed the dangling tip of his uncle's bronze tail on a ledge above his head.

"*Do you expect us to come up?*" Gyl asked wryly.

"*No, of course not. Wouldn't want you mucking about near my shelves with those fledgling wings of yours.*"

Gyl let out an unamused snort as he shifted towards the doorway. "*I haven't had fledgling wings for two hundred years.*"

There was the whoosh and snap of Wendamyr's wings as he extended them, catching a pillow of air to cushion his fall as he jumped down to the lower, center floor.

The bronze dragon was twice Gyl's size, craggy all over, with a heavy brow ridge that gave him a perpetually perplexed look. He peered at Gyl, squinting a little, then let out a quizzical hum when he spotted Hettie perched up on Gyl's neck.

"*Ah, a human guest! One moment.*" Wendamyr changed, the transformation so quick and easy that Gyl felt a flash of envy. His uncle's human form didn't show his true age, but he did appear as if he were a middle aged man with salt and pepper hair cropped around his shoulders, and brows so scraggly and heavy he could have combed them.

"Sorry my dear," he addressed Hettie in the common tongue, "I didn't mean to be rude. C'mon, boy, change. It's not polite to keep a form when you can't speak your guest's language in it."

"He can't," Hettie told him softly. Her hand was a small, gentle pressure against the side of his neck.

Wendamyr's eyebrows shot up towards his hairline, "Can't? My dear girl, what do you mean he can't?"

"I believe my lady has questions she needs answered, and I've made her wait long enough. She will speak to you first."

Wendamyr's bronze eyes raked over Gyl, his face creased in a frown. "Very well then. I suppose since my nephew can't introduce us in his current state, I'll have to do it myself. I'm Wendamyr, my dear girl." He rounded the side of Gyl's head and held his hand up to her, to shake her hand or help her down he wasn't sure.

Before his uncle could even touch her hand, his proximity triggered a confusing rush of emotions – anger and possessive jealousy chief among them. His instincts flared up again, and he jerked backward away from his uncle with a deep, gravelly warning growl.

Wendamyr just cocked his head, a look of studious curiosity settling over him. He didn't even lower his hand.

"I see," was all he said.

"Gyl, you have to let me down," Hettie told him gently, stroking his neck.

"Mine," he bit out in dragon-tongue, and even if she didn't understand the language, she caught his meaning.

"Gylharen," she scolded softly, "isn't this the man who's supposed to help me? Don't you trust him? You'll need to let me down if he and I are going to talk." It was the same voice she used the first time his instincts had kicked in without his say-so, quiet but firm.

He knew that she was right, rationally, but his hindbrain was fighting hard to overpower all reason. He wanted to twist his head and snap his uncle's hand off at the wrist, but instead he closed his eyes and lowered his front half to the ground.

"She gets off on her own... please." He added that last as a courtesy, realizing he was in no position to make demands. If Wendamyr wanted, he could transform back and pin Gyl in seconds. He was ancient, but he was still more than spry.

"As you say," he heard his uncle agree genially. "Come on down, my – er, young lady."

Hettie dismounted, using his bent forearm as a stair. "My name is Hettie."

"Pleasure to meet you, Hettie." When Gyl cracked an eye, he noticed his uncle had abandoned the handshake in favor of a polite bow, both his hands clasped nonchalantly behind his back. Hettie bowed back, almost stumbling when Gyl curled his tail possessively around her legs. She turned and gave him a *look*, and he puffed a smoke ring in response.

"I think it would be wise if Hettie and I spoke in private, don't you?" Wendamyr's tone was neutral, but the flash in his eyes told Gyl that this was not really a request. He let out a petulant whine, his tail spiraling up around Hettie's soft belly.

Wendamyr persisted, "Go on, now, hatchling. We won't get anything accomplished with you underfoot."

Gyl just tugged Hettie against his shoulder, curling his neck around her protectively.

She got up on her tiptoes and pressed a soft kiss to the wrinkly leather below his eye. "Would you like to talk to him first instead?"

Gyl snorted, affronted. He didn't want to make her wait one more second for her answers, but... oh. He was getting in the way of their conversation, wasn't he? He heaved a sigh, a billow of smoke puffing from his lungs. He dropped his tail from her body and nudged her toward Wendamyr with his snout.

"Why don't you go for a flight, nephew," Wendamyr suggested, "a few dozen lungfuls of cold, thin air should clear your head."

He didn't like it, in fact every nerve in his body screamed at him to stay put, but he turned anyway, forced himself to point his nose back down the spiral hallway and out to the mouth of the cave.

It was like trudging through treacle, but he managed to reach the spiky cave opening. It still felt good to spread his wings, despite the distance he'd already flown that day.

With a few hard wingbeats, he was in the air, that taut thread that connected him to his treasure holding him like a kite on a string.

"Will he be alright?" Hettie whispered to the older man. She wasn't sure how far her voice would carry, and the sound of Gyl's talons on the stone had only just faded.

"Oh, he'll be fine," Wendamyr waved away her concerns, "He's just matebound is all. He'll get over it."

"Mate... bound?" she asked.

Wendamyr's eyebrows flew upwards, a journey they seemed to take often, as he expressed much of his emotion with the upper half of his face. "He hasn't told you? Hm, well he is quite young, and a bit of a recluse... He may not know."

"Know what?"

"I'll speak with him first and let him explain, if that's alright. I don't want to risk misunderstanding the situation, eh? Now, Gylharen mentioned you have questions for me?"

A rush of eager energy flushed her at his prompting, and the matebound thing was immediately all but forgotten.

"Are you much of an expert on ancient magic, Master Wendamyr?"

"I like to think myself an expert on many things, my dear girl, and I myself am quite old. I would say I certainly am. What sort of magic are we talking?"

Hettie launched into her explanation, detailing her exploits from the moment she started losing control until now, and glazing over the more personal bits, especially those that involved sex. Wendamyr stood and listened in silence, the dancing of his brows the only sign he was hearing her at all.

"My, my," he hummed when she finished, "fascinating indeed."

"Can you tell me where this magic comes from?" Hettie wrung her hands anxiously.

"I believe I can," the older man nodded sagely, "but it may leave you with more questions than answers. Are you prepared for that?"

"Yes," Hettie gushed, "I'd be grateful for anything at this point."

Wendamyr gestured for her to follow, and began walking up the sloping pathway, gently running his bronze hand over the shelves as he went. Hettie followed, quickly growing impatient with his reticence.

"Are you familiar with the story of the Creator?" he finally asked.

"They teach that story to babies in daycare." She chewed the inside of her cheek. It was a story every toddler knew, the tale of the first deity and how they grew tired of living alone, and so they split their body into pieces, those pieces becoming the earth, sky, and pantheon.

"Well, there's a part of that story they never tell – perhaps because they don't know it. There was one piece of the creator left – the hand they used to rip their body apart. The Creator's new children didn't want to let their sire's power go to waste, and so they split it apart by each finger, and bestowed each finger upon a mortal creature in the form of demi-deity status.

"These gifts were wondrous. They gave their recipients in-credible power, powers somewhere between those the pantheon possessed, and what the mortals were calling magic. They did great good with them – and great evil.

"They quickly found, however, that this gift was also a curse. They had been transformed into part gods. This meant their lives were extended, seemingly endlessly. They watched their loved ones grow old and die around them. Those who didn't love them feared them. Some turned to hermits or terrorized their homelands, their sense of morality twisted with age, but eventually they all seemingly found a way to coexist or disappear. I've not even heard whispers of one for half a century or more."

"Half a century..." Hettie murmured softly, "So, what, am I a descendent of one of these beings?"

Wendamyr paused at a break in the wall, where a shimmering barrier shone instead of a window, letting a small amount of sun into the room. "Their offspring only inherit a watered down version of their power, until after many generations it behaves like typical magic. If they have any first generation descendants then they've done a much better job at teaching them to manage their magic in recent years, because I've not heard tale of any chaos magic about."

Hettie frowned. He hadn't actually answered her question. He laughed good-naturedly at the look on her face.

"From what you described to me, it doesn't seem like what you possess is watered down."

"What do you mean?" She glanced down at her hands. Her excitement and tension had her magic bubbling and buzzing under the surface of her skin, but it felt contained.

No, that was wrong. It was a part of her now. No longer was it some parasite or intruder in her magic, but rather it had grown to harmonize with her, to fill her. She couldn't say whether or not this was a "watered-down" version, as she didn't know what that was supposed to feel like.

"I see your thoughts churning," Wendamyr chuckled, "let me give you another piece of information that may make this clearer." When Hettie just waited patiently for him to proceed, he continued, "I encountered one of these beings centuries ago. I think he was grateful for some company, because he talked well into the night. He told me a story about traveling with one of his fellow blessed-folk, and how in a desperate bid to save a mortal life, their fellow had passed their gift to that mortal. The mortal lived, but the demi-god withered away and crumbled into dust on the spot. When the wind had blown away their remains, all that was left were two demi-deities – one old, and one new."

He stayed silent, face turned to the sun as she absorbed this new information.

"You think I received the original gift from one of these demi-deities?" she asked slowly.

"Like I said, more questions," he told her amicably, almost apologetically.

She stared at him, eyes wide. "So, does that make *me...*?" She couldn't even utter it. It seemed too ridiculous. Her? A *demi-goddess*?

"It seems that way," Wendamyr nodded gravely.

"I don't remember it happening," she shook her head, "I feel like I would remember."

"You may not. It's a lot of power to transfer. The force of it settling into your body may have wiped your memory. Do you have any blank spots in your personal history? Anywhere things get fuzzy?"

Hettie chewed her lip, thinking. She glanced down at her metal arm, the sun through the barrier glinting off the bronze. She hadn't thought about the fire in a long time. She knew about that night mostly second-hand from her parents recounting the tale of finding her in her nursery. She'd always thought the haze of that day and all the memories that came before it was from the trauma of the near-death experience and losing her arm, but...

"There is... one day. But it was so long ago, and I was so young. You'd think it would have surfaced much sooner, right?"

"It is possible it behaved like normal magic until you were taught to tighten your control of it. Deious magic is entropy incarnate. It would not have reacted well to being restricted. Children have far fewer rigorous expectations for themselves where magic is concerned. They are limited only by their imagination. Your youth may have made the transition easier. You will need memory magic to know for certain if that was when it happened, and that is where I can no longer help you."

"You've done a lot," Hettie's head was spinning as she spoke, "thank you."

"I can do one more thing." His smile creased his brown cheeks. He reached up to the shelf behind him, tugging down a volume sandwiched snugly between a display case and a hefty reference book. It was small, bound in rough-cut leather and hand-stitched with gut cord. "I got my hands on my demi-acquaintance's journal – won it in a game of chance. I'd be willing to lend it to you, if you make me a promise."

Hettie got a glimpse of what it must be like for dragons to feel the urge to hoard. Her eyes were pinned to that book, the need to have it suddenly overwhelming all good sense.

"Anything."

"Be careful what you promise, goddess," he teased her, his flashing eyes so much like Gyl's. "Lucky you, my request is fairly innocuous. All I ask is that you come back and fill out your own journal for my collection, particularly once you've sorted out how you received this gift."

"Deal," Hettie agreed quickly. She tamped down the urge to snatch, instead taking up and gently folding the little volume against her chest.

"Now, I think the two of us should head down to the entrance. My nephew will want to assure himself of your safety and well-being." He gestured out the gap in the wall, and Hettie finally peered outward.

Mist-ringed peaks fanned out below them, and far off in the distance the setting sun haloed a winged form. Gold flashed off of it with every sinuous movement, like the flash of minnows in a clear pond.

Gylharen was returning.

Gyl stayed away as long as he could tolerate, which was probably not as long as they could have talked for. They were kindred spirits, both scholars, and Gyl had a feeling the two of them likely could talk for days and not tire of the discourse. He'd tried hunting to occupy himself, when just flying had not proven distracting enough, but even with his belly full of fresh, hearty deer, and the water beading off his scales from the dip in the ice-cold mountain spring to clean the blood off, there was only one thing he could focus on.

They were coming down the ramp when he landed. He could hear them talking.

"Thank you again," his treasure was saying, "I have a lot to think about."

He surged up the tunnel the moment they came into view, nudging his uncle aside so he could cradle her with one claw and tug her into the curve of his shoulder.

"Gyl!" she cried, her tone scolding, but she started giggling when he pressed his snout to her temple and whuffed her hair, letting her scent flood him and soothe his frayed nerves.

"I have so much to tell you later," she whispered, reaching out to pat his snout as he pulled away.

"Come, hatchling, let's fly for a bit," Wendamyr told him as he walked by, toward the entry.

"I've only just returned," he complained, curling around Hettie.

"She has a book to keep her busy." His uncle rolled his shoulders. "You can head back up, dear girl – oh, stop that." He snapped that last at Gyl, who had grumbled a little at the endearment.

"She's not your dear anything," he groused.

"You protest being called a fledgling, but you're behaving like one." Wendamyr put his fists on his hips, elbows akimbo. "We're losing daylight here. Let's go."

"I don't want to leave her alone." He'd seen no fewer than a dozen beasties who fled from the shadow of his wings, one of which he was fairly sure was a cockatrice and had been too close to Wendamyr's home for his comfort.

"We won't go far," his uncle promised. "So either you follow, or you stay in that shape for the foreseeable future." He shifted forms at the mouth of his cave, turning his heavy, angular head towards Gyl.

"Your choice," he told him, and then launched off the edge of the cliff.

Gyl let out a high-pitched whine, glancing between Hettie and the receding silhouette of his uncle's winged shape.

"Go on," she told him. "Didn't you say yourself that there's not a creature brave enough to approach a dragon's lair?" She tilted her head, examining him, the late sun slanting into the cave flashing off her glasses. "Not to mention all the wards I spotted in Wendamyr's library. I'll be perfectly safe."

Still, he hesitated. He grumbled, butting his head into her, careful of his horns and ridges.

"Old man, don't you want to hold me again? Don't you want to kiss me and bury yourself inside me? You can't do that when you're stuck like this." Her voice was equal parts scold and sweet seduction, and he felt his cock stir behind the slit that contained it in this form.

He growled. He couldn't even tell her she was right in this form. Maybe he could teach her to understand dragon-tongue, given enough time, but he could never do the things she'd listed stuck this way, and he desperately wanted to.

Before he could second-guess himself, Gyl flicked his tongue beneath her ear and turned away from her. Her giggle chased him as he followed his uncle over the edge, snapping his wings out and climbing in the air to gain some speed and catch up. His uncle was larger than him, but his size did not equal speed – either that or he was letting Gyl catch up. Gyl drew level with him in a matter of moments.

"Good choice," Wendamyr commented mildly.

"Heavily influenced, I promise you."

"I like her," Wendamyr let out an amused rumble. *"She's got spark."*

So much spark, more spark than Wendamyr could possibly know. Gyl grunted his agreement.

"Down here." Wendamyr banked sharply, tucking his wings as he dropped between two slabs of rock. Gyl followed, emerging into a roughly circular clearing with a steaming spring in the center. Wendamyr glided right down into it, landing on its surface with a rustle of his wings like a duck.

"We left Hettie behind so you could have a bath?" Gyl asked archly.

"We left Hettie so you could have a clear head for this conversation. The hot spring just seemed like a bonus. Come on in."

There was still plenty of room in the spring, even with his uncle's bulk taking up a third of it. Gyl begrudgingly slipped into the water up to his chin, dipping his head to blow smoky bubbles with his nose.

"Do you know why it's so hard to leave her?"

Gyl thwapped the water with his tail. *"I assumed it was my hoarding instinct finally kicking in."*

Wendamyr snorted. *"You're not far off. Have you ever experienced a gestating female?"*

Gyl nodded. One of his aunts, early in his lifetime. It had

started in the late stages of her egg cycle and continued after she'd laid her clutch. She'd been restless, irritable, and territorial, snapping at any and every creature that came close, even her mate. After the eggs hardened and were much less vulnerable, she finally calmed down.

"There is something similar male dragons experience called being matebound."

"Matebound?" He had a terrible feeling he knew exactly what that meant, but he let Wendamyr explain anyway.

"When a male chooses his mate – conscious of his choice or not – in the time period between his choosing and securing the mating, a matebound male behaves toward his mate much the same way a gestating dragon behaves toward her clutch."

Gyl's stomach churned. It made so much sense, and yet it was not a comfort to know. It explained how he always inexorably knew where she was, and why his breeding instincts flared up so brightly for her, or why he couldn't stand the thought of another single person even looking at her.

But it meant that, inevitably, he'd trapped her again. He didn't know that he could bear to let her go, not now. The best thing for her freedom may have been for him to waste away to nothing alone in his castle, but even then if he had she'd still be trapped by her own wayward power.

He could not bring himself to regret any of his actions or how each one had tied the two of them together, only that she'd had no choice in the matter.

"Scale for your thoughts?" Wendamyr asked as he splashed his nephew with one wingtip.

"Is this permanent?" Did she have even a sliver of hope of being free of him if that was what she wanted?

Wendamyr hummed thoughtfully, examining Gyl with eyes shuttered under heavy brows.

"It isn't," he said finally, *"but from the few accounts that exist it is torture to break being matebound with anything but a mate bonding. You'll have to lock yourself away, because after hours of pining and longing, you'll go out of your mind and succumb to the beast, and that beast only wants one thing – to find his mate and bond her to him. Why are you asking about permanency? Do you not want to keep her?"*

Oh, he did. He couldn't imagine his life without her now – he didn't want to. But he couldn't help but think of her agony when she'd first confronted him about bringing her to his castle against her will, the anger and pain and fear that twisted her features and poisoned the taste of her on the air.

"I just want it to be what she wants too. I don't want to make this choice for her."

"Our instincts are rarely wrong, hatchling. If your body has gone matebound, it's because the two of you are a good match."

"Even so..." Gyl trailed off.

"You care about her a lot. That tells me all I need to know. She will be a good mate for you, and a good mother for your dragonets, should you want them. "

Gyl scooped water with his wings, enjoying the sluice of warmth over their leathery membranes. *"I don't even know that she could carry my clutch. She's human. Not to mention her life-span would end just after they reached maturity."* He chose not to think about that too hard. It made him itchy to think of her death.

"She's not entirely human, but we will let her tell you about that, I know she was quite eager to fill you in when we spoke.

Suffice it to say her body is capable of a great many things, bearing dragonets among them. Though most dragon matings with other species result in live births, not eggs."

"Good to know," he told Wendamyr drily. Now all he had was more questions, though they hadn't even addressed his more pressing concern yet.

"Uncle, being matebound aside, I need your help."

"Ah, yes, your transformation issue. Tell me more about it."

Gyl quickly outlined his problem, starting with his hermicy in his castle and ending with the way his matebound-induced rage had finally triggered the change, though not with favorable results.

"And now I'm stuck in the other direction. I can't hold the mortal form anymore." He blew a quick puff of flame, steaming the surface of the water.

"Obviously frustrating for another reason." There was clear amusement in Wendamyr's voice.

"Yes, yes, please mock me for my inability to get my dick wet in this form," he snarled.

"You said it, not me."

"Can you help me or not?"

Wendamyr lowered his own snout into the water, the water hissing and bubbling as he exhaled. When he surfaced, he told Gyl, *"I have heard of other cases of dragons frozen in one form, but I'm afraid your case is unique in one aspect. None of these other cases recovered, because their inability to shift seemed to be tied to their waning enthusiasm for existing in the earthly plane. They would often freeze just before they ended their lives."*

"But surely dragons have come back from the precipice of death before," Gyl sought desperately.

"*They have,*" Wendamyr agreed, "*but I've never heard of one form-frozen who did.*" His eyes flicked over Gyl again, like he was checking for some unseen wound. He pulled himself forward in the water, pressing the tip of his snout to Gyl's. "*I am very glad you are still here, nephew.*"

Gyl shivered, thinking just how hopeless he had felt in those months before he caught the thief in his vault. If he hadn't bothered trapping the thief, if he hadn't gone to town to seek an explanation for the broken trap... Well, who knows if he would even be here now.

"*I... allowed myself to be alone for too long, but I was at the bottom of a well, and I had no way to pull myself out.*"

"*Until a certain buxom beauty threw you a rope,*" Wendamyr offered.

Gyl itched at his uncle's compliment of Hettie's appearance, but he didn't feel the need to snap at him. The water truly was clearing his head, despite the insistent pull to return to her.

"*It was more like she fell down with me, and our options were either to climb out together or drown.*" He shook his head to clear the water from his ear. "*Truly, I feel we are both hovering at the precipice even now.*" Though for different reasons, and she was definitely leaning further away from it than he was.

"*Hettie mentioned you were absorbing her excess magic for a while?*" Wendamyr half-pulled himself out of the spring, folding one forearm over the other as he curled to look at Gyl.

"*I was. It hasn't been necessary in a while. Little scraps here and there, but mostly she's gotten it in hand.*"

"*And how did you feel after she would transfer this power to you?*"

How to describe the feeling? Euphoric? Inflamed? Energized? Each burst of magic left him feeling loose-limbed and satisfied. There was nothing better in the world, except perhaps the squeeze of her cunt on his knot, or the stroke of her fingers through his hair, or...

"Focus, hatchling." Wendamyr interrupted his thoughts. *"I asked a question. How did you feel afterward?"*

"Alive," Gyl settled on that answer instantly. *"Like she was stoking the fire within me."*

"I see." Wendamyr huffed a little laugh, a curl of smoke from his nostrils disappearing into the steam from the water. *"I think I understand now."*

"Care to explain?" Gyl loved his uncle, but he was suddenly remembering how frustrating the man was. He wanted you to extract each piece of information like it was a vein of ore in a mine.

"I think being inundated with her kind of magic was healing you, psychically, but the job has only been done partway. It's why when you needed your dragon form to go after her at the university your rage helped push you to reach it, and also why, now that the rage has faded some, you can no longer reach the other form."

Gyl perked up, suddenly hopeful. *"So, I should get my transformation ability back if she keeps transferring her magic to me?"*

"I think it unwise to do too much blind transfer of power. Given what she is, there could be... unintended side effects to that. However, a series of more focused transfers, or even better if she tried using her magic as a more intentional cleansing force and took it back after it ran through you, that would likely do the trick."

"*How long until I could change back?*" Gyl asked eagerly.

"*You're in new territory here, fledgling. I have no way of knowing. Though given the reaction you've already had, I'd say not long.*"

Gyl sighed with frustration. It was good news, but not as simple a solution as he had hoped for.

"*Will you explain this to Hettie for me? I can't exactly do that in my current state.*"

"*Happily, nephew.*" Wendamyr clambered the rest of the way out of the pool, shaking off in a spray of droplets that pelted Gyl like rain. "*Give me a ten-minute head start, and then you don't have to get all worked up seeing me talking to her.*"

"*I'm already worked up,*" Gyl huffed, but he agreed. He lurked sullenly in the spring, counting the seconds to each minute after his uncle had taken off.

And if he left the spring at nine minutes and twenty-nine seconds, well, he considered that an impressive feat of will that he'd managed to wait even that long.

15

Hettie never thought she'd be so happy to be swallowed by that massive front door, but when the darkness of the entry hall enveloped them and Gyl's claws scraped the stone, she thought she might throw up from the relief.

Or maybe it was just the flight-sickness. Wendamyr had offered her a tea for it, but she hadn't spilled her guts on the trip from the university to Gyl's home, nor from there to Wendamyr's, so she assumed she'd be alright.

It was a close call.

She assumed it had something to do with no longer having an empty stomach, as Wendamyr had insisted she eat (and Gyl had growled menacingly) when her stomach gurgled loudly and she'd admitted to not having eaten since the evening before, at the very dinner where she'd drugged Gyl.

"Stop moving," she groaned, her forehead pressed against his neck, "or you'll be covered in partially digested rabbit jerky."

Gyl let out a huff of amusement, but he lay flat on the ground and was still. His tail looped around and stroked a gentle path down her back. Hettie focused on her breathing – in for five counts, hold for three, out for five – until her belly was doing less rioting and more gentle complaining.

"Remind me to take the tea next time," she grumbled, swinging one leg over his neck and sliding down his forearm. He curled his neck and bumped her affectionately with his snout. She was glad to see that Gyl seemed much more at ease now than when they'd returned from the university.

She still felt an immense amount of guilt for her actions the night before, especially since they had not borne fruit. Rather, she had essentially been responsible for trapping him in his dragon form where they couldn't even speak to each other, based on what Wendamyr had said.

"Have I mentioned I'm sorry?" she asked weakly, scratching him under the chin. He let out an aggravated sound and lifted his head so she could reach the entire length of the underside of his jaw. "I don't care if you don't want to hear it, I'm still going to say it until I feel I've made it up to you."

She was bursting with the need to talk to him, to tell him what she'd learned, but, while they still had Wendamyr to translate for him, they had agreed to wait until he could manage common tongue again to share what they had discussed, though Wendamyr had necessarily divulged some of what the two of them had spoken about.

"Do you want to try doing a transfer now?" she asked,

digging her nails into where his scales gave way to leathery hide in the curve of his jaw, giving him a good scratch.

Under eyes half-lidded with pleasure with a clear second membrane pulled over them, he glanced pointedly out the still-open door, where the sky was now dark, and stars were popping up like fireflies.

She guessed at his meaning. "I know it's been a long day, but if we are going to bed to rest soon anyway... What happened to your construct?"

A couple of them had come out at their arrival, activating witchlights and closing the massive front doors. One of them was working with just one arm, the other hanging useless and crumpled at their side.

"Did you do that?" She eyed Gyl, who was carefully looking neither at her nor the damaged maid construct. "You and your temper. Poor thing. Can I try to fix it?"

He gave her a wide-eyed stare of alarm at that.

"*I'm* not the one who broke it, and it's not like you can fix it right now. If you leave it like this, it'll wear down the animation charms compensating for its broken arm." Now that she had a better idea of the true nature of her magic, she felt ready for this.

Gyl let out a heavy sigh, then gestured toward the broken construct with his nose. Hettie tamped down her triumphant grin as she flagged the construct over.

"Hold your arm out and be still," she told it. She could see the finger marks in the metal of its forearm, crumpled like an accordion under the strength of Gyl's grip.

It was strange. She'd witnessed him snap metal chain like it was made of thread, but it rarely occurred to her he could put that strength toward another being – toward *her*. She tried to picture him wrapping those fingers around her forearm and squeezing it like this, and... couldn't. As scary as he'd been that day in the shop, she couldn't imagine him laying a single finger on her in a way that harmed her. Even now, glancing over at his big, wedge-shaped head, his bony brow ridges were lowered, eyelids half-closed in an expression she would equate to the lizard version of guilt.

Even damaged, Hettie could tell his work was quite fine. All his pieces were decorated with a different motif, and this one was engraved with a motif of daisies and lemon balm.

Hettie laid her hand over the bent arm. She thought about the nature of her magic, and reached out to it. Not just chaos – life, energy, transformation. She thought of how the arm must have looked before it was crumpled, and willed it to be that way again.

Feeling the metal move under her fingers was surreal, and opening her eyes to see the construct's arm whole again was even more so. When Gyl leaned over her shoulder to inspect her work, she looked up at him silently, beaming. When she released the construct, it shook its fixed arm, like it was trying to get rid of a strange sensation, and then wandered off to go back to work.

"I did it," she murmured gleefully, turning into Gyl's cheek. "I'm really getting the hang of this."

He rumbled and nuzzled into her. If he were in his other form, Hettie could just picture him telling her how proud he was, calling her his treasure.

That thought tempered some of her enthusiasm.

"You're sure you don't want a boost tonight?" She put

her hands on his muzzle, stroking him. His rumble powered through her, shaking her to her core. She had no clue what it meant, though. It could be an affirmative or a negative.

Perhaps she could use their current language barrier to her advantage.

"So, you *do* want one, then?" She grinned wickedly. Gyl growled, yanking his head back. "Well, you should have said so. Come here!"

Gyl let out an affronted squawk, scrambling back from her. She was too close for him to navigate easily without knocking her over, his only course of action to back away as well he could. Before he could get too far, Hettie darted under his head and wrapped both arms around his neck. She took a deep breath, and for the first time not out of necessity she passed him a measured amount of her magic.

Gyl arched his neck, uttering a growling, hissing curse that she didn't need to speak dragon-tongue to understand. His breathing turned heavy, panting, and a shiver raced through him as her magic settled through his scales into his body.

She let him go and stepped back. "How do you feel?"

The look in his eyes made her shudder. He was looking down at her, chest still heaving, pupils blown wide. He took a step toward her.

She wasn't sure what made her look at his back end, but when her eyes flicked down his body, she found his cock had been extruded from the scaled slit at his groin, and it hung engorged between his hind legs, the size of a tree trunk.

Hettie had forgotten the aphrodisiac nature of her magic on Gyl. Her body lit immediately, both from embarrassment at the discomfort she'd caused him and from desire. There was no way she could take that twitching red monstrosity, it was larger than one of her thighs, but that didn't stop her from fantasizing about it.

Too late, she remembered Gyl could smell her desire. His nostrils flared and he made a sound close to a bass cat's purr. He lowered his head until it was level with her groin, burying his nose between her legs.

"Gyl," she protested, "you're going to knock me over." Gyl seemed determined to ignore her, inhaling deeply. Hettie let out a disgruntled moan, the press of his snout against her sex stimulating her throbbing clit. She clutched at his horns, nearly knocked off balance by his persistence.

When she heard the sound of ripping fabric, she tried to push him away. "Hey! I like this dress!" He growled, ignoring her, and grabbed at her skirt with his teeth. She yanked backward, spinning around and darting down the hallway, losing a chunk of her skirt in the process.

It was all for show. There was no chance of her getting away. She got perhaps a dozen steps away before the snap of his teeth in the back of her dress brought her to an instant halt. She cried out at the shredding of the fabric, and with a shake of his head she was knocked off balance, falling forward. His hold on her dress meant he could lower her down slowly to the cold stone floor. He pinned her with one foot on her back, his talons placed carefully on either side of her body so as not to pierce her skin.

Hettie was on fire. She had no idea where he was going with this, but she trusted him implicitly. Her dress was already ruined, so she didn't fight as, between teeth and claws, he made quick work of the rest of her clothing. She lie nearly naked on the stone, the heat radiating from his body keeping her from being chilled, as his massive teeth gently slid under the waistband of her underwear, tugging that last scrap of fabric from her body with a sharp yank.

"So you've got me naked. What now?" she taunted from beneath him. Her pussy was throbbing, and she could tell by the way her thighs slicked together anytime she shifted that she was dripping wet.

He shoved his head beneath her pelvis, levering her lower half up off the floor and arranging her limbs until she was ass-up on her knees, with her shoulders still pinned beneath his claw, breasts pressed to the stone floor.

He covered her body with his, the fire blazing in his belly burned against her back. Something slick and hot pressed between her legs and beneath her belly, pressing upward until the tip found its way between her breasts.

His cock.

He pressed her down more, rutting the massive thing against her belly, between her thighs. She ground down against it, the length of it rubbing against her clit as he dragged it back and forth. Her pleasured moan matched the deep groan from above her. It vibrated through her back, shaking her.

Gyl had once teased her about only transferring magic with her hands. He currently had both her arms pinned and bent at her sides, but plenty of her body was touching his cock, that soft, sensitive organ that he'd never let her transfer magic through before.

She gathered up another burst of magic, likely the last she'd be able to transfer for the day, and passed it through her lower half and into his cock.

He stiffened and groaned, his cock pulsing against her as he yanked it from between her legs an instant before his hot seed splashed onto her bare ass, dripping up her back and down over her cunt.

There was so much of it, buckets, and she was a sopping mess long before it stopped raining down on her.

She expected him to let her up now that he was done, but he kept her securely pinned. Admiring his handiwork, she thought.

That is, until something else hot and slick snaked between her legs. His tongue this time.

It was as long as her torso, and thicker than his cock in his other form. He opened his mouth wide, his teeth pricking the swell of her ass as he pressed his mouth as close to her cunt as he could get it.

He dragged the length of that tongue up and down over her pussy, stimulating her clit with its rough, slick texture.

"Fuck, Gyl!" she cried out. It was rough treatment, and brusque, but it felt so fucking good. She found herself grinding her clit down on the sinuous length with every passing stroke. And Gyl, for his part, was an even more enthusiastic diner in this form. As if she wasn't already soaked in his seed, her entire lower half was quickly dripping with his saliva.

"I'm so close," she whimpered, bucking her hips. He pressed a little harder with each lick and let out a rumble that vibrated through his tongue right into her cunt.

She nearly screamed as she came, kicking out as all her muscles tensed. Gyl gripped her waist with two claws and just kept devouring her, lifting her ass even higher so he could probe her channel with the tip of it. He pumped its thick length into her, not relenting until she came again and again and finally cried out for mercy.

"Relentless," she accused as he lowered her back to the floor. Even as a dragon she understood a chuckle when she heard one. "Am I free to go now?"

He lifted his claws from her, leaning forward to flick that wicked tongue against the shell of her ear.

"Yeah, yeah, I know, I started it. Now if you'll excuse me, I need a bath."

Gyl couldn't fit into the room he had chosen for her on her arrival, but he refused to sleep without her.

He'd tried to change back while she was bathing and greeting her chicken, but he couldn't manage. He was close, though. It was like he could tell it was only just out of reach when he really stretched for it, like Hettie in the linen closet reaching for her green sheets.

He hadn't had the rooms in the upper floors built for his size. There were ones on the lower floors, sure, but they weren't bedrooms. He'd never imagined being stuck like this. He couldn't even fit his shoulders through the doorway, let alone his wings.

Gyl let out a petulant whine as Hettie readied herself for bed, his head and neck as far in the room as he could manage with the furniture. Though he did hum appreciatively when she turned that delicious ass towards him as she dressed. He stuck his tongue out and flicked it up the cleft of those plentiful globes.

"Knock that off, right now," she scolded, "You've already devoured me enough with that thing for one day."

Gyl dropped his head to the floor, disappointed. Was she sore? Had he been too rough with her? He thought he'd managed his strength well, and she'd certainly come for him. He had felt her pulsing around his tongue, heard her crying out.

Even now he could smell her desire. When she turned to frown at him, he flared his nostrils at her.

She spared the chicken an embarrassed glance before she said, "I know how I smell. I just don't want to get messy again."

Ah. Gyl let out a smoky chuckle. She had been thoroughly coated in his fluids, so much so that she nearly slipped on the tile in the bathroom as they dripped from her. Even thinking of it now made his cock stir behind his slit.

"I'm just glad you kept it off my face. I'd never get all that gunk off my glasses."

Gyl wheezed with laughter, his tail thumping the wall in the hallway.

"You think it's funny now, but I'd have been so peeved." She was grinning too, so she clearly wasn't *currently* peeved. He nuzzled her cheek with the tip of his snout, earning a giggle from her.

"How are we doing this, then?" Hettie folded her arms, "Are you going to keep your head poked in here all night? That can't be comfortable."

He managed to convey to her that he wanted her back up on his shoulders. She clambered up, but she insisted on bringing the chicken. He carried her back downstairs to the ballroom. It was dark, currently lit only by the starlight streaming in from the arched windows that took up most of the walls.

"Down here?" He could hear the doubt in her voice. "Gyl, there's no furniture in here." She stroked Didi's head absently, her forehead pinched.

He huffed. She wouldn't need furniture if he was her bed. She wouldn't need blankets because of his internal furnace. She would see.

He had her get down, then went to the center of the massive room. He turned circles like a cat finding the right shape, and then curled up on the floor, wrapped tightly with his chin resting on his tail.

Hettie, bright thing that she was, understood immediately. She took off her glasses and set them on the flat part at the end of the balustrade on the stairs that led down into the room. "Alright, but we're going back upstairs if this is uncomfortable." She clambered up his back leg, settling in the cradle that the circle of his body made with Cordelia nestled on her belly.

"Don't squish us in your sleep, okay?" She told him once she'd gotten comfortable. He rolled his eyes, and she laughed. "You could!"

His only response was to fold his wing over her.

"Hm. Goodnight, Gyl." He felt her hand gently caress his scales. He thought she was already asleep a short while later when she peeped, "I'm glad I'm here, even if you had to kidnap me."

Gyl huffed a laugh, bouncing her a little with his exhale. He lifted his head a little so he could look at her, admiring the dark fall of her hair and brown skin against the glint of his gold scales in the moonlight.

"Every star in the sky and grain of sand on the earth was made so one day the two of us would meet, my little mate, my treasure." It was an old dragon adage, made no less true by the fact that she couldn't understand it.

"Back at'cha," she told him sleepily.

He chuckled and tucked his head in again, heart full and wholly certain, for the first time in a long time, that things would only get better from here.

16

"Just let me do it one more time," Hettie huffed.

Gyl cracked an eyelid at her, still panting from the orgasm the last magic transfer had given him. He rolled his eye slowly into the back of his head, letting his tongue loll out the side of his mouth.

"It will not kill you, don't be dramatic." She fisted her hands on her hips and glared at him.

It had been a couple days since their return from Wendamyr's lair, and the two of them had found a way for her to understand Gyl, at least part of the time, though it was mostly pantomime, noises, and context.

And tongue, there was a lot of that.

Gyl flopped over onto his back, legs in the air like a dead cockroach, wings splayed at awkward angles. Hettie laughed, she couldn't help it.

"You're ridiculous," she told him, stretching up so she could run her hands over his sides. She wandered over to his head, scratching him under the chin as she bent down to look him in the eye. "Just one more time, Gyl? Then we can be done for the day, I swear. Aren't you tired of sleeping down here?"

He rolled over, careful not to knock her flat. He locked eyes with her, neither of them blinking for a long time. When he let out a long-suffering sigh, she knew he'd relented.

Hettie threw her arms around his neck and squeezed. "You ready?" Gyl made a sound that was as close to a reluctant affirmation as she was going to get.

Hettie tried again to picture and perform what Wendamyr had described to her – using her magic as a tool and reclaiming it rather than passing a surge of it. She thought of it as a cleansing cloth, running it through him and taking away the last of the darkness and pain before she pulled it back within herself to swirl into the rest of her power, rather than leaving it within him to overwhelm him.

She felt him changing before she could even ask if it had worked. His neck shrank until her arms could circle all the way around it, and the moment he could stand on two legs his arms went around her, pressing her tightly to his chest. She felt his scales melt into smooth skin, felt his hair brush her face as he bent to kiss her.

He claimed her mouth with a fiery heat that could rival volcanoes. He devoured her, consumed her, and Hettie would happily offer herself as sacrifice, though she wished he'd given her a chance to push up her glasses. Her lenses pressed into her cheeks, getting filthier the longer they kissed.

"You brilliant, powerful thing," he murmured with

reverence when he pulled back, grasping her face with both hot hands. "What would I do without you?"

Hettie didn't answer, just went up on tiptoe for another kiss. Not because she didn't know what he'd have done without her, but rather because she knew all too well.

"Alright, treasure," he grasped her chin between thumb and forefinger, holding her face pointed towards him, "tell me what you learned from my uncle, before I give in to the urge to give you that *consequence* I owe you right here in the middle of the ballroom." He slid her glasses up to the top of her head. His eyes roamed over her face, and she could feel the stroke of them over every feature.

"There's a lot to share." Hettie's eyes stung, and she gave a watery laugh, "I was starting to worry I wouldn't get to see your stupid face again."

"I think you've mispronounced 'incredibly handsome' but I'll let it slide." He pressed a kiss to her forehead and folded her into his chest. "Tell me what you know, treasure."

"Would you believe me if I told you I was a goddess?" She pressed her cheek to his shoulder, enjoying the heat soaking into her frame. The hand slowly stroking her back stilled.

"Truly?"

Hettie took a breath so deep it made her ribs ache, taking in the smoky smell of him, before she began to recount everything she learned from Wendamyr. He stayed quiet the whole time, his chin propped on the top of Hettie's head, rocking gently from foot to foot.

"I know it sounds insane," she told him, feeling a little frantic now that it was all out there, "but it makes sense, really. I mean how else would you explain it? And there's so much more. I've been reading that diary Wendamyr lent me, and the man who wrote it was convinced he was immortal – immortal! Imagine that! I can't even begin to picture all the things I don't know about this power I inherited yet. Please say something, I feel like I'm babbling now."

"You are," Gyl chuckled, "but I'm still processing, so I don't mind."

"What do you think?" She had to pull back to look up at his face. She expected to see some trepidation there, maybe even disbelief, but instead he looked peaceful, contemplative.

"I think that this makes things vastly less complicated for me," his grin was wide enough that his fangs poked out, "but far more complex for you, and for that I am sorry."

"Are you kidding? I have answers! Any other problems that arise have a panacea to help solve them now. I feel like I can handle anything." She laughed, feeling lighter than she had in a long while. With Gyl changed back, she was quickly on her way to freeing herself of the last of the problems her magic had caused her.

Gyl hummed suggestively, "Anything? Is that so?"

Hettie heated at his tone, her sex quickly growing slick. "Easy there, you've still got to share what you learned with me."

"You know most of it," Gyl slid his hands around to her ass and yanked her upwards. With a startled squeak, Hettie lifted her legs up over his hips and her arms around his neck. He started walking.

"Wait, Gyl, I still need to know—"

"I'm about to tell you, treasure. A little patience, please." His words were chiding but his tone was amused, gold eyes flashing as he smirked at her.

"I think I've waited long enough," she grumbled.

"I agree," he told her, uncharacteristically serious, "but I'm not sure how to begin."

"You could start by telling me what being matebound is." She hadn't forgotten that word Wendamyr used and quickly navigated away from. He'd wanted Gyl to tell her, and now he finally had a voice to do so. She was almost itching with anticipation.

Gyl raked his fangs over his bottom lip, "I can, but I fear just like with everything else, doing so will leave you with more questions." They had exited the ballroom, and he carried her along the hallways, his pace slow.

"Questions you can answer?"

"More than likely."

"Then tell me." She buried her face in his neck and closed her eyes. She liked the way his deep voice rumbled against her as he spoke.

"As you wish. Being matebound makes me territorial, possessive, jealous, and pushes my instincts to the forefront. It's why knotting you makes me react the way I do, and why just the idea of you going to town and being away from me was too much for me. If I'd gone with you and some prick had looked at you cross-eyed, I'd have blood on my hands. It's not reasonable, but I can't control it as I am now."

"Wendamyr seemed to think it was common," Hettie promoted when he trailed off.

"Apparently so," he told her wryly, "and we get this way when we've decided on a mate but haven't claimed them yet."

Hettie sucked in a breath, stunned. Her? His mate? She

supposed he did seem rather attached to her, but that had never even occurred to her. She tightened her arms around his neck.

"Don't dragons mate for life?"

"They do," he confirmed softly.

"When did you choose me?" Her mind raced backward, trying to find a time before he'd been territorial over her.

"My body chose you that first time we met at the shop, I think. I felt the tie when I finally came back to myself a bit when... er, the thief got trapped."

"From the very beginning," she mused. She ignored his weirdness about the encounter with the thief. He'd already told her the tale of Rose and Spider and admitted how watching them fuck had renewed a little of his zest for life. It didn't bother her, and she'd told him that – she thought it was incredibly sexy, in fact. He seemed to think his voyeuristic streak was shameful unless it was her he was watching, but she'd never been prone to jealousy, particularly not when the encounter in question happened before she was around.

"From the beginning," he agreed, tightening his arms around her, "but, treasure, I don't want you to feel like you have to take me as your mate just because I've chosen you."

Hettie frowned and leaned back to look at him. "What are you talking about?"

"I've taken a lot of choice from you here, between choosing you as my mate and whisking you away to my castle. Mating bonds are permanent. If you agree to this, you'll be stuck with me forever. I just want to make sure it's what *you* want." His face was earnest, his eyebrows pinched as he searched her expression. She heard the questions he was really asking here. *Do you want me? Will you stay with me?*

She'd no intention of staying in this dreary castle for eternity, and that was the only hangup she had. Gyl was attentive, sweet, charming, and an absolutely incredible lover. Not to mention he was strong enough to haul her not inconsiderable weight around like she was a children's toy. Her original intention with him had been to keep him from being lonely for the duration of her stay, but somewhere along the weeks she'd been here she'd stopped thinking of it as a short stay, and started thinking of the castle as a place they both lived, together.

She imagined her life going back to normal, knowing what she knew now, and she hated the thought of it. Going back to apprentice at that shop would be like slipping back into a skin three sizes too small for her. No, she wouldn't be going back there, either.

Any futures she imagined without Gyl in them were just not appealing.

"You've not taken any choices from me, Gylharen. You've merely preempted choices I'd have made myself." She expected him to laugh or smile, but the look that crept over his face was pure awe.

"You'd take me as a mate?"

"Under one condition." She tapped the tip of his nose with one finger.

"Anything," he breathed.

"Once I've mastered this magic, we leave the castle – not forever," she added when his face fell, "not even for a long time. I just can't live here cloistered away, I can't."

His crestfallen face smoothed over into an expression of understanding, "Terms accepted. I'll go anywhere as long as you're there too."

He turned and pressed her against the wall, kissing her thoroughly. He pressed his hips into the apex of her thighs, and she could feel his hard want grind the length of her sex. She moaned into his mouth.

"I missed your cock inside me," she panted against his mouth.

His chuckle in return made a chill race down her spine. "You'll have to wait a bit longer for that, I'm afraid." He laughed when Hettie harrumphed in protest. "You see I still owe you that consequence for drugging me and running off and getting yourself captured."

"You earned a consequence too," she protested, "you told me so!"

"You can enact mine later," he growled. "Tonight is your turn."

"I think they should cancel each other out," she grumbled. The ache in her pussy was making her petulant.

"You think so?" Gyl laughed, his fangs showing. "Now where's the fun in that?"

"What did you have in mind?" She had to admit, she was curious about what he had planned. Everything else they'd tried so far had only ratcheted up her pleasure. She was hoping this would be no different.

"I think," he hummed, tucking her stray curls behind her ears, "that naughty treasures who run from their mates get their asses filled and fucked."

A strange swirl of hot and cold suffused her. She wasn't sure if she liked the sound of that, but her body reacted all the same.

Gyl leaned close, nostrils flaring, "Is that fear I smell, treasure?"

She nodded sheepishly, "A little."

"You'll like it, treasure, I'll make sure of that. My goal is to push boundaries, remember, not injure you. Consequence or not, we can stop at any time, alright?"

Hettie nodded. She trusted him. Anal sex had a reputation for being uncomfortable if now downright painful, but she didn't think Gyl would ask her to do something if it wouldn't be pleasurable for her.

Gyl let her slide down the wall, slapping her ass and turning her towards the stairs. "Good. You go prepare yourself for me. I've got toys to collect."

Hettie was nervous, she couldn't deny that, but she was also on fucking fire.

She'd taken a quick shower and twisted her hair up at the nape of her neck. She didn't bother to dress or don her glasses again, instead just sprawling on the bed and trailing her fingers over her naked body.

The bed smelled too clean. It was unsettling. Even with fresh sheets, it usually retained a hint of their combined scents. After days of not sleeping in it, the bedding just smelled like fresh lavender.

They would fix that soon.

Before she could get bored enough to start touching herself, Gyl entered the room with a box under one arm.

"So pretty," he sighed as he approached the bed, "so mine."

The box was immediately forgotten, set aside so he could palm both her breasts. Even with his hands being as large as they were, the tender flesh spilled between his fingers as he squeezed. Her nipples pebbled against his touch, and he pinched and rolled them, the stimulation just shy of pain. She whimpered, arching into his hands.

"Legs up, treasure," he whispered in her ear.

Hettie made a petulant noise, "I'm enjoying this."

"My darling, if you like, the next time we play I'll string you up from the ceiling and make you come until you dangle like a fish. This time, however, I intend to plunder your body for every dark treasure it has for me, as is my right by way of consequences for your actions, and for that I need easy access. Legs. Up."

The molten flash in his golden eyes told her he wasn't playing, but the affectionate way he stroked his hands up her thighs told her he was in no hurry. He was going to wait for her to do it on her own. It was an act of consent. He wanted her to show him she was alright with what he was about to do to her.

She lifted her legs, and Gyl tucked one arm beneath her knees, holding them up while he snagged something from the open box. It was a long leather piece with loops on either end, studded with gold hardware. He looped one side around her thigh, just above her knee, before snaking the other side behind her neck, then back down onto the other thigh. When she relaxed, the weight of her legs pulled on a thick cushion sewn into the strap at the back of her neck. It kept her legs propped up, and when Gyl adjusted the loops so the length of the whole thing was a little shorter, she also couldn't close them without curling halfway off the bed. She was stuck splayed open, bared for his use.

Gyl took one of their pillows, folding it and stuffing it under her hips so they were propped up. He ran his fingers over her sex, slick and open to him.

"So needy," he purred. "You like being strung up for me, don't you?"

"Yes," Hettie whimpered. She rolled her hips into his hand as he slipped two fingers into her cunt, stroking into her. The wet sounds his hand made as he pleasured her showed just how much desire had built up in her body.

He pulled his hand from her before she could climax, just before she peaked. She made a sound of protest, her sex clenching on nothing.

"It wouldn't be much of a consequence if I let you come just like that, would it, treasure?" His grin was salacious as his slick fingers traveled downward, massaging the dark star of muscle with the pads of his fingers.

It was a strange sensation, unfamiliar, though not one that she found unpleasant. When he pressed at her back entrance, stretching that ring of muscle, her own slick made his fingers slide in easily. Hettie squirmed at the sensation. Gyl chuckled, unrelenting in his invasion.

"Best get used to taking it back here, treasure. You'll be full of my cock before too long."

The sound that left Hettie as his fingers were buried to the last knuckle was heavy, primal. She was panting, writhing, spread open for him, and loving every fucking second.

"I'm not sure I can take you back there," she wheezed. All he had in her was two fingers, and that felt like such an invasion already.

"I'm going to gag you again if you keep doubting me," he told her. He stilled his hand in her, gently scissoring his fingers to stretch her hole. With his free hand he dove into the box again, pulling out two more items.

The first was a bottle, which he unstoppered with his teeth. He held it up over his other hand, high enough she could see it.

"This is more than just lube. It's going to loosen you up back here, to make it easier for you to take what I'm going to give you." He poured the liquid in a thin stream, and she felt the moment it hit her skin. It was warm and made her tingly, especially where it slicked between his fingers into her anus. He used the fingers he was fucking her with to spread it around the ring of muscle, twisting them until her back hole was slippery and pleasantly buzzy.

It was only then that he removed his fingers, holding up the other object for her to see.

It was made of black glass, with a wedge shaped handle he held onto to manipulate it. It was shaped like a stack of bubbles, the end one shaped more like a teardrop. Each sphere increased in size the further away from the tip it got, the largest looking like it'd fill the palm of her hand.

He slicked the toy up with his wet hand before pressing the tip to her back hole. She took in a sharp breath when the first bubble pushed in easily, despite it being a little larger than his two fingers had been. Gyl's eyes snapped up to her face, and she nodded to show him she was fine. He rubbed her clit with the thumb on his other hand as he pressed the toy in again, her ass claiming another bubble easily.

"Fuck, treasure, if you keep taking this so easily, I might not be able to keep myself from fucking this tight hole for long." He growled the words as he pressed the toy into her again, the third bubble getting swallowed into her ass with only a little more resistance. Hettie's only response was to moan, gripping the sheets with each thrust of the toy inside her and every stroke of his thumb over her clit.

There were five bubbles in total, the last two needing more gentle finesse to slide within her. Once it was seated fully, however, Gyl fucked her with it, sliding the girthiest part in and out of her until she was shaking and panting on the edge of release again. He let her climax this time, letting the toy seat deep inside her and strumming her clit until she cried out his name. She felt her body clamp down on the toy, her cunt pulsing and desperately empty.

"Good girl," he told her with a smirk. "See, it's not so scary."

"Fuck you," she puffed, still shaking.

"I'm about to," Gyl ran his tongue over one fang. "Do you think you're ready for that?" He wiggled the toy in her ass, and Hettie gasped as desire lit inside her once more.

"I think so."

"Still nervous?" He stroked his hands up the back of her thighs, "We could stop here."

"No!" Hettie protested. "I mean yes, I'm still nervous, but I want to finish what you planned for me."

"I thought you might say that," Gyl gave her a crooked smile, "I just wanted to make sure you knew the option was open."

He pulled gently on the toy, needing a little force to get her muscles to release it after her climax. He set it aside, and drizzled more of the slick potion on his cock.

The press of his broad head wasn't as easy to take as the toy, but Gyl went slow. He pulsed gently against her hole until, with a pop, he slid inside her.

Even with the potion, the stretch of his cock was a gentle

burn as she adjusted to his size, and the washboarding of his ridges in and out of her made her squirm.

"Fuck, you're so tight back here, treasure," he groaned. "It's so good. Look at what a good job you're doing, taking me," he told her as he glanced down at where he was slowly feeding his cock into her back hole. Before long, she could feel the swell of his knot press against her ass, and she shivered at the thought of taking that back there too.

He started to stroke into her, gently at first but with increasing intensity as he built their pleasure. She watched him lose his composure, his face curling into a feral snarl the longer he thrust into her until he was gripping the straps for leverage and hauling her down into his cock with every stroke.

"Touch yourself," he ordered her when she could tell he was close, "I want to watch you come undone."

She reached between them, mercilessly strumming her clit until she reached the peak he asked for, straining against the straps on her legs as her muscles tightened. She felt the clutch of her body on his cock and the empty pulse of her pussy on nothing a split second before his thrusts stuttered. He pressed himself deep within her with a growl, as deep as he could without knotting her, his hot seed filling her as she wrung him dry. With one hand Gyl released the buckles on the loops, her legs falling. He pressed the length of his body to hers, burying his face in her neck.

"That was... gods," Hettie was at a loss for words, still struggling to catch her breath as she tangled her hands in his silky black hair.

Gyl laughed against her throat, "I know what you mean."

He gently pulled himself from her, and she could feel a faint burning throb along with the trickle of his release leaking out.

He rolled the two of them so she was spooned into his chest. He nuzzled his face into her hair and told her, "Don't run from me again, treasure. I don't think I can handle it."

"I don't think my ass can handle it either," she giggled.

He laughed, but he told her, "I'm being serious."

"I know," she sobered, "but I wouldn't have had to at all if you'd just—"

"I know, I know, I share the blame. When you think up your own consequence, feel free to enact it."

"Maybe I'll fuck *your* ass."

"Feel free," he laughed, squeezing her tightly.

"You don't even sound a little nervous about that!" She squawked.

"Why should I? Did you not enjoy it?" He scraped his fangs on her shoulder.

"No, I did." Hettie's face burned.

"Then there's no need to be nervous."

"Not fair," Hettie groaned.

"I'll show you not fair," Gyl growled. He captured her hand and guided it behind her to his groin, where his cock was already hardening again.

"Already?"

"Mm. Let's go clean up, treasure. Then maybe in the shower I'll reward you for taking your consequence so well."

"Not in the ass, though," Hettie wobbled as she stood, "I think I've had enough back there for one day."

"Whatever you like, my mate," he was already behind her,

hurrying her into the bathroom, grinding his cock on her ass, "Just as long as it involves me."

17

"No."

"*Gylharen*," Hettie huffed, her hands on her hips. She must be really annoyed with him to use his full name. Usually it was Gyl, or old man.

"Can't it wait? As long as we are unbonded—"

Hettie interrupted him, "I shouldn't *have* to wait. I know we have to wait to bond until your uncle comes back with what we need to make it work, but there's no reason to put off my hunt for answers because of it." She folded her arms and glared at him, her glasses flashing in the light from the window.

Gyl let out a whine, fidgeting. They should already be bonded. They both wanted to be, but evidently there were some things surrounding the nature of bonding with non-dragon partners that could be harmful to her. The last thing he wanted was to hurt her. Wendamyr had been vague about the actual circumstances of how a mating between them would look, claiming he didn't want to give them any ideas without the proper safety precautions. He'd offered to fetch the potion they needed for it so Gyl's poor matebound self wouldn't have to deal with other dragons around his mate, but that meant waiting days – even weeks – for Wendamyr to return. Gyl hated to upset his treasure, didn't actually *want* to keep her from what she wanted, but...

"Nothing has changed since the last time you wanted to go, Hettie. I'm still matebound. Just the memory of you tied to that chair..." he trailed off, a growl rising in his throat.

She was asking to go to the Arcane University again, this time certain they could help her. Memory magic was a specialty that several of the masters there were adept in. He agreed with her, truly, but he couldn't make himself let her go, either.

"They didn't actually hurt me, Gyl," she told him, her voice softening. "They wouldn't have."

"They might have if they knew what you are. Testing and samples and measurements – those are not all harmless. You said as much yourself."

"Well, they don't know what I am, and I'm not going to tell them. I just need help dredging up some lost memories." She folded her arms, the very picture of stubbornness.

"Memories that the master who helps you will also witness," Gyl snarled. "No. After we are bonded, we will find someone else, someone we know we can trust to keep a secret."

"Gyl, that could take months – years." She pushed up her glasses and pinched the bridge of her nose. "Didn't you have dealings with Matthias Swallowtail? He's skilled in memory magic, from what I remember. You're saying you don't trust him?"

"He's a notorious skirt-chaser known for finding partners, fucking them, and then promptly abandoning them in favor of academic pursuits," he deadpanned. "So, no, I do not trust the man with your safety and well-being."

"He's a professional," Hettie pushed, exasperated.

"A professional rake," Gyl growled. "I've no doubt he'd be able to complete your request, but I don't know any of the others he'd likely have in the room, and I don't trust them."

"Is there really no way you'd allow me to do this?" Her posture started to sag, some of the fight leaving her. "If you really won't budge... I don't know that there is another way. I'm not going to go behind your back again. I've learned my lesson and I care about you too much to hurt you like that. Will you just think about it? Please?"

Oh, no. He hated her giving up even more than he hated fighting with her. The sight of her crestfallen face was like a lance to the heart.

It was her expression that finally forced his concession.

"I'll invite him here."

Hettie glanced up at him, surprised, "You'd do that? Let him into your space?"

"I don't love the idea, but I told you from the beginning I never intended to be your jailer. I have no right to keep you here against your will, not even as your mate. So, if allowing Matthias into my territory keeps you happy and is tolerable to my matebound condition, that's what we will do." He snaked out an arm and pulled her against his front.

"Will it be? Tolerable?" She tipped her head back, gazing up at him.

"I think so. Barely. As long as he comes alone and leaves his ego at home." He grimaced dramatically, "Though it shall be a trial I must be duly compensated for."

Hettie laughed, as he had hoped she would. "I'm sure we can think of something."

That was how Gyl ended up sitting in Matthias Swallowtail's office, being glared at like he was one of the master's wayward students.

"You've got some nerve showing up here after that stunt you pulled," Matthias told him, taking off his monocle and rubbing it on his shirt.

"You had some nerve kidnapping my mate." Gyl's nostrils flared, a trickle of smoke curling up towards the ceiling.

"We didn't know she was yours," Matthias murmured.

"Did you ask her?" Gyl raised a speculative eyebrow. "She told me you barely even spoke to her after you spirited her away, and not at all beforehand."

"We did not," Matthias told him stiffly.

"Not to mention I resent the implication that if she had been some other poor girl without a dragon for a mate you would have had no reticence in regards to snatching her off the street."

"We were told she was dangerous, volatile even. We thought it was safer – for everyone, her included – the way we chose to do it. I mean she wasn't even contained by the spellsilver we had on her."

Gyl bit back another poisonous retort. He wasn't actually here to fight. He dug in his pocket and drew out the leather pouch. He rolled it in his hand, letting Matthias hear the clinking of the contents before he tossed it to him.

"For the damages," he told the mage as he opened the pouch and examined its contents, "plus a little extra for services rendered."

"Services? I don't recall agreeing to perform any services."

"And it will pay for your secrecy, should you accept my offer," Gyl continued as if he hadn't spoken.

"I'm listening." Matthias perched on the edge of his desk, his posture too posed to look nonchalant.

"Hettie needs to recall to a forgotten memory. She needs your help to access it." Gyl eyed the man, giving him a quick appraisal and finding him wanting. "You owe her after your treatment of her in your care."

"I don't feel we treated her *that* poorly," Matthias frowned. He froze at the growl that erupted from Gyl, unrestrained.

"I am paying you for the service, and you owe her the time. Do we have an understanding?" He was being too aggressive, and he knew it. Matthias was a proud man, and he wouldn't be bullied into this, not even by a dragon.

"And what if I don't?" Matthias folded his arms, raising an eyebrow archly, like Gyl was a wayward pupil he was about to lecture.

Gyl took a deep breath and calmed his temper – an act that would have been impossible if he'd let Hettie come along. He didn't actually think Matthias was planning to turn him down. Gyl just needed to give him an interesting enough reason to agree to it despite the bruise Gyl had delivered to his ego when he'd nearly destroyed that tower.

"Then I suppose you'll never find out what makes her magic so strange."

There it was. He spotted the spark of interest in Matthias's eyes. He had dangled the lure, made it shiny and promising, and now he waited for the bite.

"I couldn't publish my findings if I'm sworn to secrecy," Matthias hedged, though he sounded less sure than he had a moment ago.

"Have you never learned something just for the sake of learning it? To satisfy your curiosity?" Gyl shrugged and, perhaps laying it on a little too thick, said, "I would think most scholars have – the ones who truly value academics, that is."

He caught the furious flash in Matthias's eyes before he could hide his expression.

"Anyways, you can keep the extra money either way. We will just have to find someone else to help us."

"I'll do it," Matthias barked, setting the pouch of coins aside.

Gyl smothered his triumphant grin, "But you said—"

"I asked, 'What if...?' I never said I didn't want to do it," he sniffed.

"Well then," Gyl finally let his grin out, "I look forward to your visit."

18

Hettie could feel Gyl behind her, hovering with his eyes pinned squarely on Matthias, watching where he was putting his hands.

"If you stared any harder," Matthias spoke, stone-faced and focused, "you'd burn a hole in my forehead, I'm sure." He didn't even spare the dragon a glance, as he was tunneled in on the symbols he was painting on Hettie, preparation to do what he called "memory diving."

"I'm just making sure you behave," Gyl grumbled.

"I told you I would," Matthias huffed, glancing over Hettie's shoulder where Gyl was looming before looking back at her face.

"And I warned you he's in no position to take you at your word," Hettie reminded him.

"Don't talk. You'll crack the paint," Matthias scolded. Gyl

growled. The master mage ignored him and brought the end of the paintbrush back to Hettie's face, fixing a line on her cheek she'd broken when she opened her mouth. She resisted the urge to ask how much longer this was going to take.

She was so close to knowing everything. One last scrap of knowledge, the only reasonable missing piece outside of just sheer practice using her power now that she understood it better. Who gave her this power? Where did it come from? Learning the nature of the magic had helped her so much when it came to controlling it, she could only imagine solving this last mystery would do the same.

"Alright, I think that'll do. Hands, please."

Gyl growled again, and Matthias let out an exasperated sigh.

"The hand-holding is necessary to maintain the spell. If you can think of a more innocuous way to touch her, please, I am all ears." When Gyl didn't reply, Matthias told him, "Step out of the circle, please."

The chalk circle that Matthias had drawn started to glow. Gyl's hand fell on her shoulder, and his breath tickled her ear as he bent to whisper to her, "I'll be right here, treasure."

Hettie almost opened her mouth to reply, but remembered the paint on her face at the last second and nodded.

"You're sure you want to do this?" Matthias quirked an eyebrow at her. "Knowing something is the easy part. Un-knowing it is much more dangerous. Don't answer – just grab my hands if you're ready."

She was. She grasped Matthias's outstretched hands, and instantly the world around her went dark.

Focus on what you remember, like we discussed.

She felt Matthias speak rather than heard it, like a buzz of sound right against her brain. She did as he asked, bringing to the forefront of her mind what wispy, nebulous sensory feedback remained of that day far back in her childhood.

She was standing amid a cloud of flame, its bright, wicked tongues climbing the walls and curtains of the room around her. Instinctively she wanted to cough, but she found she was untouched by the heat of the flames, the only thing she could smell the slightly bitter tang of the painted symbols on her face. She couldn't feel or smell anything in this room, in fact, just a faint pressure on her hands that she distantly realized was from Matthias holding onto her, though they were empty and slack in this vision.

A child's cry sounded from within the flames. It was sharp and strident, full of pain.

Follow it. Matthias told her, as if she wasn't already moving toward the sound.

"The flames..." She paused where the fire swallowed the doorway.

They can't touch you. This is only a memory. Move through them.

Hettie moved forward, her vision engulfed for a moment by flickering orange before she emerged into the next room.

Her memories of this place were fuzzy, but even through the haze of smoke the decorations on the walls felt like something she recognized.

This was her childhood nursery.

The crying was much closer, and it made her skin crawl with its familiarity. She found it's source, and froze.

A little girl was pinned by the arm under a massive bookcase, screaming and struggling to free herself. Blood seeped from beneath the shelf, her limb below the elbow mangled and useless. Her brown skin was raw and scorched in places, her black hair burnt short, and she had to stop struggling occasionally to cough.

"That's me..." Hettie couldn't look away from her smaller self, but it was hard to watch. This was the moment she lost her arm, and though she knew she had survived this incident, her chances of making it out looked pretty grim.

We can stop if it's too much.

"No. I'm fine." She could feel the phantom sensation of tears tracking down her cheeks but when she touched them they were dry.

"Hettie! Where are you, sweetheart?" a frantic voice called from the other room, where she'd just been standing. The little version of herself didn't answer, fading into unconsciousness.

With a concussive blast of force like a shock wave, the fires in the room died instantly. A woman stepped into the nursery, tall and slender, with long red hair she wore at a twist at the back of her neck. She scanned the room, a sob tearing from her throat at the sight of Hettie pinned on the floor.

"I know her," Hettie murmured as she watched the woman tear across the nursery, throwing herself down on the floor in front of Hettie.

You must. She's here, after all, and this is your memory.

"I think," Hettie said slowly, a memory stirring within her, "she was my nanny." Both her parents spent long hours at the university. They were a family of academics, and she'd spent her first ambulatory year waddling the halls of one campus or another until her needs and penchant for troublemaking were more than could be tended between giving lectures and conducting research. Her parents had told her that before her own schooling began that she'd spent many hours in the care of a nursing-woman, though they'd never mentioned where she'd gone after being released from their employ.

"Hettie," the woman cried, "darling, wake up, look at me." She let out a low curse and laid her hand on the shelf. The top portion crumbled away, freeing the little girl's arm.

Hettie perked up with interest. That was no spell, rather just a burst of raw magic. That was exactly what she was here for.

The woman hauled little Hettie into her lap, part of her mangled limb remaining severed on the floor. She cradled her and rocked her gently, tears in her eyes and her voice. "Stay with me, sweetheart, please."

The ragged breath from that small chest was hard to listen to.

Her nanny examined the crushed amputation of her arm, her burns, listened to the rattling breaths the girl was struggling to produce. She pushed her hair back from her face and sagged back against the wall, resigned.

"Your kind is so fragile. Too fragile, for how much you've made me love you, over and over. I will not lose another. I can't bear it." She finished the last on a sob, lifting her hand to the girl's chest, over her heart.

A glow suffused the redhead, brightening where she touched the girl. It began subtly, so slowly Hettie didn't notice at first, but that light began to shift. It dimmed in the nanny, transferred slowly into the child until the child glowed brightly, and the woman was dim.

The woman pressed a kiss to the girl's forehead and whispered, "Use it well, little one."

She looked up then, and smiled, and for a second Hettie would have sworn she was looking right at her. Then she started turning gray, cracks appearing in her skin as if she were burning away from the inside out. She crumbled away, leaving little Hettie lying pillowed in a pile of ash, glowing softly.

As she watched herself, her burns started smoothing back out into her normal brown tone. The bleeding in her arm stopped, the place where her lost limb had been severed healing over. Her breathing evened and cleared, until it seemed the smoke had never even touched her.

"She sacrificed herself..." Hettie was shaking. What an absolutely monumental act of love. She felt undeserving.

That's enough.

"No," Hettie protested on an open sob, "I want to see what happens." Her father had told her the story of her rescue more than once, but she wanted to see the truth of it for herself.

You need a break.

"I'm fine."

Your dragon is not so sure. He might actually bite my head off this time if we don't end this.

Hettie could hear the distant clamor of panicked voices. "It won't be much longer. Just a few more minutes."

Can I at least speed things along a little?

"Sure," she agreed.

The world began to move at twice its speed – flames in the doorway flickered faster, footsteps pounded on double time, the shine on Hettie's form dimmed. A group of mages came storming through the house, dousing flames. A man Hettie recognized as a younger version of her father ran forward past them all, scooping Hettie up and darting out past everyone else.

In the commotion, the ashes that were all that remained of the woman were scattered, stomped in with the charred remains of the rest of the house.

Ready now?

She wasn't sure what else she expected to see. Someone who at least looked worried for her nanny? Concerned that they couldn't find the other person who had been in this room?

"Back it up."

You want to watch it again?

"No, I want to go back, to before the fire started."

You're displaying signs of distress. You should consider ending this now.

"Take me back!" Hettie cried, "I need to see how this happened."

You know, sometimes we forget things for a reason.

"If I wanted a lecture I'd sign up for a class," Hettie snapped.

She felt rather than heard his sigh. *Very well then, but my blood is on your hands if your dragon guts me before we're finished.*

"You'll be fine." She wasn't sure, actually, but she had something else on her mind at the moment.

Fine. Here we go.

The room transformed, the scorching on the floor and furniture and scattered toys disappearing, color blooming over them as time spun backward.

Hettie could hear the gentle murmur of voices in the adjoining room. She followed it before Matthias could prompt her again.

The redhead and her small self were seated at a low table, and little Hettie was drawing in a little box of sand with a stylus.

"Now spell 'hop,'" her nanny was saying, peering over the girl's shoulder and nodding, a dimpled smile creasing her face. "Yes! You're so clever, Hettie. Your new teachers will be so impressed."

"Sandra, why can't you just teach me?" Hettie asked, scribbling through her word in the sand.

"Oh, sweetheart," her nanny – Sandra, Hettie remembered now that she'd heard herself say it, like she'd never forgotten – said as she stood, moving to an altar near the nursery door, "I manage just fine with your letters and basic figures, but there's so much more out there for you. History, music, *magic*."

"You could teach me magic," Hettie grumbled petulantly.

"My magic is different, sweetheart. I wouldn't be a good teacher. Don't you want to make friends?"

"*You're* my friend," the girl continued to pout.

"I am," Sandra agreed genially, "but little girls need friends their own age. Come do your prayers."

Little Hettie grumbled but slid off her chair and followed Sandra to the altar where the two of them knelt. Sandra lit a candle with the wave of her hand. It was just like the altar they'd always had in their home, with statues of the women's goddess, the goddess of wisdom, and the goddess of luck. There was the little dish of spirits and the glass marbles and the sticks of charmed incense they'd burn to ward off evil spirits or spoiled energy. It was all eerily the same as it has always been, had continued to be every visit to her parent's house. She had never been as devout as them, and had always given the altar a wide berth, yet here was her younger self, knelt in prayer like they always pestered her to do. What had changed?

A bell rang from downstairs, and Sandra put her hand on

Hettie's shoulder. "You finish your prayers, love. I'll be right back."

"Can we play stars and quarters when you come back?" Hettie asked hopefully.

"Of course, love. Wait for me to get it down, though, okay?" She didn't wait for Hettie's answer, rushed out of the room by the bell ringing downstairs again.

She finished her prayers, and it only took seconds for her to start to fidget. She got up and darted into the nursery, knocking into the altar in her haste.

As if in slow motion, the dish of spirits sloshed, and the candle tipped over. Hettie watched, horrified, as the candle lit the alcohol, the flame eating quickly into the altar cloth and then the wooden table. In seconds, the blaze was climbing up the drapes. Hettie could tell that at the rate it was spreading, it would take only a few short minutes for the fire to get to the state it was in at the point where she'd entered the memory.

Her younger self, completely unaware, flounced happily over to the shelf in the corner in the nursery in the next room, the heavy-duty piece of furniture loaded to capacity with books and games and toys. She reached up, hauling herself up the front of the shelf like a ladder.

Hettie didn't need to watch to see where this was going now. In fact, she didn't want to see.

"I'm done! Take me out!"

Oh, now you're finished?

"Matthias!" she cried desperately, closing her eyes hard as the shelf stared to rock and wobble.

Ending it now.

Coming out of the memory felt like opening her eyes for the

first time after a nightmare. One moment she was seeing the quickly growing fire, and the next she was looking at Matthias, still holding his hands. Her cheeks and neck were very wet, like she'd been crying the entire time.

"Is it done now?" Gyl growled from behind her.

"It's done," Matthias agreed, dropping her hands.

Hettie lost track of the ground for a moment as she was yanked backwards before she was tucked into a familiar, hard chest. She clung tightly to Gyl, her breaths twisting into ragged sobs.

"Did you learn what you needed, sweet treasure?" he murmured against her hair.

She nodded, "But if it's alright with you, I don't want to talk about it just yet."

"Of course. Whatever you need. Your services have been concluded, mage." That last was said to Matthias, Gyl's voice gone flinty.

"May I ask what exactly that was? You seem to know more about this than you did when in our care."

"Did you not just hear her say she didn't want to talk about it?" Gyl snarled.

"Right... my mistake. You know where to find me if you need any more *assistance* in this manner."

"Sure," Hettie agreed, already knowing she wouldn't.

19

Hettie was strange in the days following her consult with Matthias. She barely ate, barely spoke, and she didn't respond when Gyl would try to initiate intimacy. She'd disappear for hours at a time, and come back with swollen eyes and smelling of sorrow.

It scared him.

He was a big, ferocious dragon. Nothing should scare him. And yet looking her in the face and seeing... nothing... That terrified him, and to make things worse it was eerily familiar, as it was similar in nature to the way he'd behaved for years.

He felt helpless. He didn't know what to do. He just watched her, offered her food and affection, and waited for her to come to him.

He wished he had never agreed to bring Matthias into their home. She hadn't told him what she had seen, but the onset of this mood was brought about by that mage's confounded memory magic, he just knew it was.

Perhaps some things were better left forgotten.

After a week, when he started noticing an ashy overcast to her completion, he decided he couldn't sit by and watch her waste away.

He led her by the hand to his workshop, and his resolve was solidified by the fact that she didn't give in to her normally curious nature and ask him a thousand questions on the way.

The witchlights flickered on as they walked in. He'd been here more since Hettie's arrival, cleaning up and tinkering here and there in the moments he could bear to be away from her. The plans where he'd started designing her arm were pinned above one of his tables.

He ignored it all, taking her straight to his nest in the corner. He waved his hands to dim the fairylights that hung inside the tent-like fabric draped over it. He tugged her down into the pile of cushions, tangling their limbs and curling around her, and hoped the nest would work its magic on her.

This space had brought him comfort for many years. Despite not having used it in some time, and having freshened it up since her arrival, it still smelled strongly of him, and he hoped flooding her senses with him would do the same for her.

"What are we doing in here?" Hettie sighed, her voice small. He hated it.

"We're not leaving this nest until you talk to me," he told her gruffly.

"I told you, I don't want to talk about it. I want to forget it again."

Gyl grunted and told her, "I know, but I think you *need* to talk about it. Because unless you're planning on letting Matthias mind-wipe you, you won't be forgetting." The thought of letting the man back in their home made his skin crawl, but he'd have done it if Hettie needed more memory magic to feel better.

"I'm fine, Gyl." Hettie made as if she were going to get up, and Gyl tightened his arms on her, yanking her down.

"We both know that's not true, but you know I recognize it better than most. You're not fine, and that's okay, but I'm not going to let you do as I did and wallow and waste away until the end is just as tempting a solution as feeling better."

Hettie gazed up at him, wide eyes growing watery. Gyl thumbed away the tear that leaked down her cheek.

"I've been thinking these past few days, you know, and I realized something." If she wasn't ready to talk yet, then he was just going to keep going. "I don't think it was my voyeurism that finally brought me out of my stupor – though that was... pleasurable, I won't deny." Hettie rolled her eyes, and Gyl felt a wisp of triumph at that little glimpse of her usual self. He waited with bated breath, silently urging her to continue the conversation.

"What do you think it was, then?" Her voice was choked with tears and rough from not using it for days, but she was talking, and Gyl wanted to crow.

"Rose, the woman, she *understood* me. She and I had loneliness in common, and I felt *seen* for the first time in decades. And then I found you, and I feel like I owe that to her sympathetic ear." Please listen, he urged her silently, you don't have to do this alone.

She sniffled, looking dolefully up at him through damp lashes. "I don't know if I'm ready."

"Whatever it was that you saw, treasure, it wounded you. You can leave these bandages over the wound to hide it from the world, and it might heal eventually, but it will fester and rot first. If you rip off the bandage now, it will hurt and bleed, but you give it a chance to heal cleanly. I want you to try, treasure. Talk to me."

Hettie's face crumpled. "You're not going to let this go, are you?"

"No, I am not." He tucked her under his chin, stroking her back. "Tell me what you know, treasure."

She was quiet for so long that he thought this wasn't going to work, but eventually she took a deep, shuddering breath and sobbed out, "The woman who gave me her gift was named Sandra, and she was my nanny."

Gyl stayed quiet, afraid saying anything would shatter the glass bubble of courage she had forged, but the agony of her voice scorched his heart.

"The house was burning, and I was pinned, and by the time she found me I was dying. It was just like the story Wendamyr told me. She passed me her gift, and as she died I miraculously healed." Her voice broke and she curled into his chest, clinging to him.

"She must have loved you very much, to give you something so precious." Gyl wasn't sure what he'd said wrong, but Hettie let out a wail that absolutely gutted him. "Lover, sweet mate, take a breath with me." He pressed his forehead to hers and modeled what he wanted, taking long, slow breaths until her shallow panting evened out and she mirrored him, with the occasional shaky sob stuttering the rhythm.

"Sorry," she whispered.

"I'm not," he told her simply. "Now tell me why this woman's love has broken you to pieces."

"I don't deserve it." She squeezed her eyes closed, and tears leaked from between her crinkled lids.

Gyl grunted before he could stop himself, "I beg your pardon?"

"No, listen—"

"The hell I will. Why wouldn't you deserve someone who loved you so completely they would sacrifice their life for you? I'd do it in a heartbeat."

"Don't say that," Hettie gasped, her eyes flying open, "Don't you ever say that."

"Are you saying you wouldn't do it for me?" he challenged, "Because that sounds like bullshit."

"That's different."

"It is not."

"It is!"

"I hardly think—"

"Gyl, I started the fire!" She raised her voice over his, and when he fell silent she dropped it to a bare hint of a whisper, "I did it. It was my fault I was in danger in the first place."

A terrible understanding fell into place between them. Hettie blamed herself for this woman's death, this Sandra's sacrifice. Gyl doubted if she'd ever been responsible for the death of any living creature, let alone someone who cared deeply for her. All this time she had been grappling with coming to terms with her role in a series of events that began with a fire she started and ended with the death of a powerful being to keep her alive.

"It was my impatience that caused it," she went on after a moment, "if I had just waited for her to come back upstairs, or if I had been more careful getting up from the altar—"

"How old were you?" It was Gyl's turn to interrupt.

"What does that matter?" she sniffed.

"How old?" he insisted.

"Five, I think? Old enough I was about to go into school."

"Five?" Gyl's heart squeezed, "Sweet mate, you were a child. This is not your fault."

"Yes, it is, Gyl!" She brought her hands up over her face. "She'd still be alive if I hadn't knocked over that candle."

A candle. A single altar candle. That was what had caused his treasure so much grief.

"Listen to me, Hettie." He gripped her wrists and tugged them away from her face. She struggled against him, trying to hide, but this was a much more familiar game, one she would not win.

In a quick movement he had her pinned, straddling her thighs with both hands held above her head. She writhed beneath him, trying to yank her hands from his grip, but this was an uncomfortable truth she would hear before he set her free.

"Hettie! You. Were. A. Child. It was a terrible, unfortunate accident, but you were an ignorant child left alone in a room with an open flame. You are not to blame for this. You didn't ask to be made this. Your nanny was a demi-deious being with many centuries of life experience, more even than my ancient uncle. She'd lived a very long life, and in the moment of your greatest need she chose to save a child who'd not yet had a chance to live. It. Was. Not. Your. Fault."

She had gone still and limp beneath him, tears streaming down her temples into her hair. Her glasses were speckled, the drops caught on the lenses rimmed with the soft orange glow from the fairylights. Her mouth was slack, her lips trembling.

"Do you hear me now?" he asked, much more gently.

"I hear you," she croaked. "I... Thank you."

He sat up, releasing her wrists. She reached up and curled her fingers in his shirt, tugging him back down so she could kiss him for the first time in days. It was a sodden kiss, and she still tasted like salt and sorrow, but he couldn't bring himself to care.

"I love you," he murmured to her, "I don't care how long it takes for you to feel better, so long as you stay with me, alright?"

"I wasn't planning to... leave," she told him with trepidation in her voice.

"Good, because if you make me fight Cynyr to keep you, you'll owe me for eternity."

Hettie let out a watery giggle, "I know you're a dragon and all, but I don't see how you could fight the god of undertakers."

"For you I'd find a way." He plopped back down beside his mate and tucked her into his side. She was still stiff and tense, but he could already feel her melting into his body. Relief diffused him like tea dropped into hot water.

"Oddly enough, I believe you. Stranger things have happened." She propped her chin on her arm on his chest, gazing at him thoughtfully. "I don't even think I *could* die with this gift."

He growled. That wasn't something he wanted her thinking about.

She gave him a small smile, "Don't fuss. I'll mend. I just think I finally managed to learn more than I could handle all at once."

"No more memory diving," Gyl told her resolutely, "No more dealings with the university."

She flashed him a scathing look that was so close to her usual self that it sent a thrill up his spine. "You couldn't stop me if I wanted to, but I don't think there's anything else down that avenue regardless."

"Lucky you, I suppose. It means I don't have to tie you up anymore to keep you away from them."

"You'll find something else to tie me up for, I'm sure." The ghost of a smile flickered at the corner of her mouth.

"I always do," he agreed genially, reaching out to stroke her cheek.

"I love you, too, by the way. I didn't miss that."

"I know you didn't," Gyl grinned, "I was just happy to wait for it."

He'd have waited as long as needed for her. Centuries. Millennia. She was worth it. There was no one else in the world he wanted more.

20

There was an unspoken agreement between the two of them that their bonding would wait until Hettie had recovered from the shock of her discovery.

She spent long hours in her practice room, re-learning how to do magic with this gift, running through everything she could remember from university, with the caveat that she did the exercises the way her magic needed them to be done now, rather than how they taught her.

If she finished her work and Gyl was still engrossed in his, she would fetch Cordelia, and the two of them would find a quiet spot to curl up, usually in a plush chair in the library, and Hettie would read aloud to her, stroking Didi's feathered head, until the two of them were drowsy or a construct came to fetch them for dinner.

When the memory of that night of the fire would creep up

on her, dragging shadows in its wake, she'd creep into Gyl's workshop, where he spent his time when they weren't together, and silently crawl into his nest. There she would doze or read or just think, calmed by the smell of him surrounding her and the sound of his tinkering. Sometimes he'd hum, and the low buzz of his voice was better than any sleeping draught she'd ever tried.

And then sometimes, when the smell of him wasn't enough to soothe her nerves and she started to cry or hyperventilate, he would immediately halt all his work and crawl into the nest with her, just holding her until she calmed. He always knew, no matter how quiet she thought she was being.

They lay in the nest one day when the construct she'd repaired – she'd begun calling it Daisy, for the design on its limb casings – came in to clean. It swatted their feet with the broom as it swept past them, turning its head almost accusatorially towards them as it passed. Though that was silly – it was a construct, and constructs couldn't emote. This one, like the others, didn't even have a face.

"I swear that one has been different since you fixed it," Gyl grumbled, pushing Daisy away with one foot. It paused and tilted its head, and Hettie almost thought it was going to fold its arms and tap its foot, but it moved on instead, carefully dusting around Gyl's many partially completed projects.

"I think it's funny," Hettie chuckled. "It might be my favorite now."

"It's unsettling," Gyl grumbled, but he buried his face in her hair and changed the subject, "How are you feeling?"

"Better," Hettie smiled. She reached up and curled a lock of his hair around her fingers, admiring the cool slip of it against her skin.

Day by day her heart felt a little less heavy, particularly after the day Gyl had made her get things off her chest. She hadn't actually needed the cradle of his arms to calm down this time – she'd come in because she wanted his company, and had laid in the nest when she saw he was mid-task – but Gyl, perhaps sensing the sunshine in her mood, had put down his work and crawled into the nest with her anyway.

"I was thinking perhaps it was time for me to go see if Wendamyr has returned." He said it quietly, like he was afraid she was going to say no.

"I think so too," she agreed.

The glee that lit his face was echoed in her chest.

She was still struggling with guilt, but whereas before she'd felt crushed by the weight of it, it was now just cumbersome. She didn't think she'd ever be rid of it, but it was looking like she was going to have a very long time to come to terms with the way she'd received her power.

Gyl went to see Wendamyr the very next day. It was a necessary step in their mate-bonding, as Gyl had sheepishly admitted that he didn't actually know how dragons bonded, let alone how to do it with a human – well, semi-human. Wendamyr had promised to gather the potion they needed, for what she had no idea, and he'd likely returned from his journey days ago.

She caught the gold flash of his wings through the window while cuddling with Didi in her room. She always made an effort to spend some time with her each day, at least an hour, no matter how down she felt, but since Gyl was going to be gone for a stretch of hours, she took the opportunity to shower the chicken with her attention. Didi was actually the first person she'd told about the memory dive she'd taken. Mostly that was because, as a chicken, she could offer neither commentary nor advice. She'd needed it off her chest, and retelling the story to her silent companion had been easier than facing Gyl at the time.

Now, at the sight of her lover returning, she left Didi with a hasty apology, her body heating even as she scurried to meet him downstairs.

He caught her in a hallway on the way up, his face intense and full of fire. He dragged her mouth up to his for a possessive kiss, nipping her bottom lip with his fangs.

"Do you trust me, my treasure?" he growled when he released her. She nodded eagerly and his face softened. "Do you love me, Hettie?"

Her heart pounded in her chest as she replied, "I do love you."

"Do you remember that half-form from that day in the foyer, after the university?"

Hettie gulped, "I remember."

"Well, evidently, while dragon-dragon pairs mate bond in their big beast forms, those of us who wish to bond humanoid creatures must do so in that half form."

"Oh," Hettie's voice was small. Gyl had had some idea before he left that bonding involved the act of sex in some way. That half form had been *massive,* and since his cock seemed to change proportionally to his size...

"Don't fret," Gyl interrupted her thoughts, "and don't be afraid."

Hettie nodded, though her belly still churned. Gyl cupped

her cheeks in his hands, tipping her face back so she looked right up at him.

"Listen to me carefully, treasure," Gyl rasped, his eyes wild, pupils blown wide open, "my uncle gave me a draught to help me hold the half-form, but its making me a little feral. I have just enough control left to tell you what I need you to do, and then you will need to be swift, understand?"

"I understand."

"Mm, I know you do." He stroked her cheeks as he spoke, and she felt the catch of his talons on her skin. She could see scales creeping down his wrists in her periphery. "I need you to go up to our room and undress. You remember that potion we used for your consequence? The one that helped you to take me?"

Hettie nodded, transfixed by his intensity.

"You need to coat your cunt in it, thoroughly. Put it on a toy and fuck yourself with it if you have to, but you need to be ready for me when I catch you."

"Catch me?" Hettie breathed.

"Dragon mates play a game of fly-chase, and when the male catches her in the air, he bonds her. You and I have to do it a bit differently. When you're ready, you run, and I hunt you."

Hettie shivered, her cunt pulsing hot. "Where do I go?"

"See if you can make it to the nest. It will be more comfortable for you there than if I take you on the stone floor. I hope you don't have any more questions, because you need to go." His breathing was labored, unsteady. Scales raced along his skin, his form lengthening.

Hettie turned to go, starting to break into a jog, but Gyl let out a rough, barking warning.

"Don't run! You'll trigger my instinct to chase, and I don't want to hurt you."

Hettie shortened her strides, opting for a brisk walk. She didn't turn back, afraid even her frantic eye contact might trigger him. She waited until she was upstairs to break into a jog, padding quickly to their bedroom and snapping the door shut.

She didn't have long, she knew that much. If he was already primed enough that a few jogging steps could trigger him, he was going to come for her soon.

She shed her clothes quickly, her pussy already slick and swollen with need. The potion would only exacerbate that. She yanked open the bedside table, where Gyl had been collecting the toys they'd been using, and found what remained of the potion that had relaxed her asshole for his use. She assumed it would do the same for her cunt and his massive half-form's cock.

She started with her fingers, slicking two of them with the potion and pulsing them into her channel, but she was sure she wasn't getting deep enough that way. She rifled through the drawer again, producing the black glass bubble toy from the same night as the potion. It had been thoroughly sterilized since then, and the glass sparkled as she drizzled the potion over it. It was strange and unyielding as it slid into her pussy, but soon she felt thoroughly tingly deep into her belly.

It was hard to stop there, since the subtle heat suffusing her core was doing nothing but making her wild with desire, but she needed to go before it wore off, and from experience she knew she only had an hour or so before the effects started fading. She pulled the toy from her body with a soft whimper and set it aside, her pussy one solid ache.

Her heart pounded as she approached the doorway. It was like she could feel him closing in, already stalking her like an animal in the woods. She slipped into the hall, listening, though the rush of blood in her ears was louder than any noise she might hear.

She hurried down the hall, moving as fast as her plump body would take her. She had never been an athlete, so she couldn't run for longer than the length of a hallway before her body started protesting.

She was halfway down the first staircase when she heard the scrape of claws on stone above her. The deep rattle of his growl echoed down to her, bouncing off the walls.

She ignored her body's distress calls, nearly jumping down the last few stairs, and slammed the door at the bottom behind her. With a pulse of magic, she fused the door to the wall, rendering it useless. There was a tremendous bang and muffled roar as Gyl collided with the door on the other side.

"Ha!" Hettie crowed triumphantly, though her blood ran cold when she heard the first crack of splintering wood.

She kept going, sealing two more doors behind her. She was panting, sweating, cursing the fact that their bedroom was two floors up and the nest in the basement. By the time she got to that last hallway, her glasses were slipping down her nose, her hair sticking to her forehead, and she knew he wasn't far behind her. His growling had gotten more and more aggressive until it was near-constant, echoing down the hall after her.

"There you are, treasure." The guttural utterance was accompanied by the hiss of his tail across the stone. Hettie spared a glance backward toward the foot of the staircase, only to see Gyl's massive bipedal dragon form stalking down the hall toward her, filling the width of the space with his wings, his crown of horns scraping the ceiling.

Hettie turned and broke into a sprint.

She was only a little afraid of what he'd do to her. Most of it was just play, but she knew he'd take her where he caught her, and she wanted the reason she couldn't to walk to be because he'd fucked her so thoroughly, not because her knees were bruised purple from the stone.

She fumbled the latch on his workshop door, losing precious seconds. She got it open as he lunged for her, his claws closing on empty air as she darted inside. She slammed it closed in his face but didn't seal it, scrambling across the workshop toward the soft sanctuary in the corner.

He caught her before she could reach it, those massive, claw-tipped fingers closing around her arm and yanking her backward. She was lifted off the floor and hauled bodily up into his arms. She shrieked and kicked, and he threw her down, her fall broken by the piles of plush blankets and pillows on the ground. Her breath whooshed out of her in relief and exhaustion.

"Well done, treasure," his voice was rough, but he didn't sound at all tired, the bastard.

He stood over her, wings extended and tail whipping, and the lights that glowed in the nest made his scales glint like newly minted coins. He was so impressive in this form, the scales highlighting every carved ripple and plane of his body, down to the bulge that pressed at the slit in his groin. His lizard-like nostrils flared as he scented her, and as she watched the engorged flesh of his cock extruded from his slit, glossy and slick.

Then he pounced.

Hettie let out a startled shriek that was cut off when Gyl closed one hand around her throat.

"I will take what is mine," he hissed, his voice all feral rage. "You cannot run from me."

Hettie swallowed, mouth dry, and nodded, transfixed by the flash of sharp teeth when he spoke. Her pussy still ached, perhaps even more now that Gyl was touching her. Her nipples tightened under his hungry gaze.

She wanted him. She was ready for this.

He gripped her by the hips, flipping her onto her knees. With one brutal thrust, he filled her, and it was suddenly clear why he was so worried about making sure she was thoroughly coated in that potion. She cried out at the invasion, at how tremendously full she felt, but she didn't have time to adjust, because he was already moving, rutting into her at a pace that was quickly bordering brutal.

She clung to the bedding beneath her, helpless to do anything but cry out as his cock plumbed the depths of her cunt. As if she weren't helpless enough, Gyl shoved her top half down, pressing her breasts into the nest. He slid those deadly claws up the back of her head, twisting his fingers in her hair and yanking her head back, arching her back so her ass tilted higher for him. She let out a groan as the slight shift in position sent him even deeper. He let one out in return as her stretched pussy fluttered around him.

He was practically purring, an endless refrain that was a mixture of dragon-tongue, her name, and wordless sounds of pleasure.

She came around his cock, a sudden, fiery flood of pleasure that had her clutching at the bedding and screaming, but it was clear that Gyl was nowhere near done, as all he did in response was let out an appreciative growl and keep going.

He folded his body over hers, snaking his free hand beneath her to pinch her clit. Hettie whimpered, her pussy still pulsing from her climax.

"You'll keep coming on my cock, treasure," he hummed in her ear, "and then you'll take this fat knot."

"I can't," she whimpered. She was already fuller than she'd ever been. She didn't think she could take it.

"You *will*," he barked firmly. He kept mercilessly fondling her clit until she came undone again, tears stinging her eyes at the overload of sensation.

"Just a little more, treasure," he promised in a dark whisper, "I'm almost there. You're doing such a good job. Look at how well you take me. You were made for me." His teeth raked over her shoulder, the scrape of them making her shiver.

She could feel him losing his pace, losing what little composure he kept in this state. His breath started to catch, punctuated with pleasured grunts.

Then his thrusts stalled, his hips pressing forward. Even with the potion, Hettie felt a spike of pain as his knot pressed against her entrance. She let out a guttural groan, reaching for her magic instinctually, letting it swirl through her. The pain eased, her magic making her body pliant, and Gyl's knot popped into place within her, swelling behind her pelvic bone and locking them together. Bright spots swam in her vision as she climaxed again, her whole body shaking.

He pulsed within her, his seed pouring out into her channel. There was so much of it, she could feel it filling her, swelling her already plush belly with the sheer volume of it. She was still whimpering, her body shaking with aftershocks, when he started speaking in dragon-tongue, resting his weight on his hands on either side of her.

She felt his words washing over her like waves of flame, hot and bright but not burning her. They settled in through her skin, suffusing her with a glow she could feel all the way into her bones.

His breath tickled her ear as he bent his head to whisper, "Turn your head to me and take a deep breath treasure."

She turned her head as far as she could, bumping her nose against his scaly snout. He exhaled, blue-white flames flowing from his mouth like smoke. Hettie inhaled as he asked her, her trust in him implicit. Those flames rushed into her, burrowing painlessly deep within her, and as her body absorbed them, it was like something locked into place.

"That's it," Gyl groaned, his body folding around her, pulling her against his chest on their sides. "We did it."

"We're bonded?" Hettie couldn't help but grin. Gyl's hands in this form were too big to lace fingers with, but when he slung his arm over her waist, she tucked her hand into his palm.

"That's right, my lovely mate. You did so well."

Mate. Hettie liked that. An answering warmth bloomed in her chest. She burrowed back against him, as best she could while full to bursting with him and his seed.

Gyl rested his claws on her belly, feeling how taut and full of his seed it was. He hummed appreciatively.

"So good at taking all I have to give you, aren't you?" Hettie just hummed sleepily in agreement, and Gyl chuckled. "You'll take my dragonets someday too, won't you?"

"Mm, someday," she agreed. Though not any time soon.

She felt so full. There would be a mess when his knot deflated and his release spurted from her.

But that was a problem for twenty minutes from now. For now, she was stuffed full and well-loved, tucked against her mate. The last of her energy was finally fleeing her, and she was warm and cozy, tucked under his wing.

She fell asleep, happier than she'd been in a long, long while.

21

Gyl squinted as he looked through the magnifying glass, the tools beneath looking the size of hammers as he manipulated the joint in the hand he was building. He was so focused that his mate's cool touch on his lower back made him nearly jump out of his scales.

"All done?" he asked to cover up his surprise, swinging the lens out of the way. He twitched a drop cloth over his project, smiling a little when Hettie scowled.

"The tunnel in the treasure vault is all filled. It didn't take much to get the rock to close up. It was almost like it wanted to." She snaked her arms around his waist, pressing her breasts to his back. "Why can't I see it?"

"I told you, treasure, I want it to be a surprise."

Hettie let out a frustrated growl, pressing her cheek to his shoulder blade. "You're lucky you're cute, old man."

Gyl laughed, "Am I? What would become of me if I wasn't?"

"I'd turn you into a chicken, too."

Gyl snorted, a curl of smoke puffing from his nose. "I believe you could just about do it, too."

"I think I'm ready to try to undo Didi's transformation. Once I enchant my new arm, I think I'll try it."

It was a clear ploy to hurry her surprise along, and he smiled. He was almost finished with it, was just doing the last few fiddly connections in fact. "Well, it's almost done. I bet if you went and read in the nest for a little while, I could finish it."

He heard her eager little intake of breath as she squeezed him, "Promise you won't be distracted?"

Gyl chuckled. The past five days since their bonding had been a passionate blur. Even after the potion Wendamyr gave him wore off, and he could return to his more humanoid shape once more, the two of them had barely left the nest. The bonding flame that connected the two of them irrevocably still burned in their veins, making her just as insatiable as him. The day before was the first day either of them had put on clothes, and Hettie had come back from a visit to Didi's room and had pounced on him where he sat at his work bench. He'd likely have already been finished with her arm if the two of them hadn't been so incessantly horny. Even now he could feel the flame responding to her, his cock twitching with the start of an aching hard-on.

"If you quit pressing your breasts into me I might be able to manage," he told her smokily, craning his neck to look down at her, eyes smoldering.

A coy little smile twitched at her mouth, and she popped up on her tiptoes to kiss him. "I suppose I can comply."

Gyl listened to her rustling around, burrowing into their nest. He let himself tunnel his focus again once he could hear the regular rasp of her flipping pages.

It truly didn't take him long. He had just been fine-tuning some of the smaller details when she came in. Two hours later and he could confidently say it was finished. Really it could have been one, but when it came to his treasure his perfectionism was unmatched. Nothing but the best would suit for her. He couldn't bear to give her something and know it had a catch in one knuckle or an error in the etched pattern. He re-did several connections that normally would have been perfectly fine just because the movement felt slightly stiffer than he thought it should be.

She was up like a flash the moment he called her name, her curls in disarray from wallowing amongst the cushions.

"Go ahead and try it on," he told her, but she was already flipping the little hatch on the inside of her elbow open to reach in and release the catch that held the arm in place. Her brass arm came loose with a dull thunk, and she swung it down onto the table, holding out her mounting port expectantly.

Gyl was so used to seeing her with the brass arm, he'd almost forgotten it was a construct prosthetic. It was just as much a part of her as anything else, and that was how she treated it, but Gyl couldn't help but wonder if she ever thought any differently.

"You know, with your magic you could probably make transformations on your own body. Have you thought about making your arm flesh again? Or improving your vision?"

Hettie's eyebrows knit together, head tilting a little. Her eyes unfocused as she thought about what he'd said.

"No, I don't think so."

"Why not?"

"Gyl, if you're trying to suggest-" she started, with a growl that rivaled one of his own.

He laughed in spite of the rage that had begun to smolder on her face. "I love you as you are, treasure, you know that. I think you're perfect. *I* certainly wouldn't change you. I was just curious, is all."

She eyed him suspiciously, but she put her hackles down. "I've been in these arms since a short time after the fire, far longer than my memory goes back. I don't know a life without it. It's a part of who I am."

"And the glasses too?" Gyl tapped a lens with one fingernail. She swatted his hand away.

"The glasses too. I've had them since I started school. I like the shape of these ones. I had some heinous little square ones in my younger days." She pressed the gold frames up the bridge of her nose.

Gyl laughed and pointed the socket of his creation towards her. He held it as she guided her mounting port into the socket. He'd made the attachment specifically for her port, but he still held his breath as she latched it into place.

"It's heavy," she gave a nervous little laugh as the limb swung listlessly at the elbow, "I don't think I ever noticed with my other one."

It was because it was inert, Gyl thought, because he knew he'd made this one lighter. He'd taken every care to make this one an improvement, aside from just the appearance of it. He'd carefully crafted the joints to maintain her range of motion while improving on her frequent complaints – namely pinching her hair and clothes. It was gold-plated instead of bronze, with delicate feathered scrollwork and careful shadowing in the low areas. It was a masterpiece, his best work, and there could be no better person to receive it.

"It just needs enchanting," he assured her, "Once it feels like a part of you, you won't even notice it's there." He still held it up for her, supporting her forearm while it was still unresponsive.

She stared down at it, tracing her fingers over the lines and whorls he'd so lovingly hand-carved into every inch. "It's so beautiful."

Gyl beamed at the praise. He wanted to push her, to urge her to start her enchantment so she could really start testing it, but he'd long learned his lesson on giving her advice. He waited, as patiently as he could manage, while she admired his work, mouth absently agape.

He sensed when she started enchanting it, felt the fizzy rush of her magic through the metal. It grew warm against his palms, and whirred softly as the joints moved independently of him for the first time.

The joy on her face was palpable. She lifted his handiwork high, admiring it in the light from his work bench as she tested each joint.

"You were right," she told him breathlessly, "it feels like nothing now. I'd hardly know it was there."

The piece suited her better than he'd hoped. The gold brought out the undertones in her skin and matched the metal of her glasses. The whirling design he'd etched led the eye upward along her arm; toward her face. Not only that, but she seemed to love it. She was watching with rapt fascination the way the patterns changed as she flexed and relaxed her hand.

"You're incredible," he praised her softly, watching with a critical eye as she tested her range of motion. "I don't think there's anything you can't do."

"Woah there," Hettie teased, "let's not go there, or I'll end up with an ego bigger than Matthias's."

Gyl snorted, "Regardless. I think you're ready to change your chicken back to her real form." Cordelia, he corrected himself. While his irrational jealousy of the bird had faded with their mating, he still occasionally had to remind himself that there was a person in that little feathered body, not just a smug-looking hen.

"I think so." Her voice trembled, but there was no doubt in her face when he tipped it towards him.

"Then let's go try."

22

Hettie sat with Didi in her lap, stroking her little feathered head. She'd just explained that she thought she was ready to change her back, told her why, and she was waiting for a response from her. She twisted her little head this way and that, her comb flicking as she regarded Hettie. She gave her a slow dip of the beak that must have been a nod.

"You're sure? You trust me?"

Didi gave her a vicious peck, drawing the tiniest bead of blood. Hettie yelped and snatched her hand back, shaking it.

"Alright, alright, I get it. Stupid question." Of course she was sure. Even if Hettie fucked it up, there was no way Cordelia would rather stay a chicken than take the risk.

Hettie cradled the little feathered body in her hands and closed her eyes. She sought out with her magic like an extra sense, finding the shape of Cordelia the half-elf inside the tiny speckled body. She willed her back into that shape, pressed outward against the essence of her being until she filled the shape she was supposed to be.

The slight weight of the chicken lifted from her hands and a glow filtered through her eyelids. She opened them to find a nude, red-headed woman kneeling knee to knee with her, a gleeful grin spreading across her freckled cheeks.

"You did it!" she cried, lunging forward and throwing her arms around Hettie's neck. Hettie embraced her, eyes stinging with relief.

"I'm so sorry," she whispered. Her tears dripped into Cordelia's hair. "If I had only-"

"It's okay." Cordelia held tightly to Hettie, her voice buzzing against her neck. "I don't blame you, Hettie. You didn't know."

"You don't?" Hettie sniffed.

"Well, not anymore. For a while I refused to believe you didn't do it on purpose, that you weren't running some sort of con on your masters at the potion shop." She laughed into Hettie's shoulder, arms still tight around her middle even when Hettie loosened her hold. "But I know better now."

"I'm so sorry," Hettie repeated, "I'll do whatever needs done to help you get your life back."

Cordelia finally loosened her hold and leaned back. Hettie was struck anew with just how lovely she was. She was pear-shaped, with small, bouncy breasts and nipples that tightened into hard buds as the cool castle air washed over her. Her hips and thighs were almost as plump as Hettie's, and her belly was soft, with a little bit of delightful pooch to it. Her skin was luminescent and rosy, pale-complected and speckled with freckles on every limb. Hettie's body warmed at the sight of her, just as it had that first night.

Gyl, whom Hettie had forgotten was in the room with them, dropped a blanket over Cordelia's shoulders.

"Well done, treasure," he told Hettie with a soft, proud smile.

Hettie pressed her thighs together, belatedly remembering he could smell her arousal – more out of embarrassment than guilt. She had nothing to be guilty for. She hadn't done anything, and finding someone other than her mate attractive was not a betrayal in and of itself.

Though she was pleased to note that Gyl didn't seem jealous in the slightest. His face was easy and relaxed, and his body posture loose. The bond had really mellowed him out. A few weeks ago he'd have been snapping and snarling if a former lover had embraced her naked like that.

"Why don't we leave Cordelia to clean up and get dressed? I'm sure after all this time, she'd like a chance to take a hot bath." Gyl held out his hand to help Hettie to her feet.

"Ugh, yes, please," Cordelia groaned. "I feel like I can still smell the dust from the feathers." She tightened the blanket around her shoulders as she stood, but the gap in front didn't quite hide the thatch of red hair over the pussy Hettie hadn't gotten to taste.

Hettie looked away, face burning. Her voice dried in her throat, and she turned desperately to Gyl for what to say.

The corner of his mouth twitched upward, and he continued for her, "We will send up one of our constructs with some clothing and things for you. What do you say to dinner in two hours or so?"

"I think that would be incredible," Cordelia hummed, her eyes heavy-lidded. Hettie couldn't help but feel that the half-elf was eyeing her with considerable appreciation.

She pressed her thighs together against the pulse in her groin.

"There's a bathroom through there – but I'm sure you know that. You've been living in this room after all," Hettie squeaked. She cleared her throat and announced, "We'll leave you to it, then!"

She turned on her heel and walked briskly through the door, dragging Gyl after her by the wrist. She aimed down the hall towards their room. She needed a cold shower, or-

"Hettie, slow down!" Gyl chuckled as she marched past the bed towards the bathroom. "Come here."

She stopped but she didn't turn to look at him. She heard the bedroom door close and the chime of the bell that summoned a construct, and then the heat of his body enveloping her from behind. His arms banded around her belly, his chin resting on the top of her head.

"It's okay, you know," he hummed, continuing when she didn't comment, "that you still like her."

Hettie opened her mouth to protest but snapped it closed again. It felt disingenuous. She was very much still attracted to Cordelia. That had not changed in the two-and-a-quarter years the woman been a chicken.

"You can't deny it," Gyl told her huskily, dipping his head to whisper in her ear, "I can smell the honey filling your cunt right now."

"I wasn't going to deny it," she grumbled, "though I'm surprised you're so calm about it."

Gyl hummed thoughtfully, his hand dipping into the waistband of her skirt. "Before we bonded I was quite jealous of Cordelia, despite the fact that she was just a smug little chicken. She had given you so many firsts, and there is always something special about firsts, something that sticks. But we've had many firsts as well since then, haven't we?"

Hettie nodded. She didn't stop the trek of his hand as it slipped down over the swell of her belly, down still further to the triangle of her mons. He slid his fingers into the press of her thighs, caressing the lips of her sex.

His breath hissed and he made a sound of appreciation, "You're soaked, treasure. All this for just one glance of her naked body? She's got quite the effect on you, lover."

"And you're not jealous?" she whimpered as he continued to stroke her. She widened her stance to give him better access, eager to ease the ache throbbing inside her.

He plunged his fingers into her, tormenting her with slow, firm strokes into her wet heat. "Are you mine, treasure? Do you belong to me as I belong to you? Are we mated body, soul, and spirit?"

"Yes, yes, yes," she chanted, wilting back into him as she gave in to his administrations. She reached one arm up and curled it around the back of his neck, clinging to him as her legs started to shake. He used his free hand to shove her skirts down to the floor. Now undampened, the sound of his fingers squelching into her slick was obscenely loud.

"Then I believe there is nothing you take from me in your interest in her. I have no reason to be jealous. And you have no reason to be embarrassed. Those of us with long life spans often experiment with polyamory, generally not so close to having bonded a mate, but we can't help the timing, can we? We couldn't exactly leave her waiting while we had a sufficiently long honeymoon. Now put your leg up on the bed, there's a good girl."

Mindless with pleasure, she complied. She propped one foot on the bed frame, opening her pelvis up even more for him. He plunged his fingers deeper, grinding the heel of his hand on her clit. She mewled helplessly and clung to him.

She stiffened when the door clicked open, but Gyl's iron grip on her body kept her from pulling away.

"It's just a construct, treasure," he murmured to her. He continued to thrust his fingers into her channel as he gave the construct instructions, telling it what to bring to Cordelia and giving it a time frame for dinner. Except for his grip on her body and his fingers in her cunt, for those few minutes Hettie was completely ignored. He attended to her pleasure without once pausing or looking down at her, like she might as well have been a desk he was drumming his fingers on while he was thinking.

That tingly, loose feeling she got when tied up flooded her, and it didn't take her but a second to understand why. This was him in control again, sending a clear message with his actions and attention – *you'll take what I give you, and we'll stop when I say we stop, regardless of any interruptions.* He trusted her to communicate if she was uncomfortable or displeased, and she trusted him with the care and plunder of her body. He may have been telling the truth when he told her he wasn't jealous, but that did not mean he was afraid to stake his claim on her. Her body responded to it, her nipples tightening, her skin erupting into gooseflesh, her pussy clamping down on his fingers.

The second the door clicked closed behind the construct, his focus swiveled back to her, "What a good, patient mate you are, waiting to come until I'd finished my instructions."

She nodded, pleasure twisting her tongue, unable to do more than whimper as she ground down against his hand, meeting every thrust of his fingers with a roll of her hips.

She craved release desperately. It hovered there, just out of reach, her body tense and tingling as wave after wave of pleasure washed over her.

"You can come for me now," he told her. He pressed his lips to her neck, scraping the sensitive flesh with his fangs as he suckled it. His other hand rucked up her shirt, tugging one breast out of her stays and rolling her hard nipple between his fingers.

Her legs gave out as she climaxed, her body finally releasing the tension like a weight on a wire being cut. He held her up, pleasuring her even as her pussy clenched around his fingers, sucking at their stroking pads. He shifted, trailing his tongue along the shell of her ear as he took his time drawing her other breast out of her stays, lazily fingering her all the while.

"Do you want her, treasure?" he murmured in her ear while he was building a slow, second climax.

Hettie's brain was scrambled by the overstimulation. She wasn't sure she'd heard him correctly. "What?"

"Cordelia. Do you want her?"

"I-I'm yours, Gyl." She was pleasure-fogged, confused. What was he trying to say?

"That's not what I asked," he growled. "You are mine, there is no question of that. Do you want *her*?"

The instant answer that popped to the front of her mind

was, *goddess, yes*, but that didn't seem right. Was this some sort of test? She gripped his wrist to still his hand, turning to look at him better.

"What do you mean by that?" She frowned up into his face, trying to read his expression, which was still soft and open, to her absolute confoundment.

"I don't mean anything by it, treasure. It's just a question." He bent to kiss her, his lips hot against her temple.

"Even if I did want her," she spoke slowly, still not willing to admit her desire outright, "there's no way she'd want *me*. I stole more than two years of her life from her. She's probably ready to be as far from me as she can get."

Gyl tilted his head, gazing down at her thoughtfully for a moment. "Is that really what you think?"

"Don't you?" Her gut churned, a confusing mix of the dregs of her orgasm and new anxiety making a volatile potion in her belly.

"I know better than that." He tapped his nose with two fingers and winked.

Hettie's face heated. Had he not only been able to smell *her* arousal, but Cordelia's as well?

She swallowed, her mouth dry. "I don't know what to think of that."

"You don't have to think anything, treasure. Just know that I am not holding you back, if you want to explore."

"You're like a completely different person," Hettie told him with a laugh, "a few weeks ago you'd already be marching down the hall and threatening to roast her alive."

"Make no mistake, I am the same Gyl from before." He stepped into her space, pressing her back until the bed frame caught the back of her knees and she fell backward onto the mattress. Gyl crawled over her, straddling her hips and trailing his fingers up her belly, between the valley of her breasts, to curl around her throat. "I own you, body any soul, as thoroughly as you own me. If someone were to try and take you from me, they would find themselves at the business end of a set of very pointy teeth." Smoke trickled from his nose, curling up over his forehead and along his horns.

With a gentle squeeze he let her throat go, bending instead to press his lips to her pulse. "I do not think that is what Cordelia wants, or I would not be so glib about asking you these questions."

"I wouldn't let anyone take me from you." She addressed the first part, still uncertain how to handle the second. She lifted her hand, combing her fingers through the silky strands of his hair.

She felt him chuckle against her skin. "I have no doubt you'd be quite capable of that now. May the gods have pity on anyone who tries."

"You're not jealous." She finally reeled her mind back around to the second thing he'd said. She was repeating herself, but she had to be sure.

"No," he told her simply, winding his arms around her, "I told you, I think what you feel for me and what you feel for her are different. I do not have less just because you hunger for Cordelia. I am not a particularly territorial man, I never have been. Being matebound made me a little wild, made me feel things and behave in ways I usually would not."

"And you would let me... lay with her." Hettie had to

admit she was still intensely curious about Cordelia, and Gyl's suggestion was incredibly tempting.

"I want you to be happy, treasure. That's all that matters to me." He raised up on one elbow and grimaced at her, admitting sheepishly, "Now that doesn't mean I'm inviting you to go out hunting for other bedfellows."

Hettie punched him in the shoulder, scowling, "What kind of slattern do you take me for?"

Gyl laughed, "I'm sorry, I just needed to make sure we were clear on that front. Cordelia is a special case. Other special cases may arise, but I don't want your attention to stray unless you find some need that has been left unmet that you're looking to fulfill."

"You're lucky I don't want to mess up my pretty new hand, or I'd have punched you harder," she groused.

"But do you understand what I'm saying here?" he asked her earnestly, gently tugging a curl free from her glasses.

"You're fine with Cordelia and I fooling around because we have history, and what is between us doesn't impose on what you and I have?" She was fairly certain that was what he was saying.

"Basically."

Hettie bit her lip, "I don't know, Gyl..."

"Just think about it. I'm not going to pressure you."

"Okay," she agreed, feeling suddenly shy.

Gyl ran his nose along hers. "Come on, treasure. Let's go clean up, or we'll miss dinner."

"We still have an hour and a half before dinner!" Hettie laughed.

"I know," Gyl winked, his grin salacious, "but if we don't get up now we won't be leaving this bed any time soon."

Languid, liquid flame crept through her body in response, as it always did when he teased her. She caught the flaring of his nostrils, the widening of his pupils, and gave him a little smirk.

"We've got time."

23

Gyl watched the two of them interact throughout dinner, and there was no way Hettie could deny her attraction to Cordelia. Every smoldering look and awkward laugh brought a fresh wave of her perfume to his nose.

She clung tightly to his arm when she wasn't eating, glancing shyly up at him whenever she realized she was unintentionally flirting with Cordelia. Cordelia would glance at Gyl, face reddening behind her freckles.

It was sweet, Hettie's loyalty to their bond and Cordelia's respect for their relationship. Hettie clearly expected Gyl to change his mind at any moment and snarl with jealousy, but truly now that their bond was in place he felt quite comfortable with all of this. His claim on her was permanent, unbreakable.

He liked to watch, after all.

Hettie was obviously struggling with the idea still – and

that was okay except Cordelia was clearly starting to read Hettie's awkward reactions to her advances as rejection. With every awkward glance up at Gyl, Cordelia sank a little further in her chair. It was not at all how Gyl had expected things to go, and he almost wished he hadn't said anything at all and had let things progress more naturally. He was just afraid that if he hadn't said anything to Hettie, she'd completely miss her chance. Bards were transitory by nature, passing from town to town making their livings. There was every chance that if Cordelia left without knowing her affection was returned, Hettie would never see her again. While he knew he would be enough for her, and that she would recover from Cordelia's loss, he also knew that anything that made her sad made him anxious and fidgety.

When Cordelia commented, "It's too bad we never got to see the end of our encounter, isn't it?" in regards to some comment that was made, Hettie panicked and knocked over her wine glass, sending a ruby waterfall tumbling into her lap.

"I'm so clumsy!" she peeped, her brown cheeks heating as she blotted at the growing stain on her dress.

"Go get cleaned up, lover," Gyl told her softly. "That little table napkin isn't going to cut it."

Hettie frowned at him, glanced between him and Cordelia. He shook his head and shooed her out of her chair.

"Go on. We won't melt while you're gone."

A construct was already stepping forward to mop up the mess. Hettie stepped around it and promised – more to Cordelia than him, "I'll be right back!" She trotted out of the room with one last nervous glance back at them.

Hettie was gone for only a couple seconds when Gyl picked

up his wine glass and gestured to Cordelia, "Why don't we get some air while we wait on her? It'll get us out of the way while the construct cleans up and this dining room has a lovely view from the balcony."

"Sure," her smile was stilted, nowhere near as natural as it seemed to be with Hettie in the room.

The two of them walked out onto the balcony, the soft light of the moon bathing them in silver. Cordelia went to the railing and propped her elbows on it, staring moodily down into the mouth of her wine glass. Gyl followed, propping one hip up on the banister. He sighed, and the smoke shadowed his face for a second before the breeze blew it away.

"Look, I've got no idea how to say this tactfully, but I can tell you've got feelings for my mate."

Cordelia let out a humorless chuckle, "Don't worry yourself, lizard, I'm no threat to your relationship. I can tell she'd obsessed with you."

Gyl bristled a little. There had been another jealous lover that had called him that not too long ago, but that lover had had no reason for his jealousy, as Gyl had had no relationship with the woman. Cordelia's was well-founded, as Gyl and Hettie were securely bonded and would not be broken apart.

"Easy," he did his best to filter the growl from his voice, "I didn't bring it up to confront you about it."

"Then why did you bring it up?" Cordelia set down her glass on the railing and folded her arms.

"Because I can tell Hettie feels the same way about you, but her feelings are all twisted up with guilt – for taking two years of your life, for being attracted to you even though we're bonded. She's confused. She doesn't know how to feel about it. If you want something to happen between the two of you, you will need to initiate it."

Cordelia narrowed her eyes at him, "Who are you and what have you done with the fire-breathing beast that had to be drugged just to let her out of your sight and almost tore down a wing of the university? That's right, she told me that story," she told him when one of his eyebrows climbed his forehead, "It's easy to confide in a little feathered creature that can't interrupt you. She's told me everything, and this doesn't seem like you."

Gyl sighed, "It's not like I expect you, as a mortal, to understand, but now that we are bonded she and I have the rest of my very long life to be together. For creatures who are nearly immortal, the idea of polyamory is not that strange."

"It's not that strange to me either. You're being quite presumptuous." She picked up her wine and took a gulp, and Gyl couldn't help but feel it was to keep her from adding "asshole" to the end of that statement. His mouth twitched as he tried not to grin.

"Look, I'm not trying to trick you into admitting something. I just wanted you to know that she's interested too."

Cordelia curled her fingers around the stem of her wine glass, looking at him thoughtfully. "What if I don't know what I want?"

Gyl shrugged, "It hardly matters to me." It might make Hettie sad, but that wasn't Cordelia's problem if she wasn't interested. "Do you not have feelings for her?"

She chewed her lip, casting her eyes over the skyline where the shine of the moon on the distant ocean was cut by the edge of the mountain range. "I would be lying if I said my own feelings for her weren't conflicted. There was something that drew me to her that night, and it's still there now. That first night wasn't supposed to be anything more than a night, and it turned into two years of chicken-prison. I do resent her a little for that time she took from me – it would be weirder if I didn't, right? But mostly I'm not a person who sticks around, I never have been, and I don't know what it would mean to her if we repeated that first night just for me to up and leave."

"I mean even if you didn't want to make her any promises for the long run, if you wanted to stop by anytime you were in Serpent's Bay-" Gyl was interrupted by her sharp laugh.

"Come up here again? No, thanks. I've had just about enough of this place. It's empty and cold. It feels haunted."

Gyl didn't let that hurt his feelings. He knew the ghost of himself that had roamed these halls for far too long hadn't been completely wiped from its memory. He also knew Hettie would feel similarly to Cordelia, had hinted before even that she was not a fan of the idea of living here full-time. "We will probably have a space in town by the time you came back around."

"If I come back at all. Why are you so keen on this when your girl could end up hurt in the end here?" Cordelia wouldn't look at him, just stared out over the ocean.

"Because whatever happens, she has me. She will *always* have me. She would be perfectly happy with just me, but why would I deny her something that has just as much of a chance to bring her joy as to crush her?" Gyl tapped one finger on the side of his glass, smiling absently. "The last thing I want is for her to be hurt, but I've learned that it's not my job to control her. I can at least offer her my support and the chance to make the choice on her own, and be there for her when the fallout hits – good or bad."

He let the last of his words hang in the air, taking a sip from his glass. He wasn't going to pressure either woman in this choice. That wasn't his job. As he told Cordelia, all he wanted was to offer them the opportunity and get out of the way. Cordelia was quiet for a moment before she knocked back the last of her glass of wine and laughed.

"When I tell you I want to touch her again so badly it makes me want to cry, I really wish I was joking." When she turned to face him again, he could see the sparkling wetness gathering at her lashes. "I spent two years watching her – for more than half of it hating her, resenting her. It was so hard to hold onto for as long as I did. She did everything she could to keep me comfortable, devoted everything she could spare to it. She was clearly set to take care of me for as long as it was going to take. Even on days she was ready to give up, she never did because she didn't want to leave me trapped. She is a very difficult person to hate, and a very easy one to love."

"Cheers to that." He lifted his own glass and emptied it of its contents.

She rubbed her eyes brusquely, turning from him to hide her tears. "What exactly is it that you expect to get from this, because I have to tell you, I am a purely sapphic lover. I am not interested in you in the slightest."

"That's fair. I just... I do have one request."

"Here we go," Cordelia muttered.

"Relax," Gyl rolled his eyes, "it's just a request. You can say no." He had an idea bubbling in the back of his mind, one he hoped would be fun for everyone involved.

"Go on, then."

"I worry she may say no to your proposition, even if it's what she really wants, unless I am included in some way, at least the first time. She knows I have a propensity for... watching. I think she may be less shy if I'm in the room. I'll stay out of the act, but it may make her less nervous if I'm present."

"You just want to be a voyeur? Really? You're not looking to be the center of some fucking sandwich here?" She gave him a watery, narrow-eyed glare.

"You seem suspicious."

"No offense," she gave him a wry look, "but most men hear I only like women and take it as a challenge."

Gyl grimaced, "How distasteful. No, I've no intention of moving in where I'm not wanted. I just want Hettie to feel comfortable. I wouldn't say no-"

"Ha! I knew it."

Gyl glared at her and paused before he repeated, "I wouldn't say no if you both invited me in, but given your admission to my gender not being to your tastes, Hettie would be the one 'sandwiched,' not me."

Cordelia ran her tongue over her teeth, considering. She held out her hand. "Alright. Fine. Deal. If that's what she wants then I'm fine with it. I've done weirder for something I wanted less."

"Thank you," Gyl shook her hand cordially, "a pleasure to cooperate with you."

"So, how's this going to work? She'll be back soon. Who's going to talk to her?"

Gyl glanced back at the dining room, listening for the

sounds of Hettie's return. When he heard none, he turned back to Cordelia and lowered his voice to a whisper.

"So, here's what I'm thinking..."

24

Hettie was immediately suspicious when Gyl and Cordelia entered the bedroom together, both wearing mischievous grins. Gyl had one of his boxes tucked behind his back, and Hettie's face immediately heated with the memory of what those boxes usually contained.

"What's going on here?" Hettie glanced between the two of them, eyes narrowing. They hadn't exactly been unfriendly since Cordelia's transformation, but the two hadn't exactly seemed like pals at dinner. They seemed thick as thieves now, sharing a conspiratorial glance as they stepped towards her.

Gyl gestured for her to take a seat on the edge of the bed, and the two of them sat on either side of her.

"Hettie, we wanted to ask you something." Cordelia reached out and laced her pale, freckled fingers with Hettie's brown ones. "Your man and I were thinking it would be fun if you and I took another run at what we started that first night. Is that something you would be interested in?"

Hettie gaped at her like a fish, her thoughts taking far too long to catch up to her body, which was already heating just at the request. When she had slogged her way through the slog of emotions churning through her, she turned to Gyl and glared at him.

"Don't you dare let me learn you pressured her into this."

Gyl held his hands up in mock surrender, but before he could defend himself, Cordelia's free hand was on her cheek, steering Hettie's gaze back around to her. She smiled, a genuine expression that dimpled her cheeks.

"He brought up the idea, but I assure you there was no pressure at all to acquiesce. The choice was mine." She stroked Hettie's cheek with her thumb, her green eyes soft and thoughtful. "He wants to have a part in this, but I'll leave that explanation up to him."

"I see," Hettie rolled her eyes, "so this is for you." She'd addressed that to Gyl, but Cordelia answered with a laugh.

"That's what I thought too, at first, but I genuinely think he wants to do this for *you*."

She turned to Gyl, still holding Cordelia's hand, and waited expectantly.

"You know of my voyeuristic tendencies?" he began simply.

"I do." He'd watched her pleasure herself plenty of times now, and he'd told her about the instance with the thief and his lover.

"I don't want to deny you a single thing, treasure. I know you were uncertain about how I'd feel about this, so I thought perhaps we could combine it with that consequence you owe me and that might help."

Hettie turned to him, alarmed, "You want me to sleep with Cordelia while you watch to punish you?"

She'd forgotten about that consequence thing in the heat of their mating. It wasn't a *real* consequence, after all. Their problems had been solved with genuine apologies and a change in their behavior, not with some sexual punishment – those were just for fun.

Yet here he was saying that that was how she should think of her encounter with Cordelia. It made her mouth sour to think about.

"No, no, treasure. The seat in the audience is for my pleasure," he purred to her, gold eyes flashing, "*this* is for my punishment." He slid the gold box toward her across the bed.

"What's in it?" Hettie frowned. Relief and curiosity were overwhelming her initial distasteful reaction.

"Open it," Cordelia told her gleefully. She let go of Hettie's hand and nudged her.

It was as long as her forearm and made of a dark purple wood, with a simple hinged top that opened upward. The inside was lined with black velvet, the item inside buried under several coils of rope. She set them aside, gazing curiously at the object beneath.

It was made of a series of metal rings, welded together in a sort of curved tube, with a wire basket on one end and a wider set of rings on the other. When she held it by the wider opening, it was very clearly meant to be the shape of a flaccid phallus.

"You want me to put your cock in a cage?" She tried to picture it, and her body answered with pulse in her groin.

"It gets better," Cordelia whispered gleefully in her ear.

Gyl shook his head indulgently and said, "I want you to bind me to a chair, put my cock in a cage, and make me watch the two of you get off without being able to touch myself."

Hettie felt like she was the dragon, her very veins burning with the flames of desire.

"Isn't it evil?" Cordelia giggled, "I love it. What's even better is he thought of it himself."

"Calm down, Didi – er, Cordelia – he can break out of these ropes in a second," Hettie told her.

Cordelia's arms snaked around her middle from behind, her chin propped on Hettie's shoulder. "I think that makes it more fun. Knowing he can break out any second means he has to choose to participate. Every second he lets you keep him tied up is a promise to follow your every whim. It's actually pretty sexy. Too bad I don't like men."

Hettie locked eyes with Gyl as she spoke, and the love that shone between them told her just how true Cordelia's words were. He'd give her anything she wanted, even if it was not always him. She saw this moment for what it was, finally – a tremendous act of love, an opening of his heart and a willingness to share her.

There is nothing you take from me in your interest in her, he'd said. It was starting to feel true.

Hettie fingered one of the bundles of rope. "I guess you'll need to find a suitable chair, then." There were twin sounds of pleased satisfaction on either side of her.

"There is one more thing, before we get to that," Cordelia

told Hettie as Gyl stood to get his chair. "I am as eager for this as you are, but I just want to make sure we've no misunderstandings here."

Hettie turned to give her her full attention. "I'm listening."

"Everyone I've ever known has called me a free spirit – my family, my teachers, my lovers. Some meant it more derogatorily than others. After being locked into that tiny little feathered monstrosity for so long, the urge to wander has only gotten stronger. I'll never be what Gyl is to you, but if you've no qualms about meeting like larks every spring, I don't either."

Hettie smiled, "Goddess knows I hardly need another Gyl. One is plenty."

"I'm not sure if I should be offended or flattered," Gyl huffed, depositing his chair near the bed.

"Flattered, my love, always flattered," Hettie hummed.

"Hush, you, we aren't finished," Cordelia flapped her hands at him. "I just wanted to make sure you knew, so when the time comes for me to leave you're not left pining. You're okay with this?"

Hettie considered it. "I am." It was bittersweet, like dry red wine. And much like that wine, the taste would take some getting used to before she could appreciate the flavor. "But you'll forgive me if I pine just a little."

Cordelia smiled, and her dimple made Hettie's belly flip-flop. "One last thing."

"Anything," Hettie agreed, mesmerized.

"You can call me Didi." She leaned forward and gave Hettie a peck on the mouth, the floral smell from her shampoo enveloping her. "Now go tie up your lizard so we can play."

Grinning, Hettie turned to her mate, who stood shirtless

beside the chair. He held out the tie on his trousers with a smirk. Hettie tugged it slowly, pulling until the knot came undone, holding his pants up with the tension for a moment before she let them fall to the ground.

"You'd best hurry," Cordelia told her smokily, "If you let him get too hard that cage will never fit."

Gyl picked up the contraption and slid the larger ring at the end off. It came free with two pins poking out at the top.

"This one first, flush against the pubic bone," he told her, handing her the ring. She knelt in front of him, sliding it all the way up and over his knot, which took a little gentle wiggling to maneuver, then tugging his sac through. He handed her the second piece. "Then this one slots into place, and it locks through the loop." He showed her the padlock. She gently slid his cock into the cage, the head slipping easily all the way to the basket at the end. She had to be gentle at the base, as his knot was starting to swell a little and his entire length was already pressing up against the downturned shape. When she lined up the piece with the pins on the base, they slotted into place. When he dropped the lock into her waiting palm, she clicked that in place too.

The overall effect was incredibly erotic. Already his member strained against the metal confines of the cage, the smooth wire pieces digging into the sensitive flesh. His balls were trapped below the contraption, unable to tighten up close to his body.

"How does it feel?" she asked, glancing up at him.

"Torturous," Gyl's voice trembled, "but I believe that's the point."

With a grin, Hettie leaned forward, flicking her tongue into the spaces in the cage. A low growl rumbled from his throat, his hands twisting in her hair, as she lapped at what she could reach of his cock, and when a pearl of moisture beaded at the tip, she tasted it too, salt and musk and smoke bursting over her tongue.

"Beloved mate, if you keep teasing me like this, I'm going to lose control long before you get a chance to play with Cordelia." His chest was heaving, like he was undergoing some tremendous effort.

"You'd best sit down, then," she told him, relenting and leaning back.

She held the rope in her hands, and, on a whim, enacted her magic upon it. The bundles wriggled apart, slithering like snakes up to his wrists and ankles. She bound him to the chair, fixing him in place with knots just like the ones he'd used on her several times. His ankles were bound to the wooden feet, his wrists to holes in the arms of the plush chair.

"What a convenient design," she teased, crawling into his lap. She ground down on his lap, feeling the hard press of the metal cage against her sex through her clothes. She plucked at the ropes around his wrists, leaning forward, and asked, "Did you have some nefarious intentions for this chair, dear mate?"

"No," his voice was a hot, hungry rasp, "but I do now."

Cordelia laughed, "If you keep teasing him he's going to lose it. Come play with me."

Her belly squeezed. She bit her lip. Gyl caught her gaze and flashed her a little smirk.

"Go on," he told her.

She slid off his lap and turned to Cordelia. She'd undressed while Hettie was tying up Gyl, and she lay on her side, every inch of bare, freckled skin on display.

"Stop right there," Cordelia told her. When Hettie froze, Cordelia grinned and told her, "Undress for me."

Hettie let out a shaky breath and reached back to unfasten her skirt. It puddled at her feet, and her shirt and underthings quickly followed it.

"You're so pretty," Cordelia sighed. She beckoned Hettie forward with a crook of her fingers. Like a fish on a hook, Hettie was propelled toward the bed. Cordelia rose to her knees, trailing her hands up Hettie's belly to cup her breasts. "I always did like these."

"Yours are perkier," Hettie told her breathlessly.

"Touch them," Cordelia urged, taking Hettie's hands and guiding them up her own body. Freckles like constellations disappeared between her brown and gold fingers.

"Sorry, is my hand cold?" she asked when Cordelia shivered under her touch.

"It'll warm up," Cordelia winked. She curled her arm behind Hettie's neck and tugged her down onto the bed beside her. She kissed her, and the taste of her mouth sparked a sweet memory of that night so long ago.

Cordelia pressed her flat to the bed, her plush pink lips trailing down Hettie's neck. She suckled at the tender spots, her hands cradling Hettie's curves, gentler than Gyl but no less insistent.

She traveled down Hettie's body, suckling and kissing and scraping softly with her teeth. Her breath tickled her breasts, her nipples tightening. Cordelia closed her mouth over one stiffened bud, laving it with her tongue until the flesh was dark and red from her attentions. She repeated this with the other one, and it didn't take long for Hettie to be reduced to a squirming, panting puddle beneath her. Her thighs were already slicked with need, her sex swollen and aching.

Cordelia giggled, the sound tickling her skin as she released her nipple with a slick pop. "She's easy to wind up, isn't she?"

Hettie followed Cordelia's line of sight, glancing over at Gyl. A solid stream of smoke trickled from his nostrils. His posture was mostly relaxed, except for the fidgeting. He tensed and relaxed his calves and forearms, the ropes straining against his limbs.

"He wants you so badly, Hettie," Cordelia whispered in her ear, "Look at how hard this is for him. Are you gonna sing for him, pretty one?"

Hettie's only response was to whimper as Cordelia trailed her fingers over the lips of her sex.

"She's soaked, lizard-man," Cordelia taunted him, "Do you hear how much she wants me?" Her cunt made an obscenely wet sound as Cordelia thrust two of her slender fingers into her channel. She stroked her front wall with the pads of her fingers, finding that spot within her that made stars spark behind her eyes just as effortlessly as she had the first time.

"I'm putting a lot of trust in you here, pretty girl," Cordelia murmured to her, lowering her head, "don't turn me into a chicken this time, okay?"

Hettie laughed, the squeeze of her belly making her pussy tighten on Cordelia's stroking fingers. "I promise you'll still be a half-elf at the end of this."

"Good girl," she purred.

Hettie didn't even have time to glow with the praise before Cordelia's tongue descended on her clit. Hettie curled her fingers in Cordelia's fiery mane, rocking her hips upward into that clever mouth.

She'd thought Gyl's tongue dexterous, but Cordelia's had a delicate touch. She swirled and flicked the little pink organ against that sensitive bead of flesh, making Hettie gasp and groan with every flicker of pleasure.

"Didi," she gasped. Cordelia hummed against her, the sound buzzing her clit. "Oh, goddess, do that again."

Cordelia lifted her head, her breath still puffing over her mound, and told her, "Beg for it."

Hettie felt the gush of wetness spurt over Cordelia's stroking hand in response to her command. Her core quivered, her body tensing on the edge of release, unable to drop over the edge without the attention from her mouth.

"Please, Didi," she keened, "please, please, I'm going to come."

"Are you?" She dropped a teasing kiss over Hettie's clit. "What do you think, lizard-man, should I let her come?"

Hettie flashed a wild glance at Gyl, whose eyes were dark and intense as he watched Cordelia's fingers dipping in and out of her cunt. His gaze flicked up her hers, and he smirked.

"She's been a very good girl," he told Cordelia, his voice strained, "I think she deserves it."

"Your mate is merciful," Cordelia giggled, "I suppose I'll allow it."

Finally, she lowered her mouth back to Hettie's groin, suctioning that little bud with her plush lips.

It struck her like lightning, her climax thundering through her like a rush of water through a broken dam. Her magic rushed to her skin, and she remembered at the last moment that Cordelia was not a dragon and thus she could not absorb it. She let it race over the other woman's skin instead, lighting up all her nerve endings before drawing the power back into herself.

Cordelia sat back from her, panting, "You scared me for a second there, pretty girl." Her eyes were glassy, her limbs shaking.

"Sorry," Hettie told her bashfully. Her own legs trembled as she sat up. "Are you alright?"

"Perfectly fine," Cordelia laughed, "It felt incredible. I'm just glad I'm not a chicken again."

Hettie laughed too, "I think I have enough control now that I can avoid the chicken part."

"That's a relief, because if I was a chicken I'd have no cunt for you to taste." Cordelia gave her a wicked grin and scooted back to the headboard. Leaning back against it, she let her legs fall open, exposing the glistening pink slit at the apex of her thighs.

Hettie's mouth watered. This was the part she hadn't gotten to do that first time. She was both anxious and eager, and she knew she was going to be a little clumsy at first. Hopefully Cordelia would be patient with her.

Hettie crawled between her legs, tipping her head back for another kiss. Cordelia complied, her usual sweetness mixed with the musk of her own sex.

"Take her glasses off," Gyl commanded huskily, "they'll get dirty."

"Stay out of this, spectator," Cordelia snipped, but she did pluck Hettie's glasses from her nose and set them, daintily, aside.

With a hand on the top of her head, Cordelia pressed Hettie's face downward. Hettie kissed each freckle she passed, suckling softly at her pale skin. She nuzzled against the red thatch of hair, curling her arms around Cordelia's thighs and pressing her chest to the bed.

She lowered her mouth to Cordelia's sex, stroking up the length of her slit with the flat of her tongue. She groaned, the taste of her bursting on Hettie's tongue – sweet and earthy, addictive.

"That's it, pretty girl," Cordelia urged as Hettie got down to business, "touch me how you'd want to be touched."

Hettie stroked her tongue over every inch of Cordelia's cunt, learning the shape of it. She circled that hard bud at the top with the pointed tip, and when she did something that made Cordelia's legs twitch on either side of her head, she did it again.

"I can see you losing it over there, lizard-man," Cordelia chuckled. "What do you think, pretty girl, should we put him out of his misery?"

Gyl was trying his very best to behave. It was agony to keep his ass in that chair. He could splinter it to pieces in seconds. It would be that easy. He let his bindings dig into him, the rope creaking and popping from the tension. His cock strained against the metal, the wires digging into flesh that filled with blood regardless of the confines, and a string of fluid swung from the purpling, engorged head.

How could he not get hard, watching this lascivious scene? He always loved the faces Hettie made when she was being pleasured, so open and sweet. He'd worried for a second when he sensed her magic flowing, had almost broken free then, but she'd reigned it in quite skillfully at the last minute.

Now he was watching her please Cordelia, ass high in the air and still sopping with her arousal and release.

He wanted her so badly. He was aching to bury his cock in his mate, to knot her, to stake his claim. He had perhaps overestimated his ability to sit and watch impartially.

"I can see you losing it over there, lizard-man," Cordelia taunted, as she had been the whole time. "What do you think, pretty girl, should we put him out of his misery?"

Hettie's response was a wordless hum against Cordelia's sex that had her eyes rolling back in her head.

"You can't stand this, can you?" Cordelia locked eyes with him, "It's killing you, watching her devour me. You want her so badly. I can see it in your face."

Gyl was perhaps not as immune to jealousy as he'd originally thought. A hot wave of envy flooded him, his cock twitching against the cage in his need.

Cordelia made a smug sound, tangling her hands into Hettie's curls. "She's doing such a good job, too. Fuck, pretty girl, just like that." She let her head fall back against the headboard, eyes shuttered as she let out a wordless whimper.

He'd promised to stay out of it. He was determined to keep that promise, even with the dark fog of feral instinct pressing in on the edges of his mind.

Fight, fuck, claim.

Hettie was making the lewdest noises as she feasted on Cordelia's cunt, noises of absolute indulgence despite the fact that she wasn't even being touched. Her pleasure soothed him fractionally, let him settle back in the chair, but his limbs were still stiff, his cock nearing absolute agony.

Cordelia opened her eyes and glanced over at him, face flushed. "Pretty girl," she nudged Hettie gently, "I think your lizard may go mad if we don't release him. What do you think, will you let him have you while we finish?"

She tipped Hettie's face up with a gentle finger under her jaw. Her mouth and chin glistened with Cordelia's juices. Hettie licked her lips and glanced over at Gyl. Her eyes were unfocused, glassy, her mouth swollen. Her brow pinched as she took in the state of him.

"I'm fine, treasure," he promised her, though his voice was shaking.

"You don't mind?" Hettie turned back to Cordelia, eyes hopeful.

"As long as he keeps his hands where they're supposed to be," Cordelia glanced at him meaningfully, "then I think he's suffered enough."

"Is that what you want, treasure?" he whispered, chest swelling with hope that he might soon have relief, that soon that feral beast within him would be quieted with the warm grip of her cunt on his cock.

"Yes. I want you, Gyl." Her tone was breathless, needy. His response was immediate, tightening one forearm until the already straining rope snapped. With a wave of her hand she severed the rest, and they fell limply to the floor.

He grasped the cock cage in one hand, the lock in the other, and gave it a sharp twist. The metal snapped, the pieces falling apart with one ruthless tug. They fell to the floor with a thud, and his cock finally was able to fully extend.

"I'll get another one," he promised Hettie when she pouted down at the twisted remnants of that torture device on the floor. Maybe. If he thought he could survive another episode like this one.

Yet despite his freedom, still he ached. He growled as he stalked toward the bed, his vision tunneling on his mate, who looked over her shoulder at him with eager anticipation.

"Head down, pretty girl," Cordelia tangled her fingers in Hettie's hair and tugged her face back between her legs. As he gripped Hettie's hips, the sounds of her enthusiastic dining resumed, and Cordelia gasped with delight.

He needed to reign himself in a little. If he pounded into her as hard as he wanted he might disrupt their coupling, and while his body screamed at him to *claim* his mate, he did not want to *steal* her. He was being gifted the privilege of intruding into their time, but as much as he wanted Hettie, he still did not want to push Cordelia away.

He gripped Hettie's hips, letting his claws out a little so the dig of his fingers into her soft flesh would leave marks. He lined his cock up with her entrance, the leaking tip gliding through her slick.

Even that slight touch was agonizing pleasure after his cock's confinement. His knot pulsed, swollen and painful. He tugged her back, his length sliding into her channel. She gave a muffled moan against Cordelia, canting her hips back against each of his thrusts. With each stroke he felt the kiss of her entrance against his knot, and the urge to drive deep and lock inside was digging its claws into him.

He was losing it. The way her pussy sucked at him, gripped him, was too fucking good. He'd already been on edge when they'd freed him, and now he was so very close to the release he'd been denied.

"Oh, fuck!" Cordelia cried, lifting her hips and grinding against Hettie's mouth. "Oh, don't stop!" She devolved into wordless, desperate cries, head thrown back and body taut as a bowstring.

With a growl, Gyl buried his cock to the hilt, pressing past the resistance that always held his knot at bay. He filled her completely, his knot swelling hard and fast as his cock jerked, spitting rope after rope of his seed within her. Hettie lifted her head and cried out, drool and her lover's slick soaking the lower half of her face. Her eyes were unfocused, breaths coming in heaving pants. Her cunt fluttered and pulsed on him as her climax took her, making his own legs shake as aftershocks quaked through him with every squeeze of his knot.

When Cordelia settled, Hettie rested her cheek on her lower belly, eyes closed and face creased in a beatific smile. Gyl rubbed his hands down her lower back and over her ass, kneading her tense muscles with his thumbs.

"How do you feel? Both of you?" Gyl asked tentatively. Now that the fog of lust was lifting off him, he was starting to worry he'd overstepped and trespassed on this encounter – though his worry was assuaged when both women answered him with contented, wordless sighs. He laughed, the sharp movement tugging at the knot inside Hettie. They both moaned at the pressure.

"Can you lift her up?" Cordelia asked Gyl, cracking one sleepy eye. "I want to see what she looks like speared on that monstrous dragon dick of yours."

Gyl rumbled his assent, a sound accompanied by a trickle of smoke. "Fine with you, treasure?"

Another wordless grunt, one of general approval. Gyl banded one arm around her belly, hooking her thigh with the other, and flipped them so he was on his back, and she was straddling his groin, facing away from him. He trailed his fingers down her back, groaning as she settled her weight down on him, and his knot sank in even deeper.

"You've traded one cage for another, haven't you?" Cordelia chuckled. Gyl could feel the bed shift as she crawled forward to kneel with one knee on either side of his, face to face with Hettie.

"This one is far more pleasurable, I assure you," he told Cordelia, gripping Hettie's hips to grind her down on him. She whimpered, a sound swallowed quickly by the press of Cordelia's mouth.

"I think he deserves another consequence for interrupting us, don't you, pretty girl?" Cordelia's voice was pure mischief. Gyl was immediately suspicious.

Hettie giggled, then gasped. Gyl craned his neck, suspicious and nosy in equal parts, trying to see what Cordelia was doing.

It didn't take long to figure out. Given the angle of her arm, and the fact that Hettie's cunt quickly began pulsing and gripping on his knot, Cordelia was working her clit with deft musician's fingers. She played Hettie like a masterfully done song until her pussy tightened on him once again, squeezing his knot and sending him into an immediate second climax. He could feel the pressure build as his still-hard knot trapped yet more of his seed.

"And again, pretty girl," Cordelia urged her, her hand still working, "squeeze him tight." She kept pleasuring Hettie, even through another chain reaction of orgasms between the two of them, making Gyl's vision flash white as pleasure shot up his spine.

"No more," he begged. Everything was growing sensitive, each minute movement a live wire to his cock that zipped through his body.

"One more," Cordelia insisted, "Unless you think he's had enough, Hettie?"

Hettie did her best to glance over her shoulder, straining and twisting so she could meet Gyl's gaze. Her eyes were hopeful, pleading, and who was he to say no to her now, after all they'd been through? He nodded, already sweating at the idea of climaxing again with his body lit up the way it was.

"For a lesbian, you sure are getting off on torturing me," he panted, barely managing to form the words.

"What can I say, I guess I've found something men have to offer me after all." She laughed, the bell-like sound echoing off the walls.

"One more, but it's the last one," Hettie told Cordelia in a small, exhausted voice.

"Good girl," Cordelia praised, and she set back to work, strumming Hettie's clit like a lute.

Hettie's knees tightened on Gyl's thighs, one hand flailing backward blindly. He grasped it firmly, twining their fingers and clutching just as tightly to her as their last wave of pleasure washed over them. He felt his knees twitch, his shoulders shudder, his whole body erupt in goose flesh as Hettie's cunt gripped him again, a final climax overpowering his senses until all he could feel in the whole world was the place where the two of them melded into one, where his flesh became hers and where their fingers twisted into a puzzle that fit perfectly every time.

He spat flame when he came, he was sure of that much when his vision cleared to the sight of a black scorch mark directly overhead on the plaster ceiling. He frantically scanned Hettie's back and hair for signs of burns, relieved to find none.

Hettie squeezed his hand, a silent check-in, and he squeezed back. Cordelia wound her arms around Hettie, Hettie reciprocating with her one free arm, and the three of them stayed like that, tangentially connected through Hettie, until his knot deflated, a much longer time than it usually was, given the forced orgasms he'd had to endure.

"So will you come back?" Hettie asked Cordelia once she'd lifted off him, no doubt an awkward question to ask with his seed dripping out of her onto his thighs, but she seemed more eager than bothered.

Gyl tried to stay out of it, but he couldn't help but watch Cordelia's face for her reaction. Cordelia gave Hettie a soft smile, reaching over to retrieve Hettie's glasses.

"Will it always be like this when we have sex? The three of us together every time?" Cordelia asked Hettie, sliding her glasses up her nose for her.

"No," Gyl answered, unable to help himself.

"Only when you want to," Hettie explained, "I know this is weird-"

"Polyamory isn't new to me, sweetness," Cordelia interrupted. She flicked Gyl a look that clearly said, *stay out of this.* "In fact, I had a few lovers on the road that I hope haven't forgotten me yet. I was only asking because, as I told Gyl, I'm not interested in him. His occasional participation could be tolerated, but I can't stick around if his inclusion is mandatory. This is between me and you, but if you let me come back, you have to know you won't be the only one I visit when I come around. Can you live with that?"

Hettie nodded eagerly, and with a smile Cordelia bestowed her with a sweet kiss. Cordelia leaned around her to meet Gyl's eyes.

"And you're sure you're okay with this, lizard-man?" she asked him, "After all that, you're fine sharing her?"

"It is possible for one to love many things with their whole heart. She can love you without diminishing what love is meant for me," he shrugged, then continued thoughtfully, "I am fine with this if you cease this 'lizard-man' nonsense." It dredged up memories of a particularly obnoxious thief who called him much the same, and he'd rather not think about him unless necessary.

"What should I call you then?" Cordelia asked, folding her freckled arms over her freckled breasts.

"Gylharen," he couldn't help but grin, "or Gyl if you decide you want to be friends."

Cordelia eyed him for a long time through shuttered lids, examining him carefully. Finally, at long last, she said, with a grin, "Alright then... Gyl."

25

With her power under control and her worst blunder fixed, Hettie quickly grew restless in the castle. Cordelia departed the day after their encounter, and while Hettie was sad to see her go, it also made her heart swell to see her free again. However, it meant one less thing to distract her. Hettie never been a fan of being idle, and while there was a pool and library and Gyl, her life felt too slow and purposeless.

"I want to visit Poppy and Crystal," she told Gyl when she had reached her saturation point for her tolerance with empty hours.

"Of course," he acquiesced easily. His tail flicked lazy, his demeanor much more relaxed by the day after their mating. "Am I coming?"

"You'd stay behind?" She cocked an incredulous eyebrow. A few weeks ago there would have been no question of that.

"I'd wait in the carriage," Gyl grinned.

Hettie snorted, "You can come. They'll be delighted to meet you, I'm sure. I'd like to bring them some coin, too, to make up for all the damage I did to their shop."

Poppy and Crystal welcomed her with open arms and eager smiles.

Poppy tugged her down by the front of her shirt so she could cup her face in both hands and kiss her forehead. "I was so *worried* about you, love. Are you well?"

Hettie folded the smaller woman into a hug, "I'm very well. I missed you."

Crystal looked at her askance as Poppy and her separated. "And your... problem?"

"Completely under control." Hettie swirled her fingers in the air, producing a cloud of pink sparks that vanished into nothing.

Poppy clapped with delight, "Incredible!"

Crystal squeezed her arm, "You've done well."

"I had help." She reached back to Gyl, who had hung back discreetly for her reunion. He stepped forward and slipped his hand into hers, molten gold eyes warm as he looked at her.

"Oh, you simply must tell us everything," Poppy chirped. "Come to the back and we'll have tea. Avery!"

"Yes, ma'am?" came the muffled call from the far side of the shop.

"You're in charge of the shop for a while."

"Alone?" Avery's surprised face poked around the end of a shelf. "But we've got three orders to finish packing. And it's Saturday."

"You'll be fine, we won't be gone long," Poppy waved a

hand at her dismissively. She grabbed Hettie by the hand and tugged her behind the counter.

Hettie shot Avery a sympathetic grimace, and she received a wide-eyed look of surprise in return.

Crystal made them a pot of tea, and Poppy brought out some of her sweets from the cabinets. Hettie set about telling them the story, from the moment she'd sparked with Gyl and ruined the thieves' trap, up to the moment she'd changed Cordelia back.

They nearly refused the money, claiming at first that they were even because their lack of understanding of her magic had held back her progress for nearly two years. Hettie argued that they lost far more money in stock and property damage than would be equal reparations for the delay in her proficiency. After a moment, Gyl interrupted and insisted they take it, and while he was perfectly calm and gentle when he told them, not many people can look a dragon in the face and tell them no without a little bit of trepidation. Faced with twin walls of stubbornness, they accepted with grace.

"I suppose this will more than cover the 'help-wanted' ads we will have to produce," Crystal told her, shifting the leather pouch in her hand.

"Yes, we're going to need a new junior apprentice, I think." Poppy's eyes sparkled as she winked at Hettie over the rim of her cup.

Hettie smiled sheepishly. She hadn't told them yet, but they'd seemed to understand intuitively. "How did you know I wasn't planning on coming back?"

"This place is too small for you now," Crystal told her

sagely, stirring her tea. "With the things you can do, you have no business being apprenticed for everyday magic."

"I just don't know what to do next." Hettie glanced nervously at Gyl. He slipped his hand over her knee and squeezed.

Poppy gasped, "You should open a shop!"

"A shop for what?" Hettie frowned, "I don't really want to advertise the nature of my magic to the public."

"No, no, no, of course not," Poppy waved her hand, "but Gylharen here makes constructs, does he not?"

"That I do," he agreed genially.

"And you animated your arm, yes?"

"I did," Hettie agreed. She was starting to see where this was going.

"So, the two of you have everything you need to open your own construct shop. There's only one other in town, and I think you'd agree their work is only so-so. You'd have the business."

Hettie did indeed agree, having had her arm serviced at that shop several times and having received sub-par service at best. She bit her lip and glanced over at Gyl, who was looking at her with a sort of shuttered eagerness.

"Do you like the idea?"

"I think it's incredible," he flashed her a fanged grin, "a perfect harmony of our talents, and a worthwhile pursuit for your time. I know you've been getting restless." He leaned in and nuzzled her cheek. "I used to sell my work all the time, before I temporarily lost the taste for it. It'll be nice to make things for others again."

"That settles things then," Crystal smiled, "We wish you the best of luck, my dear, and all the happiness in the world."

"You'll come around for tea, of course," Poppy told them primly. "He's not allowed to keep you all to himself anymore."

"I think you'll find I'm very good at sharing," Gyl told them, sparing a wicked wink for Hettie. She pinched his leg under the table, her face scorched with embarrassment, but all that earned her was a belly laugh.

He'd pay for it later, of course, but it was almost worth the awkwardness for the sight of that grin.

"Now, if you want to talk locations," Poppy continued, ignoring Gyl's comment, "there's a lovely little shop down the street that just opened up..."

26

ANOTHER SIX MONTHS LATER

"How does it feel?" Gyl stepped back to examine his work, pushing his hair back from his forehead.

"The knee joint is a little tight. I'm having a hard time extending it all the way." The dwarfish man grimaced as he straightened his metal leg, a piece patinated and polished to look like antique silver, engraved with a flock of birds in flight. The man worked in an aviary, breeding birds for use as messengers and familiars, and he'd wanted the limb themed to match.

"Let me see what I can do about that," Gyl told him, kneeling beside him to get a closer look at the joint in question. He slipped a slender tool from his pocket and slid it in the narrow space he'd left in the knee joint, wiggling it until he hit the latch. The maintenance panel swung open, and Gyl stuck the tool between his teeth, reaching in with his fingers to loosen the tension. Hettie's magic thrummed against his skin as he worked, a familiar and soothing buzz.

They'd opened this shop six months ago, and were already collecting quite the customer base. They offered a variety of services, but by far their most common requests were basic maintenance and repairs – seized joints, faded animation spells, damaged parts, and problems of that ilk. Only in the last month or so had they started receiving requests for custom work. The leg Gyl was fitting was only the second one he'd completed since their shop opened, but he was hoping to get more. Since this was a passion project for him, and they didn't really need the money, it meant he could offer a discretionary discount to those who would not otherwise be able to afford his more artistic pieces.

The shop bell jangled, and a familiar freckled redhead stomped in, swinging a lute off her back and dropping it by the door with a twanging thud.

"Where is she?" Cordelia asked before Gyl could even take the tool out of his mouth to say hello. "I've had a terrible fucking day."

Gyl gestured with his chin toward the door that led back to Hettie's magic workshop, where she did much more than animate constructs. Gyl received the bulk of the work here, particularly on standard maintenance requests, so Hettie had a lot of free time for personal projects and research into the nature and limits of her magic. They kept this area hidden in the back rather than in the front workshop where Gyl worked so it was easier to hide the nature of her magic. Cordelia stormed past the shelves of parts and his work tables, pushing right pash the swinging door emblazoned NO ENTRY.

His customer glanced down at him, questioning eyebrow raised. It wasn't any of his business, but Gyl rather liked this man. They'd spent a long time discussing at length just how his construct limb was going to look, and after sitting for several fittings they'd gotten fairly friendly. He'd been uncertain about client consultations at first. He was unused to interacting with other beings, after all, but it wasn't like Hettie could do it for him. As a result, he'd been far more social since they opened this shop, and it had been a miraculous balm to the remnants of darkness hiding in the corners of his spirit like cobwebs. It was incredible to be able to gush about designs and patterns with the person who was going to wear them, and he was looking forward to the day he would see his pieces on the street.

Besides, he was neither embarrassed nor ashamed of his mate's relationship with Cordelia. She fulfilled Hettie's hunger for wildness and freedom, much like Gyl satisfied her need for safety and warmth. The half-elf had been back in town for a couple of weeks now, and Hettie was practically glowing with all the attention she was getting between Didi and Gyl.

He took the tool from his mouth and gave the man a rueful grimace, "That's just my mate's girlfriend. Don't mind her."

Gyl's sensitive ears caught a hint of their reunion, the sound of Hettie's raptured cries one he'd recognize anywhere. The honeyed smell of her arousal would filter out of the back rooms soon enough. He didn't think they were being loud enough for this dwarf to pick up on it, so he just bent his head back to his task.

"Her... girlfriend? And you're just fine with that?"

"It was my idea," he told him simply, closing the maintenance panel. "Try that."

Once the part was properly adjusted and payment was taken, Gyl sent the man on his way. He busied himself in the shop, working on another custom order with a test fitting in a few days. If he narrowed his focus, he almost didn't notice the twin cries of pleasure filtering up from the back room, though the need to adjust his trousers every few minutes ensured he couldn't quite forget them entirely.

"Daisy?" he called distractedly, "Daisy have you seen my – oh, thank you." He was cut off by the construct in question sliding the hooked tool he'd been about to ask about across the table to him.

Hettie had insisted they bring this construct to the shop with them to more closely monitor it. Something about the way Hettie's magic had enacted on it had made it strange. She'd repaired it before she'd truly gotten the hang of how her magic worked, and every day that passed since then it behaved more and more like it had a mind of its own. This was not the first time it had acted without an actual instruction, anticipating his need. Both he and Hettie had noticed it watching them, imitating their movements, often tapping on its featureless headplate like it was searching for facial features. He found it more unsettling than ever, but Hettie thought it was thoroughly fascinating. He made a mental note to inform her of this latest incident.

When the women quieted, Gyl gave them a few minutes to collect themselves before he went back to Hettie's workshop, through the swinging door and past the stairs that led to their second floor apartment. He turned the knob and nudged it open, leaning against the door frame.

"Don't you knock?" Cordelia asked with exasperation, though she was dressed except for the vest she was buttoning over her dress. Hettie, trying clumsily to lace her stays, snorted.

"Are you staying for dinner?" Gyl ignored her comment, crossing the room to Hettie. He knocked her hands away and took over lacing the garment himself. Her breasts lifted as he tugged the laces tight and tied them.

"I can't," Cordelia sighed, "I'm playing at the Crooked Crown tonight and if I don't get there early that bitchy satyr will steal my spot." She came up behind Hettie and pressed a wet kiss to her cheek. "Will you wait up for me?"

"I always do," Hettie smiled, her face still flushed. She watched Cordelia flounce out of the room, and in the shop the bell jingled as she left.

"She seemed in a better mood," Gyl commented, scooping up her shirt with his tail and holding it out for her.

"Some nasty old man groped her in the market this morning while she was busking, and then when she made a fuss about it the city guards made it seem like she was the problem," she harrumphed, letting Gyl tug the shirt over her head.

"So, I'm sure she *became* the problem after that then?" Gyl held out her skirt for her.

Hettie shook her head, gripping his arm for balance as she stepped into the circle of fabric. "There were too many guards, and they made it clear that she was going to have to either pay a 'public nuisance' fine or they'd cart her off to jail." She sneered, her distaste for the guards in question evident on her face. "They took half her afternoon's profits and humiliated her besides. She's not going to be able to busk in the market for weeks. It might mean she has to head out again sooner than she expected. I feel like she's barely been back." He caught the slight pout in his mate's tone.

"Did she catch their names? I'm sure I could speak to the guard captain." He knelt at her feet, holding out her boots. When she slipped her foot in, he laced them with careful fingers. He knew she didn't like them too tight.

"Do you know him?" Hettie frowned down at him.

"No," Gyl chuckled, "but gold makes eager acquaintances, and in case you forgot we have a lot of it."

Hettie sighed, "You know she wouldn't like that. She hates when we spend money on her. She barely let us buy her a new instrument and start her a savings account at the bank down the street." She snagged her glasses from the table, pushing them up past the bridge of her nose to the top of her head, pinning her curls back from her face.

"We'll keep an eye on the matter then. Just know that if she keeps getting harassed I'm not going to sit by and let it happen." He stood, catching her expression – one of sweet adoration as she gazed up at him. "What?"

"You're perfect. I just hope you know that."

Gyl chuckled, smoke curling between them, "I'm far from perfect, but Cordelia is part of our family – she's your lover, and my friend. I can't stay out of it."

"I wouldn't want you to," she assured him. "I love you, I hope you know that too."

Gyl heart fluttered, as it always did when she spoke to him so sweetly. He tugged his mate to his chest and squeezed her, likely a little harder than was comfortable for her, but she didn't complain. "I do know. I love you too, treasure."

"Deeper than the oceans?" She grunted, a little muffled by his embrace.

"Much deeper," he assured her, pressing a kiss to the top of her head.

"Higher than the Maw?"

"Much higher."

"Til' the day we die?"

"Far longer." He tucked his head, pressing the base of his horns into her forehead and rubbing the tip of his nose against hers. "When I am nothing but bones, and you are stardust on the wind, and our children's children's children have scattered to the far-flung corners of the world, I will still love you."

"That's a long time." Her breath brushed his cheeks, feather-light. "What if I annoy you?"

"Impossible."

"Really?" She laughed, her lips brushing his. "You don't tire of my endless questions? Or my persistent and stubborn desire to know everything, even when you find it unnecessary?"

"I made it to the other side of all that while matebound, I think I can handle it now."

"What if-"

"There is nothing you could do or say that would dampen the fire of my love, treasure. Not a single thing."

Hettie dug her fingers into his hips, straining up on her tiptoes to kiss him. He was still getting used to tasting Cordelia on her lips, but beneath that was still the taste of his mate, the sweet tang of her desire and the eager nip of her teeth on his bottom lip.

"Let's make a dragonet," Hettie told him breathlessly when she pulled back.

Gyl's stomach swooped. Jaw slack, he chased a thousand responses around and around in his mind.

"What?" was the one that fell out his open mouth.

Hettie chuckled, "A baby. Let's go."

"Right now? You're sure?" Goddess he hoped she was. Already the fire in his loins was stirring, the edges of his vision darkening as adrenaline sparked his instincts.

"I've been thinking about it, and I want them to grow up here, in this shop. We can explain away your long life, but mine? That will be difficult, considering I don't even look like I could be part elf. I look thoroughly human – and no, I won't be altering my appearance to change that. Not to mention all the people I love will age without us. We may not be able to stay here forever, and I want our fledglings to experience this with us, to know our favorite people."

"You want me to get you pregnant?" Wonder swirled with a heady, powerful urge to rut. He'd been making idle comments about babies, jokes even, hiding from her the powerful need growing in his belly for the two of them to procreate, much like his instinctual hindbrain had wanted him to before he had made her his mate. He'd refrained from being too serious about it, afraid to pressure her, but could she feel the same?

"I do."

Elation, pure and bright, lit his body. A dragonet. A tiny creature to grow and shape and bathe with their love. It was more than he could have imagined a scant year ago, yet now he could scarcely breathe for his joy.

A low growl slipped from his throat, his hand skimming

down her arm, his thumb resting on where he knew her goddess's mark lie, the magic symbol the only thing that had kept his seed from taking root for all these months.

"Whatever you say next, you'll be taking my knot regardless," he rumbled, his voice full of dark promise, "but I won't break this unless you promise me you want this, that you have no reservations."

"Not a single one." Her voice was strong and steady, her face calm and open. She was as sure as he had ever seen her.

He didn't hesitate a second longer. Black and gold scales rippled across the back of his hand as he shifted into his claws. He pressed the razored tip of his thumb into that mark, slicing through one of the slightly raised lines on her wrist, severing it. He felt the fizz and pop of the sterility charm as it broke and the mark instantly faded away. He pressed the pad of his thumb to the cut, the tang of her blood flooding his nose.

"There's no turning back now, treasure," his voice was like gravel, the beast close to the surface, "but since you've been such a good mate, I'll give you a head start."

Hettie's breath caught, "How long do I have?"

"I don't know, but you're wasting it." He smirked down at her, releasing her wrist. Her tongue poked through her teeth as she grinned, spinning on one foot to flee the workroom.

He managed to give her to the count of fifteen, once he heard her footsteps hit the landing overhead. He couldn't hold out after that, every muscle fiber screaming at him to *chase*.

"I'm coming for you, little mate," he roared, stepping out of her workshop.

He would always come for her, always, and there was not

a man, monster, or entity in the world that could keep him at bay.

THE END

Other Works by this Author

Love and Magic

Book One: *Ferrous Moon*
Book Two: *Star-Crossed*
Book Three: *Spiritbound*
Honeysuckle Wine: a Love and Magic Novella

Holiday Novellas

A Darling for a Demon: a Halloween Romance